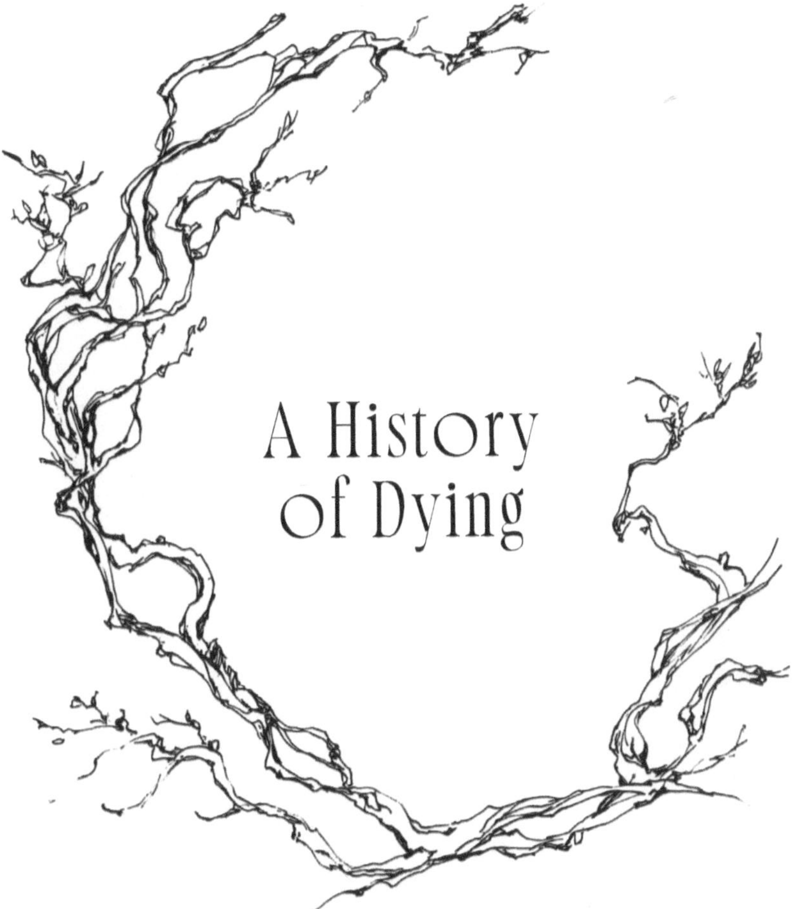

A History
of Dying

A History
of Dying

by Brooke Clonts

Second Star Press, LLC

"The Curse of the Mekori" edits by Kelley Riegert, Fiona McLaren,
Kim Autrey, and EditElle – Writing & Editing Services

Ebook ISBN 9798985171983
Paperback ISBN 9798985171990
Hardback ISBN 9798993023908
Audiobook ISBN 9798985171976
Library of Congress Number 2022921518

Manufactured in the United States of America

November 2025

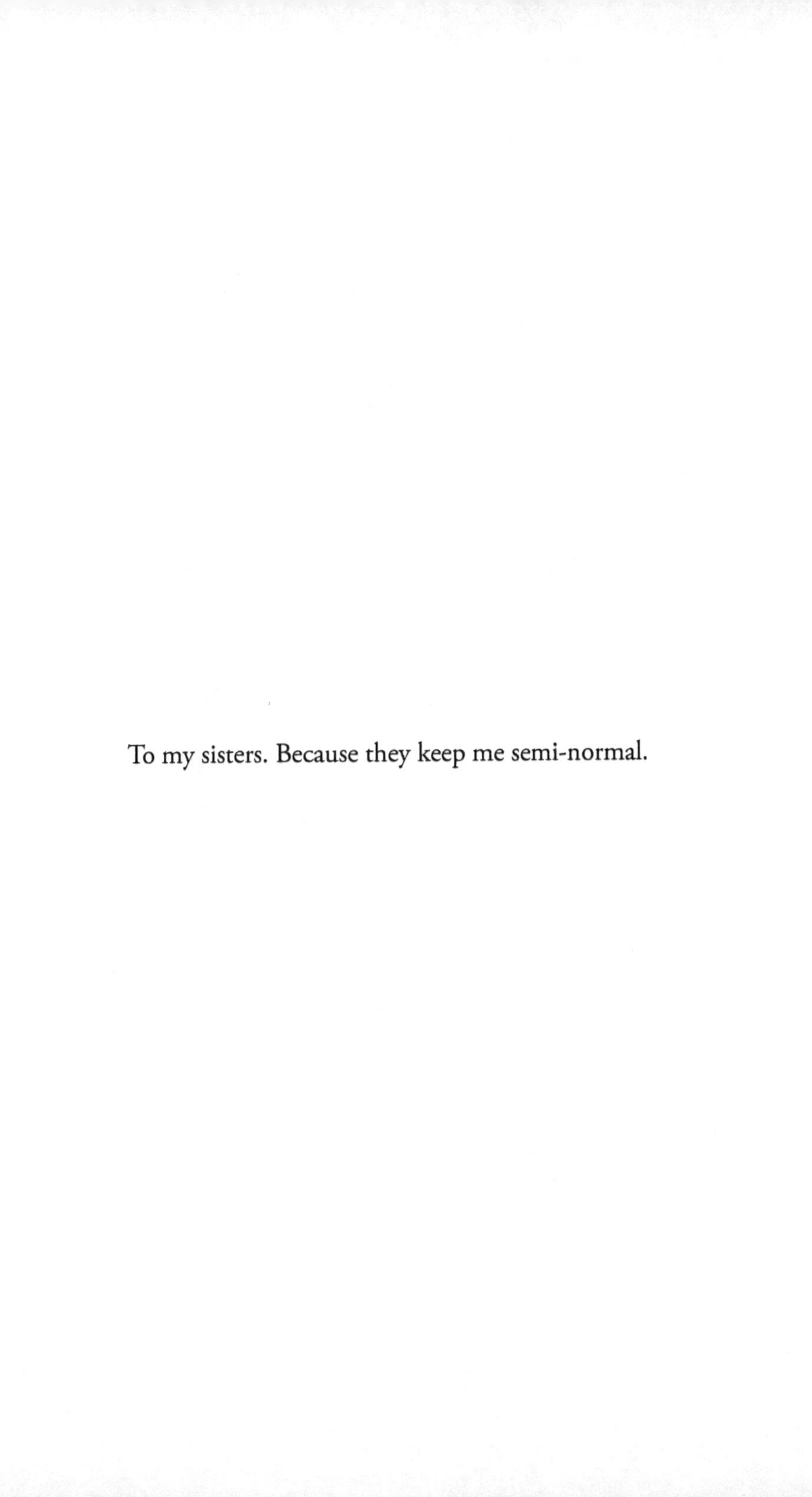

To my sisters. Because they keep me semi-normal.

AUTHOR'S NOTE

DEAR READER, this story brings in the history of the Gunpowder Plot and the Pendle Witch Trials. I encourage you to do your own research to discover what's historically accurate, and what I have twisted for the purpose of this story.

Please note: This story contains graphic violence, homicide, and instances of accidental self-harm. Please only read if you are safe to do so.

Spice Level: Light kissing only.

Language: Low levels of profanity (PG).

PROLOGUE

◆•◆

Lancaster, England—Year 1613

THE CANDLE burns low. A drop of hot wax slides down its side as Thomas Potts squints to read an account of court proceedings by the waning light.

It's too late.

He exhales and drops the document.

Opened bottles of dried ink sit in neglected corners of the mahogany bureau in his private office. Beneath his feet, a thick, patterned rug stretches across the wooden floorboards and forms haunting shapes, like outstretched hands to claim him in his misery.

Altham awaits the final draft, which means Potts can't postpone this day any longer.

Potts looks up and stares into nothingness as the candle's flame flickers. Shadow faces leer at him on the walls. Pages of words are strewn before him. "Alice Grey" and "innocent" bear scratches over the letters. blotted with ink from when Potts ruined them in a weak moment, though he could not erase them.

He finishes reviewing the last page of his record and pushes it away. The records call his employer a hero for initiating the witch trials. In the end the only witch who was prosecuted was an innocent, a young girl of no relation to the real witches who'd gotten away. She had testified against herself for practicing witchcraft and was hung. He could still remember her eyes—a haunting grey. Potts had no idea what had possessed a seemingly innocent youth to do such a thing. After the incident, he couldn't sleep for years.

The witch tree pendant, once known as the last protection against the queen witch, has vanished, perhaps forever.

The manuscript pretends victory and mentions none of this.

A chill creeps through his shaking fingers, and he closes the leather-bound book with a snap.

Finished. Done. He can alter nothing.

The door creaks open behind him, and the light of another candle brightens the room.

His son, William, hovers in the doorway, knobby kneed with wide, nervous eyes. "What do you think, sir?"

"It has been truly reported," Potts says. "It is fit and worthy to be published."

The candle sputters and William flinches, then glances toward his father. Potts stares at the candle in silence, then stands, tucks in his chair, and turns to extinguish the flame before the shadows can recognize his deceit, too. He ushers his son into the hall, leaving the room behind, swallowed by darkness.

"So, it is true? There are witches in our midst?"

"No longer, my lad." Another lie. "No longer."

CHAPTER ONE

WATER POURS IN sheets from the rain outside, the heat from the flower shop vents leaving ghosts on the windows. An assortment of fresh plants lines the shop, some in pots and others in cut and primed bouquets. The worn counter by the cash register gleams from my recent attack with cleaner. No speck of dust survives my shifts.

Customers say I can make anything grow, but today, the lilies wilt in my hands even as I add fertilizer to the water. Those same customers walk around me, but I check my phone rather than look at them.

I get off work at 8. Want to see a movie tonight?

It's the last message I sent Teddy, my ex, but he hasn't responded. We're friends now.

I wait for the three dots that say he's texting me, but they don't come.

"Beautiful necklace."

I look up.

An elderly woman with silver hair and a dozen ribbons tied to her purse gives me an apologetic smile. "Sorry, I didn't mean to disturb you, but it's a pretty tree. Where'd you get it?"

"I'm not sure," I say. Putting on a smile, I tuck my phone into my pocket and drop the pendant I was fiddling with, the tree pendant necklace I've had since before I can remember. Someone found me wandering the streets of London when I was three years old, wearing this same necklace. The cool metal pokes my collarbone. "Can I help you?"

"I'm trying to find flowers for my granddaughter's dance recital tomorrow morning. Do you mind," she squints at my name tag, "Briony?"

"I'd be happy to." I lead her toward a bouquet of carnations. "Is this what you're looking for?"

"My granddaughter prefers roses."

Me, too. They have a gothic-fantasy vibe. All mist-cloaked castles and ruby lips, the sort of beauty that makes my heart ache. I'd take them all home if I could, but roses are our most expensive flower and are usually sold out by the end of the week.

"Can I show you some of my favorites?" I indicate a few bouquets I made yesterday that incorporate roses with a few unique flowers, like marigolds and pansies. "Do you know her favorite color?"

She gestures to the purple blossoms. The ribbons tied to her purse are those same colors.

"Got it."

I sneak a peek at my phone, but the screen remains black, rather than lighting up the way it would with a new notification.

I show her several bouquets, mostly ones with sage or rosemary to ward against mishaps, but she chooses one with gardenia sprigs.

When I take the bouquet to the back, I peek at my phone again before adding a mix of purple and green ribbons to the existing stem binding. I cut the stems, loop a lavender bow around them, and tie it in a bow.

"What are the ribbons for?" I gesture to the woman's purse as I return to the counter.

"For every recital I've been to."

Sweet.

Moving to the register to finish her purchase, I hesitate.

"They're on me." I pass the bouquet to her.

"Are you sure?"

"Tell your granddaughter congrats on her recital. Tell her a fellow dance enthusiast is cheering for her."

The corners of the older woman's eyes turn up. "Thank you. I see why this place is more crowded when you're here."

I smile at the compliment, but as soon as the older woman walks out the door, I glare at my stupid, motionless cell phone. Its cold, reflective surface could light up with a notification at any moment.

With a glance around the store to make sure I'm not needed, I edge closer to a vase of roses for vibes, letting their energy stir my intent toward him, pull up Teddy's contact and click dial.

The phone rings and I pace in a tight circle. Then—

"Hello?" Teddy's voice.

Someone shouts in the background.

"Hey, Teddy. Been texting you—"

"Coming," Teddy yells back, to his teammate, not me.

I clear my throat.

"Sorry," he says, his voice edged in annoyance. "Haven't checked my messages."

"Where are you?"

"I'm at an away game. Thought I told you that."

"Oh." I stop by the window. "I thought the team got back today."

"Some of them did, but I stayed to hang out with the guys and some fans. Chilling at a motel. Be back to school Monday for sure."

A girl laughs. Another player's girlfriend, maybe? We only broke up a few weeks ago.

"Is that her?" someone calls.

"Briony, you still there?"

"Yeah," I say. "Just wish you'd invited me."

"Why? You don't even like leaving your house."

That's not entirely true.

"I'd have gone if you'd asked."

"Then you would've just been bored and miserable the whole time." He huffs into the phone, "Look, I'm missing out on a game right now, I'll text you tomorrow or something."

More laughing. Someone calls Teddys name.

I grip the edge of a flowerpot until the stand is all but holding me up. "Okay. Text me tomorrow then."

"Bye."

The line goes dead.

I stare at the "call ended" message on my screen, until it darkens to black.

Then I open my phone again. Rather than scroll through our messages to past conversations, my favorite activity when I'm bored, I open my email.

Every year before my birthday, I draft an email to a man my adoptive mom refers to as Professor Reeve, but I've never hit send. I don't need his help, but I want to know him, and I want him to know me. According to my mom, he found me as a toddler and, rather than contact social services, he located the best adoptive parents himself. My mom loves him so much for this that she named me after him, or at least based my name off his. While his first name is Bryan, mine is "Briony."

Professor Bryan Reeve.

Not only is Professor Reeve one of the most prestigious professors at a top English boarding school, but he's also a re-nowned lawyer. It's too coincidental that one of the best lawyers in England "found me" and handled my adoption case. And why choose an American family over a British one?

What if I'm the daughter of a criminal he represented in court? And I needed to disappear? When I was a kid, I used to hope I was the daughter of a princess, but my brothers made fun of me for this theory until I dismissed it.

While the professor connects with my adoptive parents every few years—the most recent call to announce the new boarding school job he was offered a few years ago as well as several awards he received—he never speaks to me.

My finger hovers over the send button, and my lip twinges as I bite down on the soft skin.

In my drafts, I don't ask questions. I don't ask for a response. I just list all the things I've done this year—minus my grades—and then sit on the draft until it curdles like cottage cheese.

Still looking at my phone, I reach for a vase of flowers to refill the water, but my fingers fumble with the edge and knock it over, pouring dirty water onto the tile floor.

My threadbare nerves rattle as I set my phone on the counter and rush to the back room, grab a rag, and hurry past customers to the slip hazard.

I wipe the spill up and turn to the windows with my handy cleaner to spray the ghosts, but the haze is mostly outside the glass, out of reach. Light from lampposts reflect off dark puddles outside.

A car turns off the road, its headlights blinding me from the parking lot as it stops.

The door chimes, and Sadie, my older sister, glides in, her dark hair in loose waves. It air-dries that way. Like she woke up in leather boots and soft pink lipstick and had no need to check the mirror twice.

She left for college a few months ago, but comes home often. Her school is only an hour away.

She frowns from across the counter. "The movie's in ten minutes. Where's your date?"

I give her a hug and hold on for a moment too long. "Good to see you, too."

She pushes me away, hands on my shoulders. "Did you invite anyone?"

I shrug and avoid her eyes. "I'm sorry, I forgot."

Except I didn't, not for a moment.

She surveys me with a knowing expression when I don't respond. "It's Teddy again, isn't it? You didn't invite him, did you?"

I look away.

Two years ago, Teddy called from his friend's phone to ask me out. I didn't think he knew my name. I stuttered several times before saying "yes." He was cute and a member of the basketball team. The day we started dating, I had a swarm of new friends and party invites.

We dated for two years, and he became a comfortable sort of "cool" stamp. Now, I just drift from class to class.

With my rag, I re-wipe the counter while staring at the floor. Sadie picks my phone up and unlocks it—shouldn't have given her the password—and laughs. Then turns her back on me.

I attempt to reach around her and snatch my phone away, but she bounces out of reach. Panic creeps into my voice. "Don't you dare call him."

She laughs again. "Don't worry, he's not worth my time. I'm just looking at this intriguing email you have. Why haven't you sent it?"

I never exited the email I drafted to the professor. "You better not have—"

"Sent." She hands me my phone. "Studying abroad is a great way to move on from past flings and meet new friends, don't you think?" She winks.

No way would she send such a message. And no way would a prestigious English boarding school accept a below average American high school student. I check my sent messages, and any hope I had drops to my toes. She really did send it.

I clutch my phone in a tight fist. "Sadie, what were you thinking? How could you? He hasn't spoken to me once, not ever. And you sent this?"

She edited the email and added to the end: "I'd really, really love a new experience like London. Can I hear more about your school? I'd be the best student," I read aloud. "Seriously, Sadie?" My voice rises as I talk, and Sadie's smile vanishes as fast as a drop of water in the desert sand. "Now he'll never want to talk to me."

Customers in the store turn with wide eyes, but I ignore them.

"I'm sorry, Bree." Sadie bites her lip. "I didn't realize this was such a big deal to you. I'll tell Ben we'll go another night. Maybe he can set you up with someone…" she blanches, as if realizing now isn't the time for that, and scurries to the door. "Never mind. I'll catch you at home." Pausing in the doorway, she says,

"I really am sorry. I just hope you know you deserve better."
Then she closes the door behind her.

As soon as Sadie leaves, I pace around the shop, hovering over customers until they rush their purchases and go. I'm done here; I want to go home. My phone laughs at me from the counter as I draft a follow-up email in my head. I'll explain everything and apologize, but as soon as I abandon my closing duties to type the message out, I can't bring myself to send another email in case I make things worse.

I drive home after my shift ends, knuckles white as I grip the steering wheel. What if Professor Reeve actually responds? I'm not sure I want him to, but if he doesn't, I'll be more than disappointed.

I'll be the best student…I sound like a suck-up.

Lying in bed, my mind won't shut off.

Sadie would say I'm obsessing.

Whatever.

Then comes the ping of a new notification.

CHAPTER TWO

MY NOTIFICATIONS alert me of a new email. My heart hammers at the email bryanreeve@burnleyschool.com; I quickly click to open it. I've waited too long for some form of contact, for some tidbit of the professor's character.

From: Chelsea Craig
To: Briony Delwood
Subject: RE: It's Me…

Briony, this is Headmistress Craig, Professor Reeve's boss at Burnley Boarding School. Professor Reeve is currently out of town, and his assistant forwarded your message to me. I've heard all about you, and I'm so excited that you want to meet Bryan and join us at our school! We have a new programme that opened up, and I think Bryan or I just might be able to get you in. If you don't mind, I'll contact your parents for arrangements. I believe Bryan's assistant has your mum's number listed in his close contacts.

Cheers!

Chelsea Craig
Headmistress, Administration
Burnley Boarding School, UK

I stare at the signature at the bottom. For being a colleague of Reeve's and not Reeve himself, Chelsea Craig sure responded quickly. Especially when Reeve never reached out himself. Perhaps she doesn't know Reeve keeps his distance.

Maybe Reeve won't ever see my embarrassing message? Nah, he probably will.

What if I went to school in England? What if I had the opportunity to research my heritage? That would require me to actually go to England, which is unthinkable when I'm comfortable where I am. Of course, I can't go.

I exit the email and stomp up the stairs to the breakfast table to show my father, who reads what Sadie wrote with a solemn face.

"Sadie sent this?" he asks. His tangled beard, the color of freshly churned dirt, nearly touches his collarbone. He's a big guy, the kind of big that makes other men shrink when he enters a room. But his brown eyes and skin are warm.

"Yes."

"We'll talk about this after you get home from school," he says.

"Why not now?"

My dad hardly needs to look up, though he's sitting and I'm standing. "I said *after*."

"Fine."

I go to school, but Teddy isn't in algebra. I check the cafeteria at lunch. Nothing. At home, I'm the first to the table for dinner.

Family pictures cover the walls, and there's a wood carving of a momma bear.

I tap my fork against the stained wood, its surface rough and pockmarked, just as the last few weeks of my life have been.

My family gathers, and I stare at the email rather than look at Sadie, even as the steam from my bowl of soup ebbs to nothing.

"What's wrong with you?" My brother, Henry, pokes my arm, but I ignore him. He's short, with messy hair that never lays flat, and an annoying smile that never dies.

My older brother, Xander, sits on the other side of Henry and watches me with more interest than I like. Long black hair hides half his face, and his fingers have fresh scabs from too many hours on his guitar, probably to impress girls. He goes to the same college Sadie does and returned with her for a short visit. Something about his roommates expecting him to do his own dishes and finding a pile of dirty pans in his sheets. Guess he needed a break.

I still can't believe Sadie sent that email.

Henry prods harder. "Spacing out again?"

I shove him off. "Stop touching me."

"Leave your sister alone," Mom says in the breezy voice she uses when she's said the same words a thousand times. She has short hair and a long, straight neck that she uses to her advantage when she's angry. Her firm mouth brings severity to every word.

Mom and Dad eat slowly, raising their spoons to their lips and blowing, as if life hadn't tipped on its side. Henry returns to his food and I dig my nails into the wood, waiting.

"Kids, you're free to go," Mom says as she rises to put her bowl in the sink.

I stand so quickly my chair tumbles backward and crashes to the floor. "What about that email?" I point an accusing finger at Sadie. "What about what she did?"

Henry scurries into the living room, probably to wreak havoc in the room my mom just cleaned. I'm glad he's gone.

"I'd like to stay," Xander says, a smirk lurking in his expression.

Dad ignores him and turns to Sadie. "Sadie, I don't know what you were thinking. I think you should apologize."

"I'm sorry, Bree," Sadie says. When she looks at me, her face is downcast, her shoulders slumped in a perfect picture of misery, but it's not enough.

"Why did you send it?" I demand.

"Now, Bree—" Dad begins, but Sadie interrupts.

"It's all right, Dad." She averts her eyes and talks to the floor. "Bree has a right to be mad. It's just that you're always waiting around for someone. It hurts to watch. I just wanted to fix it."

My anger thaws at the sincerity in her voice, and I'm angry at myself for not holding strong.

Sadie picked my outfits when I went to my first dance. Even my first date. The first time Teddy took off to hang out with his friends rather than call me, she told me to hang out at some other boy's house and tell him about it afterward.

This last year, Sadie's smile became fringed with ice when she saw Teddy, though Teddy does his best to charm her. He charms everyone else without effort.

"I'm glad you two have worked things out," Dad says with a smile too broad for my current level of forgiveness.

Xander leans forward as if to remind us of his presence. "If you end up going to your special school, Bree, you'll want to look into the dress code. And you'll need new pants. Jeans are an obvious sign you're American." Xander visited England for a few months after he graduated from high school, and he's overly proud of the fact.

I can't tell if he's teasing, but I take note.

Mom returns to her chair and steeples her fingers beneath her chin, her elbows on the table. "Of course you should meet Bryan. I'm sorry we didn't set something up for you two sooner. Not sure about you going to school there but we could figure out some kind of meet up if you wanted."

The professor has no biological relation to me, but he's the only connection I have to any other life outside Colorado. How could they want me to meet him?

Mom and Dad stand, and Mom squeezes my shoulders before leaving the kitchen.

My cheeks burn.

Sadie waits until they're both gone, with Xander following them out. "Bree?"

I look up.

"I am sorry, really," she says.

I nod, though I wish I could take the email back and pretend none of this happened. Little do I know, solemn dinner conversations are inescapable for one such as me because one week later, Sadie returns home for one last visit before her semester picks up again. Mom sits beside Dad at the head of the table, and dismisses my brothers with a wave of her hand. As I stand to go, she clears her throat. "Briony, Sadie, can you both stay a minute? Dad and I need to talk to you."

Sadie casts me a questioning glance but I shrug.

Mom turns to Dad, and there's something off in her voice, the kind of off rail that sends trains careening over precipices when they've lost hold of the world. "John?"

Dad strokes his chin. "After Sadie sent your email, I got a call from the Headmistress of Burnley Boarding School. She was interested in you, Briony. Excited, I'd say. She didn't know the professor rescued another kid so I guess that means there's somebody else with a similar story."

Professor Reeve found another kid? Too unlikely to be coincidental.

I lean forward, the edge of the table biting into my ribs. If I had names I'd stalk Facebook and Instagram pictures all the way back to the embarrassing albums they posted in junior high, though they likely call it something else in England. "Really?"

"Yes but she didn't give me details. I guess the school is opening a program for students with disabilities and other learning difficulties."

Disabilities?

"ADHD isn't a learning disability."

Mom's frown deepens. "Just listen," she says.

Dad continues. "Bryan's assistant mentioned she could get you into the program if you want to go, bad grades or not, and you'd get to meet the professor. You'll spend a year in the country you're from, and you'd be in a situation to kick your grades up, so you can go to college."

I don't know where to look. I've never heard of anyone I know being sent to boarding school. That's something they do in old classic books, not in real life.

How does a single drafted email come to this?

Even Sadie stares at Dad with wide eyes, as if she didn't quite expect her joke to go this far. Her mouth hangs open, a smudge in her pink lip gloss.

But I still have a choice. They aren't forcing me to go. I simply have to say no.

"What do you think, Briony?" Dad reclines in his chair, his ankles crossed above his muddied boots. "Mom and I already talked, and we've agreed this could be good for you."

Mom grimaces. "Hardly. Your dad had to do some convincing

but I think he's right."

"If the school doesn't see effort on your part," Dad continues, "they'll send you home, so it'll be up to you to make this work."

I study the wood patterns on the table. I have always wanted to go to England; I've always wanted to meet the professor. But I can't leave my home, Sadie, my family, my job, or Teddy. Boarding a plane to another country has a lot of unknowns. I've never flown in a plane.

"I don't want to go."

Sadie's face relaxes.

"But maybe," I add. I'm not sure I want that door to close. Not completely. "I'll…I'll think about it."

CHAPTER THREE

THE OPEN DECISION of going to England paired with Teddy's recent indifference haunts me as I take my math test at school the next day. It takes all my energy to focus on the questions.

Some of my favorite stories originate in England. Every few months, I reread *Jane Eyre* through the night, but it doesn't fill the need to go to England myself. With a struggling lumber business, my family never spends money on travel.

England is much more interesting than math problems.

After what feels like several hours, I hand my test to Mrs. Allred, and she holds up a hand while she scans my answers from behind winged glasses, her hair pulled into a tight bun. I divert my eyes to the organized bookshelves and scrubbed-clean chalkboard behind her desk as she writes a score in red ink and circles it. She writes the score down for her own records and hands me the paper back, but I don't look at the red.

"Thank you," I mutter.

As my teacher's eyes slide away, I toss my test into the trash.

"Briony?"

I cringe at Mrs. Allred's exasperated tone as I turn and meet her eyes, wishing I could escape out the door into the empty hallway.

The eyes of the other students rise. Many desks are empty as most of the students have finished and gone, but heat still creeps up my neck.

I pretend not to notice the attention Mrs. Allred has drawn to me. "Yes?"

Mrs. Allred's gaze slides to my fingers where I fiddle with the chain of my tree pendant necklace. I force myself to stop.

She beckons and turns on a fan, so the room is filled with a subtle whirring noise. My feet are stiff as I force them to move toward her.

"Briony," she begins in a low voice so no one else hears, "if you don't try a little harder, you'll be nothing more than average." She taps her paper where she wrote a "D." "This grade is below average. Is that what you aspire to be?"

At least it's not a failing grade, like my last test. If she expects nothing, she won't be disappointed.

Mrs. Allred waits for my answer, but when none comes, she sighs. "All I'm asking for is a little effort. It won't hurt you to try. You've only got two years to impress colleges. Or maybe you don't care to go to college?"

I don't, but she doesn't need to know that. Working at the flower shop is enough for me, and maybe one day I could own my own. Maybe.

"Yes, of course."

"That's good to hear. I expect to see that reflected on your test scores from now on."

I nod and turn my back on her. She doesn't dismiss me, but she doesn't call me back either. Hurrying down the hall, I find my locker and twist the dial. My fingers remember the code before my brain does. The mechanism clicks, and as it swings open, my books tumble out onto the floor.

The hairs on my neck rise. I flip around and a girl across the hall turns her face away. To her right, a few feet back, a boy does the same. I face my locker again and pick up my books. Sure, the hard covers smacking the floor was loud, but not that loud.

As I swing the metal door shut, Abbey, one of my friends who shares this hour of my schedule, stands behind it. I jump, laughing as my heartbeat settles. "Were you trying to scare me? Cause you succeeded."

She grins, but her smile looks forced, like she's dreading Spanish even more than I am. She's wearing her usual oversized hoodie and beanie, with dangly earrings that sport Teddy's favorite band. "Absolutely, I was. Are you ready?"

"Let's go."

My phone buzzes, and I glance down at a message from Teddy.

Sorry, just been busy. I haven't been avoiding you, promise.

My stomach drops. No mention of getting together. Not even a "see you at lunch."

I tuck my phone into my pocket and sling my backpack over my shoulder.

Abbey follows at my side. "Who's that?" she asks.

"Teddy."

She nods.

More stares stalk our progress down a hallway decorated with only gray walls and cement floors. I used to think people didn't know who I was. Perhaps I imagined it.

"I've caught three people staring. Are they looking at you, Abbey?" I ask. "Did something happen you haven't told me?" I jostle her shoulder, but she doesn't laugh. She's usually more chipper.

"I don't think they're staring," she says, too quickly.

I look sidelong at her, and she avoids my eyes.

As we round the corner, just a hundred feet from Spanish class, Abbey abruptly stops and thrusts out an arm, so I'm forced to stop, too. I follow her gaze, and the top of my ex-boyfriend's messy brown hair sways over everyone else. I smile at Teddy, especially at how tall he is. He used to be shorter than the other kids in our classes, but he shot up his freshman year.

A thin girl with bluish-black hair stands at his side, a few inches away, but close enough to touch him. My heart skips a beat at them standing together. The happiness I felt at seeing him dissipates.

My feet slow.

They aren't holding hands. They aren't even looking at each other, but there's a soft expression on Teddy's face that he used to reserve for me.

Abbey's eyes are wide. "I think we should skip Spanish today," she says in a panicked voice. She looks from one side of the hall to the other.

Teddy leans toward the girl and whispers in her ear. She smiles shyly, her mouth moves, and she steps away to disappear into a classroom.

He didn't kiss her, but acid burns my tongue.

"Briony…" Abbey's hand touches my shoulder, and I brush it off.

My forehead is burning, my cheeks, even my neck. "Just stay away from me."

"I didn't know how to tell you," she says.

Teddy turns and steps back as he sees me. His face pales, and the soft expression dries up. "Briony, what're you doing here?"

Judging by his expression, he one hundred percent has been avoiding me, until now. Must've forgot my Spanish class is only a few doors down the hall.

He walks toward us, his eyes flicking between Abbey's and mine. "I was just walking a friend to class, that's all."

Sure.

He opens his mouth and closes it. "Honestly, I didn't know how to tell you. You're just so nice, and you don't have a lot of friends. I knew you'd take this hard." He holds out a hand. "Forgive me?"

I stare at his open palm, his long fingers. I used to hold those hands between classes. They made existence in high school bearable.

Can we really be friends? I meet his gaze one last time, and the answer stares back in his eyes, blue as forget-me-nots.

And I walk away.

CHAPTER FOUR

I SIT BY MYSELF at lunch the next day. Two tables down, Lynn sits by Teddy. My insides clench as he wraps an arm around her waist and draws her against him. They look good together. Easy.

Eyes settle on my back, and their gazes beat against my skin. I can't eat my lunch at this table every day like I used to. Last year, I sat in this exact spot day after day, and it's only the beginning of the new school year. Teddy knows my habits.

I can't spend all year avoiding him. If I stay, I'll break a little more every day. But there's a solution. I can leave him behind. Far behind. An ocean behind.

So I stand and leave my lunch untouched, hurry out the door onto the grassy hillside. As I stop to breathe, my chest rises and falls like I ran a marathon. The air sticks in my chest as if I not only lost that marathon but tripped over the finish line.

People stop to stare, and I turn my face away. I run down to the parking lot, jump in my car, and rush home. Street signs pass, and I roll the windows down, let the wind whip my face. When I pull into my driveway, I pull myself together.

Mom's in the kitchen—I can spot her from the window, but I

can't get past her to the stairs without her seeing.

That doesn't stop me from rushing in.

Mom chops chicken at the counter, a collection of herb jars lying open in disarray, a simmering crockpot with steam that whistles from the lid. Pots and pans hang above her head from an industrial rack.

"I want to go," I say as I stop in the kitchen entryway. My hands clutch the frame so hard my fingers hurt. I'm breathless from running. I think I'm sweating, too. I'm hot everywhere.

She glances up, and her eyebrows rise. "What?"

"I want to go to England, to that school."

"The boarding school?" Her brows almost disappear into her bangs.

"Yes I want to meet the professor. I'll get good grades, and I'll put in my best effort. When would I leave?"

Mom gathers the chopped meat into a pile. "You do seem eager. Why the change of mind?"

"I thought about it, and I really want to go."

"You'll do your very best?"

"Promise." I'll promise anything to never set foot in my high school again.

"Let me talk to Dad." She sighs and puts the knife down. "I don't like you leaving, but it could be good for you. Dad and I will arrange it. The headmistress thinks this is the perfect program to help you turn around your grades for college."

Mom doesn't know I have no intention of going to college, but now isn't the time. I swallow the guilt from letting her hope, and nod quickly.

"I can pay for the flight," I say.

Finances are tight for my parents, and it's not like I do anything else with the underwhelming savings from my part-time job.

I've worked at the flower shop since early this year. There was always something peaceful about working with the flowers. My boss won't be happy to lose me, but they'll find someone else.

Mom fiddles with her apron strap. "Are you sure?"

"Yes."

She nods and brushes her bangs out of her eyes, while the creases around her mouth deepen, making her look older than her fifty years. "Start thinking of what you need to pack, but don't pack yet. We'll need to find out if they can make the transfer. I'm sure their year has started."

This requires me to leave my family behind, but I can write and talk to them.

I hesitate, but go down to my room and scan the closet for anything I should bring. There are old, dusty USBs—dance tutorials I'll never finish—hidden in a box. And never-worn slippers.

I stuff a duffel with pictures of Sadie and leave the ones of Teddy. Maybe I should tear those up or toss them out, but I'm not ready for that yet. Don't need much. I just need to get out of here.

My skin prickles and I glance over my shoulder as Sadie enters. "You're back again?"

She leans against the wall beneath my bookshelf. "Never could sneak up on you. You've got eyes on the back of your head." Her hair's in a fashion pony without its usual flounce, as she bends over my bag and folds in an ochre beret hat with a few plaid skirts and sweaters alongside my sweatpants. "Heard you were leaving, and I had to say goodbye. Drove back for tonight. I wanted you to know—you leaving home wasn't my intention." Her voice softens. "But I imagine you'll need some new clothes."

"Mom told you?"

She nods.

I walk to her and give her a hug, bury my face in her shoulder and try not to break in half.

"I'm sorry, Bree." She holds me tight. "I love you a million—"

"Chocolate covered strawberries," I finish with a broken laugh.

"You never liked Teddy as much as you think," Sadie says. "Transfer to a different school here. I'm sorry, I know this has been hard for you. I just wish you weren't fleeing the country because of him. You do know that leaving isn't going to fix anything, right?"

"I know." I don't want to fix it. I don't want to deal with it, or him, at all.

Maybe I'm overreacting, but I can't imagine anything worse than another afternoon in the cafeteria across from Teddy and Lynn.

Sadie pushes me back, her hands on my shoulders. "Mom and Dad think this'll be good for you. It would be selfish of me to dissuade you if they're right, so I won't try. But I'm sorry if I had a hand in making you leave. In fact, I'm more than sorry. I'm pretty pissed at myself, to tell you the truth."

I give her the best smile I can muster, though it hurts my cheeks. "Write to me."

"I will." She takes the beret hat back out and slides the band over my hair until it's snug on my head. "This is a good look for you."

CHAPTER FIVE

TWO WEEKS LATER, I'm at the airport. Finding the correct terminal is one thing, but transferring at JFK is a beast. By the time I arrive at Heathrow, I think I finally understand how terminals work. I follow the neon signs, pretending to know where I'm going. The pretending gives me the courage to smile at people as I pass glass windows featuring jeweled purses. The polished floors gleam under incandescent lights.

I take a train marked Burnley School and sit on faded seats, one suitcase balanced on my lap. My heels tap against the floor as I rise on my toes and lower again.

Squished houses and cars with narrow license plates flash past, then trees—plane trees with peeling bark. I've never seen them in person. Willows. Vines gripping old stone walls like claws.

I must have been staring out the window for hours before the train stops, and a bottle rolls across the floor, clinking. A middle-aged woman stares at me across the aisle. Our eyes meet, and a chill chases away my exhilaration. Everyone else is quiet, staring at the ground. Most of them wear jeans, not the stiff dress pants I bought five pairs of.

I'm going to kill Xander.

When a horn blares, everyone stands. The doors squeal open, and I file out after the crowd onto the train platform.

A bitter wind whips through my thin jacket. I pull it tighter around me. In the distance, a spire pierces clouds that thinly veil a timid sky. I drag my suitcases toward it, toward the terraced houses and smoking chimneys surrounding its base.

I've left my mountains for flat grass and the occasional rolling hill. Every plant is so green, so alive. Humidity clings to my clothes, and dew seeps into my fabric shoes. Nothing like the dry freeze of Colorado.

I walk faster, following the curve of the sidewalk. I want to breathe it in and make it all familiar.

The spire grows as I near, revealing a network of stone buildings at its base. A moss-colored river loops around the perimeter, its sluggish flow like a modern moat. Trees dangle lush leaves over a bridge that casts a long reflection.

Unease slithers down my back as a guy in a charcoal hoodie strides toward me, hands shoved in his coat pockets, shoulders hunched. He's tall and solidly built, with copper-auburn waves escaping his hood.

He's big enough to drag me away without effort.

I shouldn't have left the main road. No one would look for me if something happened.

Why cover his face?

I'm being paranoid. Everyone wears hoodies. I force my shoulders to relax.

He doesn't step aside, so I keep my gaze forward and watch him from the corner of my eye.

Then he looks up and smiles—reassuring and warm.

He's young, my age or a year older. His gaze carries a quiet intensity, but his eyes twinkle when he smiles. So familiar, though I've never met him. Maybe he reminds me of my brothers when they tease me. Or some actor I had a crush on.

The edge of a rock catches my foot. I trip. My carry-on tumbles and splits open, and books scatter onto the grass, soaking up water.

The boy crouches, rights the suitcase, and gathers my belongings while I brush off my dress pants. My cheeks burn as he examines a book before tucking it inside. "Your books are ruined," he says in a thick British accent. "It's a shame. I like this one." He points to *Northanger Abbey*.

I'd die happy just to hear him read a few pages aloud.

If Sadie were here, she'd laugh at me for going from terror to infatuation in 3.2 seconds. If this is a trap, I'd walk right into it.

"You've read it?" I take the suitcase handle from him.

"Yeah. It's clever. Everything Austen writes is."

"Oh, wow. I feel the same." I want to say more, but my voice catches. I'm sure all he sees is a lost American with an unmanageable suitcase. "Thanks so much for your help."

His hazel eyes have gold flecks.

"You're welcome. I'm Julian, by the way." He offers his hand.

I shake it, and electricity shoots through me. It's more of a painless, tingling jolt, but I stifle a gasp as I say my name, "Briony Delwood."

Julian's brows pinch. "Can I walk you to wherever you're going?"

"I'm not going far." My voice is still strained. Maybe it's static from the grass or the station. Or nerves. I want to ask if he felt it, too, but that might sound weird.

Julian reaches for the larger suitcase. "May I?"

"Uh, yes. Please."

I step back as he takes the handle of my suitcase and mute

my mother's warning voice about strangers. He's clearly another student here. Refusing his help would be weird.

We continue down the sidewalk side by side, the rumble of the suitcase wheels drowning our footsteps. "Thanks for your help," I say. "Really."

Julian nods. "Where're you from?"

The dress pants were supposed to make me blend in. "Colorado. The accent gave me away, didn't it?"

He grins.

"A little. And—" He points to my dress pants. "You're dressed up for travel."

I look down. "My brother told me everyone here dresses formally. Said jeans would shout 'American!'."

Julian's grin widens, but he doesn't laugh. "I think I'd like your brother."

The suitcase rattles behind him. "Is Colorado closer to California or New York?"

"California. Definitely."

"I'd love to go to California. Bet it's warm where you're from."

I never thought anyone in a place like England would consider my home interesting. "Warm in the summer, sure."

He frowns slightly. "How far is Colorado from California, then?"

"Fourteen hours, maybe?"

His eyes widen. "Not close at all."

I studied English maps and train schedules before coming, and everything did seem a lot closer here.

"It's a long drive, for sure." I've made the drive before. Threw up a bag of licorice in the back seat and haven't eaten it since, but I leave that story out.

A trace of cigarette smoke drifts from groups of students chatting by the roadside. Ahead, a gate towers with spikes of weather-stained stone. We near and the details sharpen: a crest with griffins marking the entrance, a gold clock, and Latin text carved above it.

Cavete virtutem eorum qui nunquam moriuntur.

Julian glances sideways at me. "Burnley's quite different from other schools. One perk is our uniforms are more relaxed, unless you're in Reeve's honorary program. Muted colors. Nothing too short—that sort of thing."

"I read the dress code." I hesitate. "There are houses, right?" I'm not sure how they group girls and boys in their dormitories. "Which are you in?"

"St. James."

I try to hide my disappointment. "I'm in Sharona."

We pass a kid in a hat and sweater, reading under a tree. By the time we reach the gate, the crowd thickens. We enter a courtyard with a statue at the center, and a chapel looms with carvings webbing across its steeples like age-old vines.

Someone bumps my arm, and I stumble into Julian. He steadies me as two more people shove past. I lead him out of the crowd to a patch of grass, so I can fish for my map.

Julian eyes the rumpled page as I tug it out and smooth it.

"Do you need the administration desk?" He points to tall doors with flaking paint. "It's just inside Wilbur Hall, through those doors. Will you be okay from here?"

"Yeah, thanks."

"I've got to work, but I'm sure we'll see each other again. It was very nice to meet you, Briony."

Not just "nice" but "very nice."

"Nice to meet you, too."

"Welcome to Burnley." He waves and leaves for the gate. The

crowd of people part, then engulf him so only the top of his head surfaces.

Without him, I'm swarmed by unfamiliar faces. Voices are louder. Everything towers, casts long shadows.

I shake the feeling and follow a trail of wet footprints into Wilbur Hall. Voices echo against marble. I shrug off my sweater, droplets splattering the floor.

The room smells of polish and old paper. The heavy, carved tables are made from stained wood. Portraits of scholars in matching white wigs, like old women with perms, hang between sconces.

At the far end, a gold plaque reads, "Administration."

Two women stand behind a desk. One smiles and drums her fingers.

"My name's Briony Delwood," I say. "Transfer student from America. Am I in the right place?"

Her eyes brighten. "You are indeed. We've been expecting you."

She takes my papers and hands me a brass key and class schedule. "Down that hall and up the stairs. You're in Birdie's Court."

"Is the headmistress here?" I ask. "I'd love to meet her."

I should thank her for getting me in, but I also want to ask if Bryan Reeve is around. I bite my tongue before vocalizing the last bit. If he wants to meet me, he'll come.

"She's not, but she's excited you're here. Professor Reeve gave her the seats to fill, and you took the last spot."

"Does he know I'm here?"

"I'm sure he does."

My stomach is suddenly queasy as I follow the attendant's directions. Through a library, past more offices, up a set of stairs with polished wood banisters to the third floor of Birdie's Court.

At door sixty-two, I pause, flex my fingers, and unlock it with the key from the attendant. The knob is cool brass. Then I hold my breath and push.

The thick wood creaks as it swings inward. It's heavier than I expected.

A musky smell greets me. River sounds drift through the window. Inside is a small, cozy writing desk, a springy bed wedged into a corner, and a narrow fireplace of soot-hardened stone, framed by peeling wallpaper.

A bed. I haven't slept in almost twenty-four hours.

My eyelids sag like shelves heavy with books. I sigh, drop my suitcases, and collapse on the mattress.

Tap, tap.

I bolt upright. It's barely past midday, but all I want is sleep.

I stand, rub fatigue from my eyes, and open the door to a curvy girl with long lashes, wiry hair the color of burnt oak, and a scatter of acne scars on her cheeks. "Are you Briony?" she asks—definitely not British.

"I am."

She beams and extends a hand. "I'm Noelle. I heard another American was coming. I'm the only one, besides you. From Flori-da." Her gaze flickers past me at the bare room and crumpled bed. "Just got here?"

"I did."

"Well then, I'm officially your first friend." Noelle steps around me into the room, plops onto my bed, and bounces a few times. The decaying wood frame groans. "Mine's stiff as a board. Not all rooms are singles, you know."

I sit on the edge of my desk chair, trying to look relaxed. Like a normal, friendly person. Even if I'm a bit wary of new friends so soon after Teddy and my not-so-great friends at home. "Thanks for coming by."

She smiles like friendship is effortless. "Do you have your class list yet?"

"They gave me an itinerary." I tuck my hands beneath my legs.

I want to know how long she's been here, if she has fun, if the classes keep her up all night studying.

"What classes do you have?"

I hesitate. I haven't looked yet, and I don't want to admit I'm in a special program. "I heard there's a botanical garden," I say instead. "I used to manage a flower shop. Do we go often?"

Her eyes light up. "You can go anytime. I'll take you. You should totally see it."

A smile squishes my cheeks.

"I'd love that."

"I'll put it in my calendar." She reaches into her purse and pulls out her smartphone. "When would you like to go? I can't go tomorrow night. There's a store opening I have to check out. How about after? Monday at 5:30? You'll be out of class by then, right?"

"Yeah, sounds good."

"Can I get your number?" She waits with a finger over her screen.

I recite it, then add hers. Good thing I got an international phone plan.

"I'll see you around," Noelle says, "Cafeteria, library—sit with me anytime."

She stands.

"Of course."

"I'll be looking for you," she says.

When she's gone, I lean against the wall, grinning like an idiot. Maybe this change is not just good, but necessary.

Everything's gone smoother than I dared to hope. Maybe I overthought things—it wouldn't be the first time. My introduction to the professor could go well, too.

Reeve might even answer my questions about my birth parents. I'm old enough now. A couple years from being a legal adult. Would they be ashamed that I only got into Burnley Boarding School with a special program?

I'll just leave that part out.

CHAPTER SIX

I'VE JUST CLAMBERED into bed when another knock shakes the room. My exhausted limbs tense. The knock isn't soft like Noelle's, but hard and urgent enough to rattle my insides.

Wish I had a peephole. I shoot to my feet and swing open the door. A man faces me, pale and trembling, his fury sharp enough to slice the air.

"What are you doing here?" His hands ball into fists.

My stomach drops to the bottom of my chest cavity, where I wish I could curl up and hide.

"What do you mean?"

Though he seems to think he knows me, I don't know him, and I certainly don't know why he's here looking at me as if I did something wrong. He looks too old to be here anyway, at least college age. "I think you're at the wrong door."

A drip of perspiration slides down his face. If his face wasn't so contorted, he might be handsome. "You must leave this place. Now."

"I think you have the wrong room." I try to close the door, but the man grips it tight.

"I have the right room," he says through gritted teeth. "You must leave."

His eyes drop to my neck where my fingers twist the chain of my necklace, and his face droops, leaving behind an exhausted shell of a man. As if the very sight of the silver tree pendant unraveled him. I drop the necklace faster than a burning coal.

He releases the door with one hand and massages his forehead. "I sent you to America for a reason. You shouldn't have come."

Wait… That voice—I've heard it before, on speaker across a crackling phone line.

"Professor Reeve?" I take an involuntary step back. He's far too young to be the man I've heard so much about. The professor would have to be more than twice my age to be old enough to handle my adoption.

"Yes," he says simply, as if his name isn't one I've heard all my life.

I envisioned my first meeting with the professor so differently. An offer to show me around. An embrace, maybe? He might have smiled, at least. Mom and Dad never showed photos of him, and none exist online, though I searched for years.

I imagined a different man, short with spectacles and a long beard. This man is tall and lean with a crisp, fitted suit. His cleanly shaven cleft chin reveals a square jawline, a straight nose, and proud, twisted lips. And wavy, black hair.

Professors shouldn't look like models on a T.V. set, nor should they be college age.

"Why did you come here?" Professor Reeve demands.

I gesture at our surroundings. "For school. Why else do people come here?"

"You could've gone anywhere in America." The color drains from his lips. "Why this school?"

This is a man who calls to check on me every few years. Even if he didn't want me at Burnley Boarding School, he shouldn't be this angry.

I look down at my feet, rather than let him see shame creeping into my face.

"To see the country I'm from," I whisper, instantly wishing I'd said something braver.

"You're serious? This is a vacation for you?"

"I, uh—wanted to meet you." It stings to admit that, but I doubt he'll accept sightseeing as a valid reason.

"Meet me?" he scoffs. "Whatever for?"

I want to slam the door, but I don't. Instead, I look up. He won't get the pleasure of thinking I care. "Fine then," I say, my face growing hot, "I want to know where I come from. That's all."

Reeve rolls his eyes. "You didn't come from anywhere. If you met your parents, you wouldn't see a single resemblance. Their names wouldn't tell you anything you don't already know." He pauses to take a deep breath. "No, there's a better way. It's not what you think. Look, I'll refund your tuition money. I'll buy your plane flight home. I have connections at different schools in America. I'll get you into whatever school you want."

"I just got here."

"You're in danger here. You need to leave."

I haven't seen or met anything to cause me concern, except the professor himself.

"What do you mean, danger?"

Professor Reeve yanks a phone from his pocket and taps the screen. "There are no flights tonight you'll make in time. I'll buy your ticket for first thing tomorrow morning. Be at the airport at six, and I'll send the confirmation email to your mother."

"I'm not going."

"I can force you to leave."

He's right. My brain scrambles for something to cling to. I could throw a fit and destroy my room, except I couldn't force myself to ruin something so beautiful. I could leave a terrible review. Would anyone care?

"Then I'll find a different school in England that'll accept me," I say, "and I'll leak to the press that you kicked out one of your special education students before they could even start, for no reason."

His eyes narrow.

I'm not sure my threat holds weight, especially here in England, but I let my words sit between us, watching his face for how they land.

He keeps his expression neutral.

"Al—" he coughs, "Briony." His voice deepens. "I need you to trust me."

I haven't done a lot in my life to be proud of. I never played sports, never received any plaques at work. But I'm proud of myself for flying to England on my own, for starting at a new school, knowing no one. I wouldn't have considered doing this a few months ago. Now I'm excited to be here. I'm ready. I'm not going home.

"No."

"What do you mean, 'no?'" His eyebrows rise.

I open my mouth, but a weight settles on my chest. Words retreat. What if he's right? I shouldn't have come.

My brain becomes a vacuum, my throat bending to its silence.

Teddy said I'm too nice to be honest with, but I don't want to be nice. Not right now.

Then the words burst out. "Why should I trust you? I don't know you. You've never bothered to speak to me."

"I did," he shoots back. "I kept contact through your mother and planned to visit when you were older, even looked at positions at Colorado Universities, but enough of this. What can I do to convince you to leave? Money for college? For your family?"

I'm angry, I'm tired, but worse, I'm disappointed. It's a disappointment that bleeds through me and makes me wilt, like a cut flower. "You can tell me where I came from and why you want me to leave."

A muscle in his jaw twitches. "I can't do that—"

"Then there's nothing else you can do."

"If you won't talk to me, I'll call your mother."

"Call her then."

The professor lifts his chin and stares down at me. Then he stalks down the hall.

I close the door slowly and lie in bed again. Stare unblinking at the ceiling, my shoes still on.

So, Teddy takes off with someone else, and I decide to flee the country and hope the professor who never bothered to talk to me will be excited to see me? It's laughable.

Unless said danger has something to do with my past, and my parents were criminals after all. The kind with enemies. Then why doesn't Professor Reeve just tell me that?

Or the danger is flunking out of a British school after struggling through my American one, and there's no returning from the double shame.

If I left, it would give the professor what he wants.

I wish I had Sadie with me. There's a seven-hour time difference between Colorado and London, which means it's morning there.

The room feels smaller with every thought.

I snatch up my phone, and the metal edge digs into my ear as it rings.

"Briony? I'm skipping class to talk to you." Sadie's hushed voice is as good as a balm. "Is everything okay? You've only been gone a couple of days. How was your flight? Have you worn those clothes yet? Did you get any compliments?"

The dam holding back tears cracks a little.

"I'm fine," I lie. "But," my voice hitches, "now that I've heard your voice again I miss you too much to stay."

"Briony." This time, Sadie's voice is stern. "You spent thousands of dollars to get out there. You can't turn around and come home. Give it a couple weeks, okay? I doubt you have the money for the flight, and you know Mom and Dad can't afford it."

"You don't understand. I met the professor, and he doesn't want me here. He came to my apartment and told me to go home the moment I arrived."

Static cackles through the other end as Sadie sits in silence. She must think it's bad, too.

"That doesn't make any sense," she says at last.

"I shouldn't have come out here. He doesn't want to get to know me."

"You have no reason to stay, then? Thought you wanted a fresh start."

Julian and Noelle come to mind, but I'm not sure they're enough.

Sadie takes my silence for a response. "So what if the professor's a jerk? You'll barely see him. You need to push through this, Bree. Whatever your professor thinks. He'll love you if he gives you a chance. Don't make a rash decision to leave. Give it a few weeks."

I hesitate, take a deep breath. Maybe she's right. Opposition exists wherever I go.

"I miss you."

"Miss you, too."

I end the call and sprawl on my bed, but now I can't close my eyes. My conversation with Reeve replays in my head, louder each time. He doesn't want me here. He doesn't want me.

What if he comes back and tries to kick me out again?

The light outside dims and muted shouts across the river quiet. A squeak from floorboards out in the hall sends me upright so fast my head spins. No knock comes, and I rub my aching eyes.

I check the door's lock, put a chair under the knob, and stack my suitcases to barricade the door.

My phone taunts me from the desk beside my bed. I could call Noelle, the girl who visited earlier, but I hardly know her. I'd rather die in a hole.

I squeeze my eyes shut, and open them again. My arms are so heavy. So are my legs. My breathing starts to slow, until I'm not in bed anymore. I'm standing alone in a room of stone, a noose dangling from the ceiling above my head. Smoke stings my nostrils, but when my eyes fly open, the burning smell evaporates. Just a dream.

My breaths come in short gasps, as if I've just run the mountain trails behind my home in Colorado with a bear behind me. Except I'm in England, thousands of miles away.

No, I don't want to die in a hole.

I dial Noelle's number, and my finger hovers over the green phone icon.

Just do it.

She acted so friendly. Surely, she wouldn't mind. I hold my breath and hit call. The phone rings.

A sleepy voice answers, the airy lilt Noelle tries so hard to maintain gone. "Hello?"

I almost hang up, but steady my hand. Noelle herself makes this sound so simple.

"Hey, Noelle, this is Briony." My voice quivers. "We met a few hours ago. Would you mind staying with me tonight?" I swallow. "I'd love some girl time, and I could use the company."

Noelle doesn't speak for a long moment. Does she think me childish? I wouldn't blame her. "I'll bring some blankets," she says. "Be over in a few."

I exhale. "Thank you so much. You're the best." Whatever she thinks, she's coming. I won't have to face the night alone.

CHAPTER SEVEN

I LET NOELLE into my room and shut the door behind her. Too bad I don't have chocolate bars to make tonight feel more like a party and less like Noelle babysitting.

She dumps her blankets in a pile on the side of my bed and kneels to arrange them, her hair creating a sheet over the side of her face so I can't read her expression. Or how she feels about staying with me tonight, rather than sleeping in her own bed.

I fold my arms, standing beside my bed rather than sitting on it. "Thanks again for coming."

She flashes a charitable smile. "You're not the first to get homesick on your first night here."

"Did you?"

"No." She arranges her blankets and pats the layers before laying down.

"Oh." I finally allow myself to sit down and look at my hands. "I never asked but what brought you to Burnley?"

She plumps her pillow. "I didn't want to go to the same private school my brother goes to. And I watched this show where a girl goes to a boarding school in England, or at least I think it was

England, and meets hot vampire boys. So, I asked my parents, and they said 'yes.'"

"Have you met vampire boys, then?"

She laughs. "I keep an eye out."

I try to imagine Julian with fangs, but it doesn't suit him. As I pretend to check for vampires under my bed, Noelle laughs again, this time with her head thrown back.

"You joke," she says, "but when the day comes that I finally meet my vampire boy, he'll fall so madly in love, he'll want me around for eternity. And when he bites me and gives me that porcelain skin, I'll have all the other vampire boys chasing after me, and I'll be a heartbreaker. That's the dream."

"That's quite the dream," I say. Heartbreaker instead of heart broken. A nice role reversal. "Breaking hearts and taking names. My boyfriend and I broke up before coming." He went quiet until I got the hint. I tried giving the silence a voice, tried to bring back something that wasn't there. "It's a big part of the reason I came."

"I've never had a serious boyfriend. I'm too picky, but I asked a guy out here a few months ago."

"You asked him out? I'm impressed. I'd never do that."

"Why not?"

Isn't it obvious? Maybe not to her. "Because that takes courage. And confidence. I'd worry I'd get turned down."

"I've been turned down." She shrugs. "Their loss."

The threads of my bedspread are unraveling beneath my fingers. I drop the tassel and tie a knot where the threads have come loose.

"That's brave of you." I fish for something else to talk about. "So, you don't like your brother much?"

She turns over on her blankets so she's facing away. "He's fine."

"One time, my brother hid five alarms in my room that went

off a minute apart. Had me scrambling around in the dark to shut them up."

"Sounds like a brother."

"I didn't pack any jeans either. He told me not to and I was dumb enough to listen."

"We can go to Primark. It's cheap and they'll have jeans. I haven't shopped there myself, but I've heard about it."

And then we could tour the city I've heard so much about, the very streets where Professor Reeve found me. "We can grab food, too."

"Unless you like Thai or Indian food, food's mediocre. Makes me miss the restaurants my parents used to take me to. We went out all the time. Mostly to meet people. Big names, usually."

"What about the bread, cheese, and chocolate? I've heard the yogurt is good, too." I strain to remember what else my brother raved about. That might have been it.

"They're fine. But my parents imported better stuff at home."

"Oh?"

My siblings and I ate squished peanut butter sandwiches my mother hauled around. There were six of us.

"Sounds incredible," I say.

"Connections are important."

"I'm not a big name, but I hope it's worth you coming here tonight."

"Of course, it is. I got to know you so much better. But you never told me, what fictional species is your dream boyfriend?"

I picture Julian. A human? But that's not what she's looking for. "A leprechaun. Because they're short, chubby, and green."

Tears spring to Noelle's eyes as she laughs again. "Gold digger."

"Send the money. Postmarked to my address, please." I chuckle into my hand. "Don't think I could actually do that, even to a leprechaun."

Noelle snorts. "Don't, they wouldn't feel bad for us."

There's a bitter note in her voice that chips at my smile.

"Did anything happen with the boy you asked out?" I ask.

"Not really. I don't have the best dating history, but he seemed a decent choice. Don't think he likes Americans so it didn't work out." She shrugs.

I let the conversation fall to a comfortable silence and lay back on the bed. Noelle shifts under her blankets.

"What happened to your boyfriend?" she asks.

I flinch. "Mine?"

"Your ex, yes. Unless you'd rather not discuss it."

She did so I guess I can, too.

"We dated a long time." I falter, but as I start again, my voice gains strength. "We drifted apart, I guess. He stopped calling. Weeks would pass where I wouldn't see him. I'd text him, and he wouldn't respond. Figured he'd eventually tell me what was bothering him. Thought it had nothing to do with me and something to do with things going on at home. Truth was…he didn't care anymore."

She pulls her blanket to her chin. "You'd think when they got to know you, they'd like you more, not less. You love the people you're familiar with and comfortable around. But it doesn't work that way."

She said she hasn't dated much, but this boxes up my experiences in reinforced steel packaging.

"Have you had that happen?" I ask.

"I've had everything happen." She sighs. "But yes, we move on and get over these things, but I do wish…" She pauses and takes a deep breath. "I know it's terrible, but I hope that one day they regret not liking me. When that day comes, I'll be more than good enough, and it'll be too late."

Sometimes it's nice to be chosen, rather than left behind.

Noelle turns over in bed. "I'm tired," she says. "Let's call it a night."

I fold my arms beneath my neck, staring up at the yellowed paint on the ceiling. "Thanks again, Noelle, for making me feel so welcome here."

"Of course." Her pillow muffles her voice, and I smile.

I'm oceans away from Teddy.

But then there's Reeve scowling from the darkness.

I fall into a fitful sleep, my dreams a mix of past high school drama and boarding school professors with red report cards. The low murmur of voices outside my door kickstarts my heart, but they're young girls, giggling about something. Girls who probably don't even know my name.

Then, the sun creeps into the sky, highlighting spider webs outside my window.

The tranquility won't last, not when Reeve comes again. But Noelle and I are behind a locked door.

My eyes, heavy as a thick blanket, close.

Julian's sitting beside me, eating lunch. He tells me we have the same classes.

"I'm here to leave it all behind," I tell him. To become someone new.

He leans toward me, whispers in my ear, "Me, too."

Bang, bang.

The door shakes, and I lurch to my feet, my bedspread falling to the floor in a puddle.

CHAPTER EIGHT

✦ • ✦

"WHAT THE——" The floor groans as Noelle rolls over. "Who is that?"

The sharp thuds come again.

"Don't know."

But I think I do.

Panic creeps in as I straighten my pajamas and crack the door open. Professor Reeve stands on the threshold, a woman beside him. The woman wears baggy pants with a loose t-shirt, her hair twisted into a tight bun, her expression both confused and annoyed.

I force my face smooth. "Yes?"

The woman smooths her shirt. She must have slept in it. "Hello, Briony, I'm your superintendent. Professor Reeve said you've been told to leave the school. I must ask that you pack your things and vacate at once."

The pounding of my heart almost drowns out her words.

"On what premise? I've done nothing wrong."

"I asked her to go." Professor Reeve gives me a hard look. "That's reason enough."

The woman continues, voice weary. "Professor Reeve has asked you to leave, Briony."

"I'm not going." There has to be another threat I can make, even if it means going to Chelsea Craig, the headmistress, directly. "If you force me from this room, I'll stay with someone else." I open the door a little wider, so Reeve can see Noelle sitting on her blankets with the covers pulled to her chin. "You can't kick me off campus without reason. You're not the headmaster of this school."

Reeve's eyes narrow as the superintendent glances between us.

"You can go," Reeve says to the superintendent. "I'll speak to Miss Delwood in private."

Noelle shifts on her blanket pile, and the professor's eyes flick to her. "Who are you?"

"Noelle," she says in a small voice.

"Return to your dorm."

Noelle stands and edges out the door, leaving her blankets behind. I can't expect Noelle to stay, not after the professor gave such a direct request. But the bravery I mustered knowing she was behind me deflates as she turns the corner.

I clench my fists at my sides.

"Come with me," Reeve says as soon as Noelle's gone.

So he can dump my body in a dumpster?

"No, thank you."

Reeve takes a step closer. Too close. His eyes bore into mine.

I take a step back, but his mouth moves, and my feet freeze in place. Words tickle my ears, but I don't understand them. All I can see are his eyes, the pupils widening until I'm enveloped in soft darkness. My shoulders relax, then my back and legs.

I blink, and there are walls around me, blurring into people moving on my left and right. A car door slams shut. Buses pass, then hedges, a parking lot, marble floors, a lineup of suitcases, then red seats. Chiming speakers, bright and two-toned, as an announcement crackles through. But I might as well have cotton in my ears.

My arm lifts a piece of paper, and a woman accepts it.

"Welcome aboard."

The woman wears a neck scarf tied in a bow, pearl earrings, hair smoothed back. I walk down a hallway, and people pass by. Posters of planes hang on the wall. I slow as an attendant stops in front of me. "Excuse me, miss, the plane is about to depart. You need to get on and find your seat."

"Plane?"

My brain pounds, and the world whirls around me.

"Yes, you need to board your flight."

I inhale, and memories from this morning sharpen. Professor Reeve's livid glare is stamped behind my eyelids. "I'm not supposed to be here," I say slowly. Professor Reeve came to my room, and now I'm at an airport?

I'm at an airport...

"What did you say?" the attendant asks.

"How did I get here?" I struggle to keep the anger out of my voice.

He wouldn't have drugged me...would he?

The attendant cocks her head. "You walked in a few minutes ago. Are you okay, miss?"

This has gone too far.

"Your boyfriend asked me to escort you through security and to your seat."

"Who?"

The attendant gives me a concerned look. "He said he was your boyfriend."

Gross! "Is he still out there?"

"Do you need him?"

"No, I'd just like to know if he's there."

The attendant shrugs. "He said he'd wait until the plane takes off if you need anything. He's just outside security."

My head hurts, but I push the pain off and lower my voice. "Please, ma'am, help me? I can't board this plane. I just started school here, and he's trying to force me to leave." If the attendant can get me out of the airport without Reeve seeing, he won't know I didn't board. He'll find out eventually, but I can deal with that when the time comes. By then, I'll have had enough time to reach out to the headmistress.

The attendant's lips purse. "I suppose I can't force you, and we have a few on standby that would love your seat. What would you like me to do?"

"Tell me where to exit the airport, somewhere he won't see."

Two more attendants enter a side door and collapse strollers. The attendant glances over her shoulder at them. "Let me talk to my coworkers about this. I'll be right back."

I give her my best tight-lipped smile. "Thank you."

The attendant stops her coworkers with a wave of her hand. As she approaches them, the female attendant glances sideways at me while the other purses his lips.

My head pounds, and the tension in my neck moves into my shoulders as neither attendant responds to the first. Then one nods, and the other opens her mouth, though I'm too far to hear what she says.

Pointing somewhere to my right, the male attendant motions like he's saying to take me back. To Professor Reeve?

The tree pendant on my necklace digs into my skin as I squeeze it.

I want to stay so bad that it hurts. Noelle was so kind and welcoming, Julian, too. But it's not just that. This is where I need to be. I feel it in the weight of my necklace, in the way my skin soaks up the moisture in the air.

Inclining her head, the first attendant turns toward me and beckons me to follow. "This way. I'll take you past security where he won't see us. Just stay behind me."

"Thank you, thank you." I hurry after her, dragging my suitcases behind me.

She takes me down the gangway, and we re-enter the main building. Signs speckle the walls as polished floors reflect them. Suitcases roll. Cell phones flash.

The attendant leads me through a side door. "He's over there." She indicates the front of the security line with a nod of her head. "So don't go that way." Then she points overhead. "If you follow those signs, you should be able to find train stations, buses, or whatever else you need."

"Thanks again."

She nods. "Good luck."

I follow the signs but don't breathe easy until I've squeezed onto a train. The doors beep as they close, and I find my seat. The train slides from the platform and I lean my head against a hand-rail.

That really just happened. And despite everything, I'm still here.

After another exhausting series of trains to Burnley School, I call Noelle. My cell phone buzzes against my ear as I drop my suitcase beside my bed and run a finger along the intricate designs carved into my writing desk.

It's like I'm a reflection of myself watching my life unfold, waiting for the film to run out.

"What happened?" she demands the moment she picks up.

My hands shake and I can't sit down, so I pace from the fireplace to the window. "He tried to force me to leave, but I'm back. I'm not going anywhere."

"So, you're in your room? Stay there. I'm coming over."

"Okay," I say.

Within minutes, Noelle walks into my little room without knocking. Just like the first time. "You have to tell me everything."

I explain it to her, ending with my train ride back. "I'm so tired. I don't even know if I trust myself to remember. Half of it's a blur."

She drums her fingers on my desk. "And you still want to stay? Why?"

"Why does anyone want to stay?"

She gives me a disbelieving look. Maybe most people don't care to stay. Or are here because their parents and grandparents went here.

For her, staying is escaping her brother. Or at least, it seemed that way when she talked about it. Me? I left because of Teddy, but I'm staying for me.

"Fine," I say. "I just really like it here. I like you, this room, everything."

Noelle drops herself, once again, onto my bed, as if my admission reestablishes our familiarity. "How do you know Professor Reeve?"

"He knows my parents."

Her eyes track the path my feet carve into the chipping tile. "Really? All the way out in Colorado?"

"Yep."

"Are your parents rich?"

Reeve paid for my adoption because my parents couldn't afford it, or at least that's what they told me. "No, why?"

Noelle plays with her sleeve. "He's the jewel professor at one of the top boarding schools in the country, and a renowned lawyer. So yeah, he knows everyone worth knowing."

"Guess he knows people not worth knowing, too."

"Then why does he hate you so much?"

Her words make me pause.

"He said he means to protect me."

She arches an eyebrow. "From what? Overeager boys?"

He never explained anything beyond the "danger" part.

"Vampiric schoolboys?"

Noelle chuckles, until her expression turns thoughtful.

"I've seen Reeve around school," she says, "but I've never spoken to him face-to-face. He keeps to himself and his honor students. The headmistress lets him do whatever he wants. I never expected to have such an…interesting experience with him."

That makes two of us.

I turn to the window. The river weaves through the grass like a molten snake while giant chestnut trees spread scraggly fingers over the water. Clouds cast long shadows and wring life from lush colors. "I didn't expect to meet him that way, either."

The floor creaks as Noelle stands and bends to pick up her blankets. "I can't believe he bought you a flight home. That's insane." She shakes her head. "I'm heading to bed. Thanks for my blankets."

"You don't want to stay?" If Professor Reeve returns, I'll be alone.

"Uh—" She folds her blankets. "Not really. I didn't sleep well last night, and I have class tomorrow."

I bend to help her and her eyes flick to the scars on my wrist, a question in her eyes.

White scars, like veins, spider across my wrist, and I pull my sleeve to hide them. I've had teachers invite my parents to private conferences to express their concerns, but I've had these scars since I was found. The marks have faded, and people rarely notice them anymore, but when they do, the conversation is always awkward.

Teddy asked me about them once and never brought them up again. Though I suspect he paid attention in case they got worse.

I give my typical answer. "Telangiectasia—that's what my doctor called it. A vein issue." Maybe I'll buy a few rope bracelets to hide them better.

Noelle nods, but her brows remain furrowed.

I gather the rest of her blankets and pass them over. "See you at breakfast."

"See you."

Noelle hauls her blankets down the narrow hall, the smell of fresh polish on the floors, alongside a clinging dampness that I suspect never fades.

Professor Reeve thinks I left, so he shouldn't come tonight. If he does, I won't answer the door, but I can't ignore this forever. There's only one thing to do. Sitting down at my desk, I draft a quick email to Chelsea, the headmistress.

She might side with me over Reeve. She was the one to get me in, after all.

Hi Chelsea,
This is Briony again. I just arrived at school, and Professor Reeve tried to force me to leave...

I backspace every word until the greeting.

I arrived at school today and have every expectation of loving it here and doing well in my program. My only concern is that Professor Reeve doesn't seem to be excited about my arrival. I hope you know that I intend to be a contribution to the school, and I hope you'll explain this to him as well.

—Briony.

I hesitate for only a moment before sending the email, and Chelsea's response comes within the hour.

Briony, I assure you Professor Reeve is very excited about your arrival and has every hope you'll be an asset to our programme. There's no need to worry.

Chelsea Craig
Headmistress, Administration
Burnley Boarding School, UK

I scan her words again and again. Does this mean she spoke to him? I'm not sure, but at least the headmistress is aware and can intervene. Whether or not she will is a different story.

No incidents occur that night, so when the sun brightens the sky the next morning, I meet Noelle in the great hall for food, ready to walk confidently down the tables where not a single face resembles Professor Reeve. However, what I actually do is creep like a spider down the tables and double-check each face to make sure Reeve isn't among my peers.

The cafeteria is more like a cathedral, with oak beams, tall, arched windows, and half-burnt candles. Just not as quiet as one, not with the combined conversations of dozens of students.

Noelle spoons food onto her plate as I slither into the chair beside her. "You can stay with me if Professor Reeve is a jerk again."

I snatch a slice of toast, take a few bites, and eye the crowd. "He can yell all he wants. It's whatever."

"I'm sorry you didn't have more time to tour the school before class."

I drop my toast onto my tray. "Yeah. Me, too." I hoped to have a day or two of the weekend to tour the place, especially the gardens. Instead, I sat in cars and trains.

"We'll make up for it this week, don't worry," she says.

I force a smile as she digs into a pile of yogurt on her plate.

She swallows, gives me an encouraging grin. "I have to go to class, but I'll see you later?"

"Sure, thanks."

Noelle stands and a passing boy smacks the back of her head. He's in all black, with a thin tie and polished boots, his face long and thin, cheekbones razor sharp. "Hey, Ramen hair, did you brush this morning? Can't tell." He and his friends laugh, and the group of them leave.

At least her hair isn't slick enough to fry chips.

I should have said it, but I sit frozen.

Noelle's eyes are shining, but her cheeks are dry.

"Noelle, are you okay?"

"I'm fine." She hurries off, smoothing her tresses as she goes.

My fingers are stiff as I clear my plate. I dump my leftovers in a garbage can and tug a map from my pocket to locate my first class. If only I could resurrect the excitement I had when I first arrived, but I move slowly out the door and across a courtyard to a dull, red-brick building that stands out like a bruise against the fabulous architecture of Burnley School.

I speed up a little, reach for the doors, push them open.

There are a few students in the hallway, but none have Professor Reeve's sleek black hair. The classroom door stands half-open. I peer inside. The room is a wide half circle with rows of chairs and a long, thin desk that mirrors the shape of the room. There's a vacant seat at the far end, probably where the professor sits.

I shake out my trembling hands and move forward. No one gives me a second glance as I sink onto a plastic chair, and I'm grateful for it.

There are quite a few people in the room. I scan each of their faces, but their life struggles aren't in the shapes of their noses or the thickness of their eyebrows.

The teacher enters from a side door. Her brittle brown hair has streaks of gray, woven into a thick, loose braid. She faces us, and smiles. Crow's feet deepen at the sides of rich amber eyes. She seems nice. So long as she doesn't make me feel special in a way I don't want to be.

"Welcome to your British studies class. Here we learn about the history of our great country." Her eyes find me, and gleam.

She turns and writes on the board. Two dark holes appear in her graying hair, and the curves and craters become the glaring features of Professor Reeve. Round, black pupils constrict, and a voice whispers, "Why are you here?"

As I force myself to blink, the vision of Professor Reeve vanishes.

I look around at the other students, but they're focused on the professor now talking about hunter-gatherers and Germanic tribes.

I can't decide if I'm going crazy or if Reeve is literally haunting me.

The teacher turns to face us. "Does anyone know the answer?" She shakes the stick of chalk in her hand, but I don't remember the question.

I've never hallucinated before. I used to have nightmares about suffocating and fires. In fact, I've been terrified of small rooms, flames, and being followed my entire life, but I've never seen a dream or nightmare so clearly.

A bead of sweat trickles between my shoulder blades.

I shrug my shoulders, but the feeling lingers.

Papers ruffle as the students around me bow to retrieve notepads from their backpacks. They open them and scribble notes, so I do the same, writing as fast as my fingers can go. So, if my brain doesn't pick up on the words, at least my notes record everything.

The girl in front of me writes a few lines and draws pictures. Little flowers growing over stylized block letters. Fairies leaping from one letter to the next with sharp little features and detailed wings. Like the fairy garden figurines we sold at the flower shop.

The grandma who bought flowers at the shop before Sadie came…did her dancer like her flowers?

The boy on my left coughs into his hand, and I jump.

Gripping my pen tight, I hurry to scribble the last few words the teacher spoke. It'll make sense when I review my notes later, I hope.

Then I bite my tongue to stay on task and keep writing.

Class ends, and I stroll down the sidewalk to my dormitory in Birdie's Court. I have thorough notes, so I should be prepared for the next class. And I haven't seen Reeve yet, which hopefully means the Headmistress talked to him and I won't have any more issues with him going forward.

My phone flashes with a notification.

Noelle: Are we still going to the gardens tomorrow?

Before Professor Reeve ruined every waking moment, I looked forward to going. Now I've all but forgotten. I hurry to type out a "yes," but as I look up, the bottom of my stomach plummets.

Professor Reeve stands across the lawn, eyes narrowed beneath the brim of his fedora.

My heart sticks between beats. I hoped to avoid him for a few days, but at least I planned what to say.

He has no business kidnapping people. I ought to report him to the authorities. He's a Class A jerk.

I can do this. I can confront him. I can be mature.

He shakes his head slowly, lips pressed into a firm line, eyes never deviating from my face.

I open my mouth…and run.

CHAPTER NINE

I N MY ROOM, I swap out my ugly dress pants for one of
Sadie's plaid midi skirts, add the slouchy beret, and stuff a rain
jacket in my purse. Noelle should arrive to take me to the Botanic
Gardens any minute.

No knock comes, so I perch on my bed and open *Northanger
Abbey*, the book that fell in the mud when I met Julian. I read a
whole page, but the words don't stick as my attention continues to
drift towards the door.

Then the anticipated knock comes. Not loud like Reeve's, but
soft and singsong-y. I leap to my feet and swing it open. Noelle's
hair hangs thicker than the day before, longer. The dark color
shines as rich as melted chocolate. She beams at me. "Excited?"

"Did you dye your hair? It looks good."

"No, I went to that new store on Mill Road, Mystic Cosmetics.
Didn't try the shampoo until today though—like an hour ago.
Their formulas are like magic. I'm not sure how it all works, some-
thing to do with collagen." She combs her hair with her fingers.
"They're a big brand in the states, started on the East Coast. Or
maybe it was France, I dunno."

I close the door behind her.

While I don't frequent cosmetics stores, I love fancy soap bars with bits of not-soap floating inside. Especially when they're flowers.

"A decent hair dye would go a long way with you. I'll take you there," she says. "I like your hat though."

Mousy ash hair is what I get for buying cheap drugstore shampoo.

Noelle talks about the different products Mystic Cosmetics sells while we walk out Burnley gate to the closest bus stop. Red and orange leaves have fallen into the road's craters, last night's rain making them shimmer against the black asphalt.

A double-decker rolls to a stop, two doors squealing open.

It looks like a regular bus, but with a spiral staircase that leads to a second floor. A few students sit at the far end, backpacks on their laps. None look familiar.

The bus moves as we sit down, and the driver pulls into traffic on what I still consider as the wrong side of the road. My heart does a somersault, but no one else moves. Eventually, I'll get used to the difference—I hope.

Traffic rolls in the direction the bus moves, students biking alongside us.

My teetering heart steadies as Noelle rummages through her purse for her lip gloss, and I force myself to look out the window, past the cars. There's an inn on the corner, with flowerboxes beneath the windows, and wooden tables holding collapsed umbrellas.

What kind of flowers though? They're white, with tiny petals. Pansies?

"Briony, are you listening?"

I jerk at my name.

"Did you hear what I said?" She crosses her arms as I scramble for a way to pretend I hadn't accidentally tuned her out.

"Sorry, I got distracted."

Noelle sniffs. "There are two parts to the Gardens," she says. Very slowly. "The outdoor gardens and the indoor. I thought we could tour both."

"I'd love that."

The bus sways as it stops in front of a glass greenhouse framed by black weathered iron. So much glass that it's a wonder the building stands without additional reinforcement. Some panes are cracked, others fogged, with climbing vines and trees and foliage at the base.

Inside, we enter a fresh, humid rainforest that immediately opens my lungs, and a smile tugs at my lips. What I'd give to take this place home with me.

Noelle drags me toward the first exhibit where a sign says, *Rotheca myricoides*. It's native to Uganda.

"The purple leaves are my favorite," she says.

A smooth, plastic sign illustrates the flower in its natural habitat. I snap a photo with my phone. The pictures it takes are small and pixelated, but it's better than nothing.

"It's beautiful."

"Do you have a favorite flower?" she asks.

"Roses."

"Any particular reason?"

I raise my shoulders. "They're pretty." Dark and creepy in some settings, thoughtful with a sense of longing in another. Romantic.

"If you like thorns," she adds.

"What?" I strain to remember what I said.

"Roses. They have thorns." Noelle faces the purple flower again.

Not completely harmless then. "Right. I just like the look of them."

She motions me to the next garden, and I follow her to a fresh array of plants and flowers, more tropical than the last.

One of them is labeled as the "titan arum flower." A bloom whose tallest petal stands a half foot shorter than me. Must be over five feet tall. It reeks, too. Something like rotting flesh that leaves a nasty taste in my mouth.

Noelle chuckles. "Prettier than it smells." She scans the other greenery. "Want to try the outdoor gardens?"

"Do you really need to ask?"

She laughs as I follow her out glass doors to grounds filled with winding gravel paths and old stone steps softened with moss. There's even a pond lined with white foxgloves.

We follow a line of boxwood hedges trimmed into perfect squares and circles, down to a garden called "The Scented Garden," as indicated by a quaint wooden sign. The whole place is crammed with florals that shame even the most expensive perfume companies. Pink petals with purple veins. Welcoming yellow bell flowers. Allamanda? I can't be sure.

"There's a bench over here somewhere," Noelle says. "I wouldn't mind sitting down for a minute."

We leave the pond behind, and approach a willow tree, its knobby trunk thick enough to hug without touching fingertips. At the base is a pot of ghost orchids. Pure white, almost translucent petals that glow in the darkness. An incredibly rare flower.

"I can't believe they have these here." I stop to smell them, and to touch their delicate, spidery petals. Magical.

"Alright, come on," Noelle says with a touch of impatience. "We're getting close."

I straighten with a sigh and follow.

"Just around this—" Her voice dies.

Julian, the guy I met walking through Burnley's gate for the first time, inhabits the cozy bench Noelle described, a thick book in his hands. Loose strands of untidy hair hang over his forehead, and the sleeves of his cardigan are rolled up. His eyes dart across the pages, and his brows knit together, a question squished between them. With his left hand, he twists a silver chain around his neck. Unlike my necklace, it's thick, tarnished and weathered.

I falter, too, heat springing up my neck as I fix my hat and smooth my hair.

"The gardens are meant to be quiet," he says without looking up. His tone is polite, not rude. But also disinterested.

"Then why're you talking?" I ask.

He looks up. "That you, Briony?" he asks, tucking his chain inside his shirt.

"Yeah. Me and Noelle."

Noelle's face is pale, but she shakes herself. "Of course, you two know each other."

Noelle surveys the gardens for any other benches. "Come on, Briony. Avoid him. We'll find some place else to sit."

When I don't move, she glances between us and rolls her eyes. "I think I'll just go to the bathroom for a minute. I get the feeling I'm not wanted."

"What do you mean?" I try to reach for her, to make her explain herself, but she stalks off.

"Toilet's the other way," Julian says, but too late. She's either too far to hear, or she doesn't want to listen.

"She'll be fine, I think," I manage to say.

He slides down the bench and pats the empty space beside him. "Sit by me?" His book is on his other side, hidden from view.

I sit and adjust my skirt. "What're you reading?"

He hesitates but flips the book over, so the title faces up. *The*

Holy Bible. King James Version. Then he looks at me and waits.

I bite my lip. "This is how you relax?"

The twinkle in his eye flickers out, and his goes rigid. "Some people get their enlightenment from scripture. Can't knock that."

"That's not what I meant," I say, sobering quickly. "Just didn't expect it, that's all."

His shoulders ease, but only a little. "What did you expect?"

"Sherlock Holmes, maybe?"

He laughs and I laugh with him. "I'll have you know—Sherlock is one of my favorites."

"He's a proper icon, for sure." He pauses. "Been enjoying yourself? The first few days, and all."

"They haven't made me stand on a stool with a sign yet." I chuckle, but his brow scrunches. "Like Lowood, Jane Eyre's boarding school." Clearly not my best joke. "Sorry, it's not funny if you don't get the reference."

Recognition lights his eyes. "Is that what you were expecting?"

"No, not really." I need a reset button. "It's not so bad here," I say at last. "But there was this creeper who snuck up on me my first day."

Julian's eyebrows shoot up on his forehead. "It was the hoodie, wasn't it?"

"Possibly."

He laughs. "I'll never creep again." The hand closest to his Bible twitches.

"What part are you reading?" I ask.

His smile stills. "Nothing exceptional." And awkwardness snaps back like a rubber band. "What brought you to the gardens?"

"I asked Noelle to show them to me."

He drags his fingers across his book's leather cover, his name inscribed in the bottom corner. Then he picks the Bible up and flips it over. "I'm reading about Solomon. Something about having his brother killed."

"Yeah?"

"There's some odd stuff in here. Decent bits as well, though."

I chuckle. "Think I remember asking my dad questions about that." I remember the night well. My dad sat on his recliner by the TV, and my mom scolded him for the mud on his shoes. And I pushed his old Bible onto his lap. *It was a different time,* he'd said. "Dad's a Christian, too."

"Are you?"

I gesture to the plants surrounding us. "This is my religion if I were to have one. Connection. Harmony. Growing roots to draw water, to catch the sun. There's a certain magic in it."

He leans back against the bench, grinning. "How old are you?"

"Old enough to drive and young enough to still get harassed by my brothers."

This time, he laughs, and the smile lines linger, the twinkle in his eye returning to half-mast.

"Ever worry you've spent your whole life working for something, believing in something, that was wrong?" he asks.

Usually, I'm the one overthinking things.

"How old are you?"

He laughs again. "Touché." After a pause, he adds, "Hope I'm not boring you."

"You're not," I say.

"Just feels like I know you already." He squeezes his copy of The Bible, but then his eyes dart to the far end of the garden path as Noelle returns from the bathroom. She's so quiet, I'm not sure how he noticed.

She stops a few feet away. "Glad you two are such good friends," she says. My face warms as Noelle hugs her purse to her side. "Well, let's go, Briony. I'm ready. Nice to see you, Julian." Her voice is cold.

I'll have to ask her why later.

Julian inclines his head.

Noelle clutches my arm and I allow her to drag me down the walk, glancing just once over my shoulder for one last glimpse of Julian. He's still sitting on the bench, Bible on his lap, but he has his necklace out again, and he's twisting it absentmindedly. It's an old cross, thick, with engravings that I can't make out. Definitely not a vampire.

"If you want to avoid Professor Reeve, you'll want to avoid Julian, too. Julian's in that exclusive program of his," Noelle huffs. "Besides, there are lots of hotties. Don't sell yourself short."

Reeve and Julian are two completely different people.

"You don't like him." More a statement than a question.

"He's fine, I guess." But she doesn't look at me as she says it.

She pushes her way out the glass doors. "They all know each other. I heard Reeve made a special request to get Julian in."

A special request? "Huh. He certainly didn't do that for me."

"No." Noelle smiles a little. "But at least he isn't still trying to force you to leave the school."

We walk to the bus station, a small bench with a glass overhang and crooked bus sign with the schedules. Noelle tugs at her hair as she studies it. "Fifteen minutes till the next one." She turns to me. "No time tonight—I think the store closes soon. But do you still want to go to Mystic Cosmetics? I'll introduce you to Jane and Ellen."

"Sure. Remind me who Jane and Ellen are?" I'd go see the store if only to understand why her eyes light up every time she mentions it.

Noelle puts her back to the sign and leans against it. "The owners. There's a tonic for weight loss I'd like to try, but it's expensive. And I heard they have stuff for acne, too."

"I have a sister who had acne," I say. "It took time for hers to clear up, but it did, and the treatment was affordable. I can call and ask her about it if you'd like?"

"No, thanks. I'll try the tonic. Everything at the cosmetics store works. And not only does it work, it works in seconds. What're your plans for next week? We'll plan a day to go. This Saturday I have a group project I can't miss, and I'm meeting a friend for lunch."

"Next week? Let's see. I think I'll go to class, eat some food, sleep a little, and do some extra important walking around my bedroom."

Noelle scrunches her nose. "Sounds busy. Think you can squeeze me in?"

I give her a teasing sigh. "Guess so."

I'll clear my schedule for anyone who'll keep me company.

"Good. Let's go to Mystic Cosmetics and watch a movie afterward. Make a night out of it."

Air hisses from the brakes as the bus lurches to a stop on the side of the road. We climb aboard and find our seats.

Noelle asks, "You're thinking about Julian, aren't you?"

"What? No." But I spoke too quickly.

"He's a bit weird, but if you like weird, I know a close friend of his."

"I thought you weren't a fan of Julian."

She picks at her nails. "I told you I asked a guy out. That was Julian. He turned me down, but I've thought about it, and just because things didn't work between us, doesn't mean they can't or shouldn't work out for you. I can get over the awkwardness of it."

But can I? There's probably a friend code I'm breaking somewhere.

"Um…that's nice of you. But are you sure?"

"I'm sure. So, you want me to set it up?"

If she's willing. "Yeah," I say. "Thanks."

She half-smiles, and I have the oddest feeling that I shouldn't have accepted.

We return to Birdie's Court, and I climb the stairs to my room, waving goodbye to Noelle as I open my door. Then I check my email for any messages from home. A new message flashes on my screen. I click, and a single sentence from Professor Reeve greets me.

You should have gone home.

CHAPTER TEN

"**B**RIONY? I GOT A VOICE message from Professor Reeve about you coming home. What happened? Please call me when you get this. We're worried."

Stop. I cut off my mom's voice with the push of a button. I don't have it in me to tell her the professor wants nothing to do with me. I avoided the topic with Sadie, too.

I drop my phone, let it bounce on my bedsheets, and pack my backpack. My morning class is in one of the newer buildings. I weave through Birdie's Court, out the nearest door, across the grounds, and toward sheets of glass that stretch upward, giving the building's structure a sharp, modern profile that contrasts the worn brick and stone around it. I enter through the building's glass doors and climb the stairs, a view of the grass grounds in every direction. At the hallway intersection, I stop to peer around the corner.

Gleaming floors reflect student artwork on the walls, but no shiny black hair or fedora. No Professor Reeve.

"I admire amateur artwork, too, but usually from a less irregular angle."

I spin around, my heart in my mouth.

Julian grins at me from the top of the staircase. "You see it much better when you stand directly in front of it."

He's still wearing his chain, but the cross is tucked under a brown shirt and houndstooth blazer, with just a sliver of silver poking out.

"You scared me." I press my hand to my heart and lean against the wall for support.

"Just—what did you call it? Creeping? Same old."

I shake my head, my heart still slowing. It's me doing the creeping this time, but I don't want to explain why. Honestly, I'd rather not talk about Reeve at all.

He gives me an odd look. "Where are you headed?"

An easy question. "Biology."

His face brightens. "That's where I'm going. Join me?" He turns so I can walk beside him, sticking out his elbow like he plans to escort me.

I playfully slap his elbow away. "Very gentlemanly of you, but I can walk myself."

"Ouch. Proper knock-back." But he's still smiling.

I walk beside him into the classroom, and then follow him to the back corner.

"Mind if we sit here?" he asks. "I'm a bit weird like that—like to see everything."

Julian sits but his eyes dart around the room from one door to the other, and then down the lines of students.

"What're you doing?"

He looks at me. "Not certain what you mean."

"You look like you expect a bomb to go off. Should I be concerned?"

He relaxes into his chair, as if to show me I'm wrong. "If I thought a bomb would be going off I'd not sit and wait for it to happen. Would you?"

"No," I say.

The overhead lights dim and a professor in a turtleneck and vest strides forward, thinning hair combed back. "Quiet please."

Julian repositions himself and rests his chin on his fist. His tousled hair sweeps over his ears and around his face, the color somewhere between brown and copper. His jawline is sharp, expression intent, a gaze that's both kind and weighted. Like he considers everything he looks at with gravity.

I look away before he spots me studying his profile, and scribble notes. The professor starts a slideshow on a project, and Julian sits up straight, twirls a pen in his fingers, but doesn't write a word.

"Were you listening?" I ask as the professor finishes and turns the lights back on.

Julian stretches. "I was."

"Aren't you worried you'll forget what he said? We have a test on this."

"I'll remember." He stifles a yawn and stands. "Thanks for the pleasure of your company. Perhaps I can convince you to join me again." He flashes a smile. "Will you?"

"I will."

"Good. I have to run. Errands and such before my next class. But I'll see you around?"

"So soon?"

"Unfortunately, yes."

I sigh and tuck my notebook into my backpack as he gives me a final wave and shuffles between the chairs to the door. I make it down the hallway and halfway down the stairs before a hand grips my shoulder.

"I need to speak with you," says Professor Reeve's familiar, agitated voice.

I whirl to face him. "How dare you talk to me after what you did? I should report you." I want to smack him and run from him, but I'm too scared and angry to do either.

Annoyance ignites his eyes and then vanishes like he jerked a shade over it. "For what?"

"For harassment. Kidnapping me. Take your pick."

The professor straightens his black fedora. "I made a mistake. I'm sorry, I shouldn't have forced you, and I'll not do it again. I realized what I did wasn't the best approach, so I decided to give you space and think long and hard about how best to explain. Now that I've come to a resolution, I have something important to show you. Please, come with me."

He's joking, right? After what happened with the plane tickets?

"I'm not going anywhere with you."

He takes a step toward me. "Please."

"No."

Despite my determination, my feet move without my permission. I can't scream, no matter how hard I try. I've never heard of a drug that controls limbs. If there was such a thing, there's no way to give it to me. Unless it's something in the air.

"I need you to understand," he says as we leave the building and step out onto a stone pathway.

I grit my teeth. It's the most I can do.

He directs me to a rounded structure with windows reflecting gray clouds, each framed in black metal. It's crisp, new, and modern, like the building my biology class was in. One of few newer buildings, and an ugly glass blot against the gothic architecture surrounding it.

We walk through a set of glass doors to an enormous door. It's the sort of door that makes you hesitate before knocking—tall, dark, and paneled, with brass handles and a faint smell of polish. Inscribed into the gold surface of a plaque is the name: "Professor Bryan Reeve, BA, BCL, LL.M, DPhil, PhD in History, PhD in Political Science."

Professor Reeve opens it and waits while I fight to control my feet, but my legs continue until Reeve closes the door behind me. He tosses his hat at the coat hanger, shrugs off his suit coat, and hangs it on a rack.

My legs buckle, and I reach for the wall to catch myself. "What was that?"

"What do you mean?" He leans against the wall, hands clasped.

"I don't want to be here," I say between breaths. "You forced me to come."

"I never touched you. You came of your own volition. And I have video cameras to prove it." He points to two cameras mounted on the wall above our heads. "You should feel safe knowing these are here, too."

He owns the footage, so I'm not safe at all.

"I'll call the police and tell them what you did. You'll lose your job."

He arches an eyebrow. "Will I?"

"Yes."

A smile quirks his lips. "Go ahead. You can borrow my mobile to phone them." He sets his cell phone on the desk. "It's there if you decide to use it."

He's right. No one would believe me. I survey the office. There has to be a way out.

Diplomas and awards cover the walls. His mahogany desk is organized with pencil holders, a fancy bottle of brandy, and tidy compartments of papers. A nameplate announces the professor's identity in gold letters.

He motions to a cushioned chair. "Are you going to sit down? I have no intention of buying you another plane ticket."

I don't want to sit down, but I'd rather bend my knees on my own, so I lower myself into the chair. My right index finger throbs from twisting the pendant on my necklace, but I keep twisting anyway.

The professor has too many awards. The plaques date back to 2008, 2010, and another 2010. One faded diploma says 1980. Perhaps it belongs to his father—another pretentious jerk, no doubt. The man pacing the carpet doesn't look a day over twenty-five. "You should be older."

Professor Reeve's mouth twitches. "How much older?"

"I don't know." At least twice my age, not a man who can fit in with his students. "Why do you want me to leave?"

"You're in danger."

"From what?"

He shakes his head. "I can't answer that."

I bite back my frustration. "Why bring me to your office, then?"

Professor Reeve sits down, and his eyes bore into mine. "I'd like to try one more time to convince you to go home. Is there nothing you want?"

I clench my fists. "You can tell me why I'm in danger."

He glares at me, then exhales. "There are," his face contorts, "persons here who would harm you should certain circumstances come to pass. And these circumstances cannot be prevented at this school without constant diligence on my part, which I haven't the time for."

"Yeah, that tells me nothing."

He shrugs, and his eyes flit to the silver necklace hanging from my neck. "I learn from my mistakes. There's nothing more I can say."

"Do people not like Americans here or something?"

"Potentially." His face remains smooth and impassive, but his eyes move to my neck again, to the pendant I can't stop twisting. "Can I see your necklace? I'd like to study it."

"Why?"

A muscle in his cheek twitches. "Please," he says, but his tone is condescending.

"You've given me no answers, no explanations. And you want me to give you my jewelry?" I've worn this necklace since before I can remember. I'd feel naked without it. If I were to give it to someone, it wouldn't be him.

"I'd be willing to make a trade." He unlocks a drawer in his desk and pulls out an old piece of parchment.

I crane my neck for a better look. "A trade for what?"

Professor Reeve holds the parchment in his hands with the surface turned so I can't read it. "I've done a fair amount of research on the history of Lancaster, particularly in the fifteen and sixteen hundreds. That's how I discovered you."

He holds out his hand, palm up. "Give me the necklace, and I'll explain what the letter is."

I hesitate, and study the fine lines in his open palm. I've had this necklace for so long, but the professor must see through my stubbornness to the desires my necklace could never fulfill.

"I'll give it back," he says, "and you'll get no further without this trade. I promise you."

My hands shake as I unclip the necklace, and hold it in my fingertips. I better not regret this.

"Explain first."

"Fine." He takes a breath. "I found you when I was doing a study. I'm renowned for the findings I made in that study—for the

Lancashire Witch Trials. You are a descendant of the woman who wrote this letter."

I'm not sure what I expected, but witch trials wasn't it. And still, I wait for him to continue.

Professor Reeve reaches for his desk drawer. It glides open. Then he reaches inside, takes out a letter, and sets it in front of me. There's a name written in curling script.

Alice Grey.

I lean forward, arm hairs prickling, and my chair squeaks.

The name is simple, unextraordinary, and I swear I've heard it before.

"How do you know we're related?"

Professor Reeve inspects me, a line between his brows. "I took a few blood tests and established it."

"You have DNA from this Alice Grey?" I tried DNA tests before, and they could only tell me of an Anglo-Saxon ancestry. No parents. No grandparents.

"I do."

"But if you know that much, can't you find out who my parents are?"

"Briony, if your parents wanted you to know them, they would have left me a name, not to mention they wouldn't have abandoned you to wander the streets. Will you give me the necklace now?"

"Not yet." I shake the chain, so the pendant dances. "Why were you studying this woman, the woman I'm related to?"

"The purpose of my study," Reeve says, slowly, like I'm scraping the words out with a scalpel, "was to determine whether the records of the witch trial are correct. Alice Grey was supposedly released before the trials, though I found accounts that claimed she died in prison. There are no records of her having children before the trials and no records of Alice Grey's life after the trials. You proved some of the records were wrong, and it became my goal to discover what really happened."

He picks up a pen from his pencil holder and bends the plastic with his fingers. "You were left on my doorstep, which is why I sought a home for you. I don't know the reason your family left. I don't know who they are, either."

I set the necklace on his desk by his nameplate. He answered my questions, even if his answers were unsatisfying. "Listen, professor, I don't want to go back home. I swear I'll do everything I can to keep my grades up, so I can stay."

Silence stretches.

Then a knock sounds on the door.

"Come in," the professor says without taking his eyes off me.

A stunning young woman with vivid red hair steps into the room. Her emerald eyes have puffy circles, and black mascara streaks, as if she's been crying, but her eyes are angled, too narrow and sinister for sympathy.

The professor clutches his chair. "What could you possibly want from me now, Jane?"

The woman stops, eyes flicking to me, though she doesn't bother to hide the mascara smudges on her cheeks.

"This isn't one of your usual students," she says in a low voice, cocking her head to one side.

"Briony, it's time to go," the professor says quickly. "Take that with you. Read it and meet me here tomorrow night. Same time."

Jane's expression transitions from sad to suspicious faster than I can leave the room.

I clutch the letter as the door closes, leaving the necklace behind. It's just a necklace, but I rub the skin where the necklace used to be. It just feels…wrong.

As the distance between me and the glass building grows, I breathe easier. Reeve asked to see me again tomorrow but hasn't forced me to go home. Not yet.

And he gave me a piece of my past.

I stride through Birdie's Court and unlock my apartment door. Despite the piles of homework on my desk, I dump my books and papers, shove everything aside, and tug the old parchment from my backpack. At the bottom corner is a date.

—*1775*—

Ink stains. Parchment preserves.

Beneath the earth and tombstones at Moorhill Cemetery are mounds of piled bodies. A past incarnation lies among them. I will remember her if no one else will. How could I not, knowing her fate parallels my own? I will relive the horrors of her life in full.

In another time, yea, years before this woman was born, a younger woman walked the ancient paths of England. So prominent was her character in our story that my tale ceases in significance.

Her name was Alice Grey.

Many an eye would follow the belle's foot-steps as she crossed the forested expanse of rural Pendle, growing more agreeable with each step and every swish of her skirts.

Affluent men courted her as she came of age, despite the disparaging situation from which she emerged. Even the prominent judge, Altham, could not ignore her—he who passed through Pendle on business countless times.

Much changed in the years before the witch trials.

—Marguerite Dye of Birmingham

The letter stops with strange suddenness. The scrawled date and name at the bottom contrast the careful writing at the top while the more hurried script in the last paragraph shows a different hand finished the letter.

Just a few crumbs from a cookie I've been smelling for years.

I reread the paragraphs, rearrange the words, chew on each letter, until my eyelids are heavier than the fireplace stone.

I've never heard of Marguerite, and she couldn't be my birth mom if the letter was written in 1775. She might be an ancestor? While the letter mentions Alice Grey, it doesn't say much about her.

I tuck the piece of garbage into a drawer in my desk, only to take it back out and smooth it flat.

If Reeve thinks Alice is so important, I'll do some research.

CHAPTER ELEVEN

The next day, I have history class again. My teacher has her hair up, strands of gray escaping, with her usual pencil skirt, sleeves rolled to her elbows. According to my schedule, she's known as Professor Karina.

A half circle of students sit in a tiered lecture hall, all facing the lectern, all quiet. Not even the tapping of pencils—the worst distraction.

"It's time to turn your assignments in. Please, pass them to the students on your right, and I'll collect them on the aisle over here."

Sweat cools my back as she points to the far side of the room and clasps her hands.

There wasn't an assignment…was there? I scan the room, but everyone has their papers ready. Pages crinkle as they're passed from one hand to another.

Not again.

If my chair would melt, I'd happily drown in it.

I must have tuned her out when she gave her instructions last class. But I can't miss my first assignment. I've been to every class since I arrived.

Maybe if I talk to Professor Karina, she'll give me an extra day, but then I'd have to admit I wasn't listening. She wouldn't like that. There's no way to tell someone nicely you weren't listening without offending them. Or them thinking you're making excuses.

The teacher picks up the piles of papers, and my neck gets hotter as she moves further away, until sweat prickles my forehead.

Even if she's offended, I have to try.

I close my eyes and inhale.

The teacher starts her projector with a remote, and I force myself to pay attention. But my heart sinks as she talks about Germanic and Anglo-Saxon tribes and kingdoms. How they settled Britain. How the land became "England" after the Roman Empire's decline.

I'm listening, right?

"We'll talk about the important queens and kings, even the mythical ones," my teacher says. "Starting with our famous King Henry the eighth."

She shows us slideshows of artifacts in museums, and we discuss styles during King Henry's reign, and how styles changed through the years. I hope we go to a museum.

After the lecture, the projector flicks off, and the lights turn on, throwing the room into tungsten yellow.

I stand and hesitate as rows of students file out the door. The teacher waits by the first aisle, her eyes roving over her students until she finds me. I'm tempted to duck under the desk, but she beckons. After a moment's indecision, I push toward her.

She waits as I descend the stairs, still holding her remote in one hand. Her sleeves have fallen to her wrists and she rolls them up again.

I stop a foot away. "I'm sorry, professor. I didn't do the assignment. Must have missed hearing you talk about it. Is it possible for me to still do it, even for half credit? Will you tell me what I can do? And what the assignment was about?"

"Do call me Karina."

"Thanks, I will." She seems kind, but I wait to pass final judgment.

She meets my gaze. "Your name is Briony Delwood, right? My SEN student?"

"Uh, yeah." Perhaps she didn't hear my questions.

"I have a few students enrolled that I keep track of." She hands me a sheet of paper with a brief paragraph detailing the assignment. "This should help. I'll make a point of doing the same for all future assignments."

Really?

I stare at the slip of paper before taking it. "Oh." My brain must have stopped working, because I don't even thank her, just silently add the paper to my bag.

She sets her projector remote on the lectern and tucks a stack of papers under her arm. "I'll see you next class then." Then she just leaves, without a backward glance.

I make my way to the library, steps slow and deliberate. She should have given me a scolding. Most teachers do.

The walk is longer than expected, and my stomach growls from having skipped lunch. A branch cracks in the trees behind me, and my heart skips a beat. With a glance over my shoulder, I scan the trees, but no one seems to follow. Still, I give the woods a wide berth.

No one would care to harm me. I'm a nobody.

But my arms prickle.

The library rises in solemn stone, its façade weathered by centuries of rain and ivy. Arched windows climbed toward the gables, their panes leaded and uneven, while grotesque gargoyles hide beneath the roofline.

I push through heavy wood doors and stride down the hall, past shelves sagging under the weight of forgotten knowledge, their spines cracked, gilded titles faded. The silence is broken only by the creak of floorboards and the rustle of turning pages.

A room with computers calls to me—a place to write the essay I missed. I find a computer table surrounded by more bookshelves that has everything I need. So I sit down, login, and type. I type about each of the wives of King Henry, why they died, and why he killed them. I type until my fingers ache.

Once I finish the last line, I turn to my browser.

England adoption records. Results list the government's website. *For all adoptions outside of England and Wales, call the General Register office (GRO).*

I once submitted a request for contact to discover the names of my birth parents, but I wasn't old enough. I'm not eligible now either, but I have another small lead.

Alice Grey.

I type the name from Professor Reeve's letter and pages of results pop up. The townsfolk of Pendle accused Alice of witchcraft in the trials. Professor Reeve mentioned something about this. Some sites claim the judges acquitted her; others argue she died.

I keep digging. At the time of the trials, King James wrote *Daemonologie,* a book that basically stated God would never allow an innocent to be accused of witchcraft. The trials spread.

A young girl with the surname of Device supposedly cast a spell on a peddler named John Law. She was the granddaughter of Demdike, an unpopular woman, who made a living off begging and extortion. Grandma Demdike feuded with another infamous old woman, Chattox, who Demdike claimed stole from her family. These two families dragged each other into the witch trials.

Another one of the accused was Widow Nutter, a woman who owned a tempting parcel of land.

The witch trials became a convenient way for the local magistrate and lawyer to take the land they wanted and rid themselves of local pests.

Alice was a girl caught in the crossfire. She was accused of witchcraft, but was related to neither Chattox nor Demdike, owned nothing, and had little to do with any of the feuds.

This all happened in the 1600s, and somehow Reeve has Alice's DNA?

It makes no sense. When I meet with him tonight, I'll ask him to clarify.

I open Ancestry.com, and login to my old account. A few years ago, I did a DNA test, but it only said I have Anglo-Saxon ancestry, which I already knew. Still, a link to the results shows on my profile, next to an empty family tree.

I search for Alice Grey, and then a family branch to follow. My chest hollows.

Nothing.

A video call alert pops up on my phone's screen, and Sadie's photo appears in the corner. I jab "end." Later.

I pull out my notes from class, review everything I learned and quiz myself on dates, until my is brain leaking the information I'm trying to spoon-feed it.

At this point, it doesn't matter if I stay five hours or one.

I leave the library and pass through Birdie's Court to the great hall. Carved arches fan like spider webs, and the scent of roasted chicken saturates the air. A vacant table beckons amid the lineup of students eating their lunches.

"Briony!" Noelle waves while her other hand balances a tray piled with leafy greens. Behind her stretches the lunch buffet.

She makes a beeline toward me, and her hair shimmers with each movement; longer, thicker, and darker than the previous day.

I attempt to imagine my hair as a silky chestnut brown, but the image falls flat.

"You weren't in your room earlier," Noelle says. "I tried to find you. You could answer your phone, you know. Ran out of shampoo. Want to come with me to Mystic Cosmetics? I told you I'd bring you Saturday, but do you want to go this afternoon instead? Like right after lunch?"

"Sure."

"Ellen makes the best shampoo. Get your food and meet me at the table." Noelle points three tables away. "I'll be over there." She hurries off.

I load my food and sink into the seat Noelle saved. Going somewhere with a friend, even a makeup store, would be a good respite from homework and worrying about Reeve. I still have a few hours before my appointment with him.

Noelle tucks a hair behind her ear. "Are you okay?"

Apparently, I wear my feelings like an emo t-shirt.

"Yeah. Just have to meet with Professor Reeve tonight."

"Why?"

"Wants to show me something, I guess."

"And you're going?"

I shrug. I don't want to explain everything. "I am, but can you make sure I make it home afterward? If I don't, look for my body somewhere by the law building." I let loose a hollow chuckle. Reeve wouldn't actually hurt me…I think.

Noelle grimaces. "That's not funny, Briony. Let's get going, so you're back in time."

I stand with my tray. The cosmetics store has to be better than Reeve's office.

CHAPTER TWELVE

I ride the bus with Noelle to Mill Road. When it stops, we step off onto a narrow street with Victorian brick houses, the occasional awning, terraces, brightly lit signs, and chained bikes outside shop doors. Several stores open their windows to admit the fresh evening air. Most of the streets I've seen in Burnley are varying shades of modest brown, but splashes of muted, vintage colors bring life to Mill Road.

Noelle pauses on the sidewalk. "Coming?"

"Yes." I hurry after her.

A purple awning bears the words, "Mystic Cosmetics," in black, spiky letters with a gnarled vine that twists upward into the upper stories. Huddled about the window, young men press their faces to a wide crack in the glass where fumes escape to swirl into the sky. Not a single guy steps into the store. They just linger around the threshold.

The number of boys far outweighs the number of girls.

"Isn't this a cosmetics store for women?" I ask.

"It's for both," Noelle says. "But you're right, it's usually women you see shopping here."

We circumnavigate the group and make for the door. A spoon sways from a knocker with strange symbols inscribed into the convex side. Dried parsnip hangs from the handle.

Inside, dozens of fruity scents churn in the air. Bars of soap organized by color decorate rows of wooden tables. Bundles of lavender, basil, dill, and chamomile dangle from the ceiling, some fresh and others dry. A circular counter stands in the middle, covered with old-fashioned pots and silver spoons. A clock with an oval face chimes, elaborate eyes painted onto its hands. Perched on top, a raven cocks its head, its three tiny black eyes sending a shudder through me.

Is it a mutant raven? A fake, robotic one? I'm not sure, but its beady eyes look too real for comfort.

About a dozen women crowd in the far corner behind a sign that says, "Demo today only. Make your own soap. Sign up for lessons now." A girl leans to sniff a platter of soap bars with dried herbs drizzled over the top. All the women in the store are beautiful with long, thick hair and perfect skin.

I touch the freckles on my nose, peel off a strand of mousy hair stuck to my cardigan.

Noelle tugs on my arm and wheels me to face a young blonde woman behind the counter with glossy hair, ivory skin, and ice-blue eyes. In one hand, she stirs a concoction over an electric stove. If she didn't run a cosmetics store, I'd have guessed she was a girl in her teens, too.

Something squishy strikes my foot.

Scrieeee!

A rat darts out the open door as I stumble sideways.

Noelle steadies me with a smile. "Don't mind that. It happens."

I don't trust myself to speak. The little hairs on my skin refuse to flatten, and I can't stop eyeing the crow while it watches me. My hand goes to my necklace, but it's missing from my neck.

I'm overthinking this. The store owners must have added the crow to set a mystical mood. It's in the store's name, after all. So perfectly normal. Not like I'm afraid of rats.

I laugh aloud, but the sound comes out hollow.

Noelle steps toward the blonde woman. "Hey, Ellen, I came to get more of your hair product."

"I'm making it now," Ellen says in a tone that would make anyone hide under a rock.

"No rush, I can wait."

"Excuse me." A man wedges around me and rubs his fingers on the counter. His eyes track Ellen as she crosses the room and reaches for more lavender. The men outside the door continue to watch, barring the exit.

Ellen turns to him, a bundle of dried lavender in her hands. "Are you here to buy?"

"No." The man tugs on the neckline of his shirt. "But—"

"Tell me your name."

His expression brightens. "Tom."

"Out, then." Ellen returns to her pot of bubbling product.

The man's face falls. He shuffles his feet, sticks a hand into his coat pocket and looks around. When he finally leaves, the door slams shut behind him. The young men around the window step back, crane their necks, and regroup.

Ellen holds her chin high. "Just blonde hair to them," she mutters.

"Who're you looking for?" I ask.

Noelle shakes her head to silence me, but it's too late.

Ellen's eyes fix on me and narrow. "What do you mean?"

"You asked for his name," I say. "Are you expecting someone?" Clearly not a Tom.

Ellen sniffs, but her haughty expression relaxes as she returns to stirring. "Julian Bristol, or at least that's what I hear he calls himself. Seems every man comes to see the Bierley sisters, except the one I care about. I don't suppose you know him?"

Julian?

I glance outside at the gawking men and my gut twists.

"No," I say.

Ellen's upper lip curls back and she leaves her pot, thrusts aside a set of curtains behind the counter and vanishes.

Noelle stares at the shifting drapes until they calm. "That was weird," she says.

The drapes stir again, and Ellen returns with a box of supplies under one arm.

"Oh, you're back," Noelle says brightly. "I'd like to get cover-up for sensitive, light skin and try it on my friend here."

I don't remember discussing this. "That's nice of you, Noelle, but I don't have the money for—"

"I'll buy." Noelle winks.

Ellen points to the far wall, and Noelle follows her silent direction to study the different hues of foundation. I suppose if Noelle wants to buy the cover-up, it's her prerogative, but I hadn't thought I needed coverup so badly.

I wander the perimeter of the store. Near the door, women with bruises for eyes glare down at me from vintage frames. It's high fashion. A low, circular table displays stacks of soaps with dried herbs sprinkled over the tops. I pick up a bar and turn it over to read the ingredients.

Bloodroot, mandrake, lavender, wormwood, fingernail...

It's a joke, of course. I set the soap down, and a spider crawls from a crack in the pile, almost brushing my hand. A squeal tears from my lips, loud and high-pitched, before a sharp elbow shoves me aside.

Ellen sweeps the spider into her hands and dumps the black, sprawling ball of legs into her pot. She stirs with her spoon, and a loving smile caresses her face.

I'm hallucinating, of course, so I pinch myself to make it stop.

Ellen's spoon knocks against the side of her cauldron. "Would you like to learn how to make those soaps?" she asks. "We're selling lessons."

Noelle claps her hands. "Will you teach your secret recipes?"

"Yes." Ellen waves a hand over her pot, and the scent of lilac fills the room. Lilac—love, innocence, youth, and the lingering presence of the past. "But only to a select few. If you bring Julian Bristol, I'll give you fifty percent off."

The spider's gone, so there's no more need for pinching. I let the smarting skin loose. "But why Julian?"

"We saw him earlier this week at the Botanic Gardens," Noelle says.

Ellen's red lips spread thin over white teeth, and it's like someone dumped a bucket of ice on my head.

"He used to be quite the gentleman," she says.

"Used to be?" I have every reason to believe Julian still merits the word, archaic or not.

"Ugh! You have the worst taste in men," says a voice behind the back curtain.

Ellen goes back to stirring. Did I imagine the voice?

"Tell you what," Ellen says, "bring him today, and I'll give you seventy percent off."

"Today?" Noelle's brow pinches. "I don't have his number."

"Not my problem."

Noelle can't be serious. Julian would have no reason to come here. He's too kind to dupe for Noelle's vanity and pocketbook.

"I'll try to find him." Noelle pauses. "Would I get a discount on the products, too?"

I grab Noelle by the hand, the same way she grabbed mine at the Botanic Gardens, and tow her outside before Ellen replies.

"Certainly," Ellen calls as the door chimes shut.

We leave the purple awning and the door with the dried herbs behind until the fuss of the store admirers blends into the general noise of the street. As I stride toward the bus stop, my cheeks are on fire. Even if we wanted Julian to come, he wouldn't agree to it, would he?

Noelle stops beneath the bus sign. "I don't know why you were so anxious to leave. You acted like you'd seen the devil."

I flinch at her words. "There's something wrong with that place."

"Look," Noelle says, "we'll go back and get some stuff for your hair. You could use the color boost, and we'll have a discount." She pulls her phone out of her purse as compact cars rumble by. Beside me, a pole supports a plastic case with missing person pamphlets. Someone pasted a photo of a kid with bright eyes and two overlapping front teeth.

I don't want to be analyzed like an art project she wants to paint over.

"I'm not going back there."

Noelle purses her lips and jabs at her phone's screen.

I wait for her to finish before asking, "Are you friends with Ellen?"

"She's nice."

I bite my lip.

Noelle drops her phone into her purse and sighs. "I don't know where Julian lives. How could I have known to bring him? And how am I going to convince him to come? Maybe you can talk him into it?"

Ellen, in all her blonde beauty, would wait in the doorway for Julian to arrive, long curls spilling over her shoulders. Those chilling eyes would devour him in a glance.

"I thought you didn't like Julian," I say.

"I told you I'd get over that. I decided to forgive him. Anyway, you like him, so I have to like him, too." She pauses, eyes fixed on a point somewhere behind me. "I know someone who knows him. She'll know where he lives."

"I can't go back. I have to meet with the professor."

"Forgot about that." Noelle opens her phone, maybe checking her calendar again. "We'll bring him back another day. Maybe on a group date. Fifty percent is still a good deal and any guy will go anywhere for a pretty face."

"I'm not going back. This whole thing is weird."

"I don't think it's weird, but if that's what you want…" Noelle watches a car drive by. "I still think a group date would be fun. Maybe not a date, but a hangout. I'd like to introduce you to my friend Mika, too."

The tension in my neck and shoulders ease, just as the bus appears down the road and draws closer with traffic.

"If we do that, I'll have time to give you a makeover. Then when we go out, everyone will see how pretty you are."

Maybe I'm overacting and maybe she just wants to help. A makeover wouldn't be so bad.

"Sure, but no going back to the cosmetics store."

Noelle rolls her eyes, but nods.

CHAPTER THIRTEEN

The professor stands outside his office door, fedora and suit coat already on. Like he's about to walk down a runway, not dirty-floored tile hall. I can smell his cologne from ten feet away. An old-world scent with sandalwood, lavender, and a touch of musk. Probably expensive.

Maybe he has somewhere to be and doesn't intend to stay long. Please, let it be so.

I hold out the letter. "If this is all you've got, I'd like my necklace back."

"No to the necklace." He locks his office door. "And the rest of the journals are at the library."

"The rest?"

"Yes, like the one I showed you." Professor Reeve strides toward the doors that lead outside and motions for me to follow.

If I went, I'd be alone with him, following him to dusty rooms in far corners of the library. I shudder at the thought. What is his knowledge worth?

"The library isn't far. We can walk together." He glances over his shoulder. "Coming?"

I take a step, and this time, I command my own feet.

Reeve gives me a dazzling, irritating smile.

We walk along a path that borders a biking trail where tall hedges become lofty, overhanging trees. Then a brick tower emerges over the tops of the highest branches. Trees part, and there are the gargoyles, crouched, wings folded, peering out with hollow eyes. The library guardians. Defenders of books, not teenagers with unknown backstories.

Every step of the way, I watch Reeve out of the corner of my eye.

"Why do you need my necklace?" I ask.

Reeve casts me a look and changes the subject. "I found a collection of works made by a man with a guilty conscience—the same man who recorded the history of the witch trials I told you about yesterday. His name was Thomas Potts. He collected journals from the ruined homes of those that died, and I've added a few entries I discovered on my own. When you put them together, you get a clear picture of what happened."

Will Thomas Potts explain the need for my necklace?

The professor walks beside me into the lobby and beneath a cream-colored, arched ceiling. Fine lines intersect on golden stars while antique cherry bookshelves whisper of dusty volumes.

Reeve continues up two flights of stairs to a door in a remote corner of the third floor.

He unlocks the door and ushers me into a room with an arched window of stained glass. Bookshelves reach to the ceiling on either side, a single wood desk between them. The desk has two large leather books, side by side, and there's a scanner and printer on the opposite wall. One of the books has a black cover with a gilded tree and runes. The other is a simple brown.

Professor Reeve picks up the black book and motions to the

other. "I put this in here for you. It can't be taken out—it's too valuable—but you can come anytime you like. You won't be able to read it in one sitting." He lifts the brown book and opens it to the last page. Then an awful ripping sound makes me flinch as he tears a page out and stuffs it into his coat pocket.

"Why tear it?" I ask, "If it's so valuable?"

"It's very valuable. You are correct." He hands me a small brass key. "To access the room."

I grip the metal in my fist, caught between curiosity and a sinking sense of caution. "Can I copy them?"

"Yes, it won't hurt the book. You can take the copies home, too."

"Will it tell me who my birth parents are?"

The professor's eyes bore into mine. "It'll tell you who you are. And when you make the connection, hopefully, you'll leave."

"But—"

"When you're ready to leave, come to me. I'll get you wherever you want to go, the moment you want to go. This is all I can do, short of strapping you to the seat of a plane and calling all the powers of hell to hold you there." His mouth jerks into an almost pained smile. "Believe it or not, I care about you, Briony. I'd like to keep you alive."

My throat goes dry.

With his black book tucked beneath his arm, Professor Reeve turns to go, but I call after him. "What about that one—the one you're holding? Don't I need it, too?"

Professor Reeve pauses in the doorway. "The book on the table is sufficient."

"What are those characters on the cover?"

"A language few know."

I'll have him know I've smacked my brothers for being less

needlessly cryptic. "And you know it?"

A smirk steals over his lips. "I do." He closes the door behind him.

I have homework to do, and I can't be late on another assignment, or Professor Karina might not give me another chance. Professor Reeve told me to scan each page. Then I can take the scans home. That's what I'll do.

But instead, I trail a finger over the book's soft leather cover, stained with age. I ease it open to a description written in fancy calligraphy.

The compiled works of Thomas Potts.

A collection of true accounts in an attempt to right a terrible wrong.

All works have been honestly claimed from the homes of victims

or given by the families of those accused.

Other accounts have been provided by the son of Magistrate Nowell,

in his later years of service.

Though I know none will believe this account,

I feel I have done all I can to atone for mine part in this heinous transgression.

A note at the bottom says, "The Pendle Witch Trials and curse of the Mekori." I grab the letter from Marguerite Dye out of my backpack where I'd tucked it when the professor refused to take it back. The signature matches the more recent handwritten note.

I put the letter down and check the clock on my phone. I have time before the library closes to read a few pages. I'll make the copies before I go.

Above the first letter, a preface written by Thomas Potts spans the page in curling script.

I did not believe in witchcraft until the trials here in Lancaster. Read and be warned lest you be accused of witchcraft or fall and become one of the devil's followers yourself.

I continue to a journal entry further down the page.

—June of 1603—

I crested a hill overlooking Trawden Forest.

Blue haze drifted over the tree line, a crowd of dancing ghosts. The road descended into the trees and disappeared, though my map indicated the road should lead to Cox Colne, the local alehouse.

I glanced behind me. There were no figures in the distance, no crunch of feet, no cracking of whips, no gunshots. And yet, I still heard them echoing between trees.

My horse, Dantes, pawed the soft dirt and let out a low whinny. I had but one thing to collect before my escape. We wouldn't stay long, I assured him.

Still, I brought out my cross. The smooth metal usually gave me a sense of bearing.

I pause at the mention of the cross as a sense of meaning grips me, the image of Julian in the gardens stark in my mind. But lots of people wear crosses, especially when this letter was written. It may mean nothing. So I dive back into the letters.

Dantes pranced back and forth. I dismounted, clasped my hands, and prayed with an earnestness I have never before known. I prayed for the Catholics. I prayed for the Protestants. I prayed to rid our government of the evil that infiltrates it. I even prayed for the king, though, in my heart, I have not forgiven him.

When I remounted Dantes, I spurred the horse into a landscape of boughs and muttering breezes. Branches creaked and skeletal leaves fluttered to rest in a grave of deteriorating mold. Creatures slithered through needles as a crow sprang from the canopies and squawked.

I leaned forward and rubbed Dantes along his neck, but a soft mew made me pause. A black cat slunk through the dead foliage, its tiny legs keeping pace with the horse.

I laughed at myself, at how such a slight thing could make me so uneasy, but my mirth rang hollow through the forest, and I let the sound die.

A woman's voice came from behind, asking me to pardon her intrusion. It seemed she appeared from nowhere. Before me stood the most beautiful woman I ever beheld, carrying a broom, which was strange, for she had nothing to sweep but dead needles. She wanted to know if I was from Colne.

I answered that I was foreign.

She had long locks that flowed like a golden waterfall down her back, fine jewels and ruffles about her neck, and a smile as pale as the glittering moon over the Basque Coast.

I dismounted Dantes, stooped to kiss her thin fingers, but my lips met stone, and I pulled quickly away.

"A lady's hands are always cold," she said.

I planned to travel to Cox Colne Alehouse

for the night, I told her, and that, on the morrow, I should continue to Liverpool.

She offered directions, but I had a map and knew the way.

Out of politeness, I asked her name. She answered with Ellen Bierley.

When she asked for my mine, I gave her "Guido." She wanted to know where I hailed from, if not here.

I come from many places; nonetheless, I considered Flanders and Spain home for many years.

She observed my face closely as we spoke, and she asked a number of questions, said she does not often find gentlemen in her path, especially when in Samlesbury, her place of residence. She wished I would stay longer, and asked if I had seen a child with yellow eyes.

"No," I said. "We both seek that which eludes us."

Ellen smiled, but without warmth. "I know what it is you seek."

"And what is that?" I asked.

"To be remembered for your faith and virtue. For you are virtuous, are you not, Master Guy Fawkes?"

A bird somewhere overhead chirped a warning crescendo. "Guido," I corrected her.

She said she would keep my secrets. Yet she repeated my worries in the exact phrases I thought them. If I had the sword I seek, I might have ended her then. Instead, she extended her hand and asked for my map.

I reached into my saddlebags, but instead of a map, found parchment folded into the crude shape of a cat. I crushed the little feline in my fist.

The sacred path—gone.

Clutching my crucifix beneath my coat, I told her I must go. Quickly.

Her face hardened as I urged Dantes on. She demanded I stay, but I continued with Ellen's eyes boring into my back.

I did not expect to find a living soul until Marsden. However, several miles down the road, an old woman stirred at the foot of a wizened tree, begging for coin, her crumpled legs surrounded by empty and broken bottles. Wrinkled fingers clawed the air while a milky white film covered the old woman's eyes.

She said her daughter was lame. Indeed, her daughter sat beside her, meeting my gaze with unbalanced eyes. I drew several small coins from my pocket, but the elder woman seized my coat, pleading for milk, though I promised I had none.

A figure emerged from the trees with ebony hair, calling the woman by "Demdike."

Even the remote towns of Lancaster are infected with the devil's handiwork.

I ripped my coat from Demdike's grasp, remounted my horse, and the two of us fled, ready to fly to the shores of Liverpool. Save that my business was yet unfinished.

We didn't slow until the dim silhouette of the alehouse appeared across the road.

—Guido

I touch the name, *Ellen*. "Guy Fawkes" sounds familiar, too. Surely, the reason Reeve wants me to read these will become clearer as I read further.

"Excuse me, the library is closed," says a snappy voice from the doorway.

I twist in my chair to face a woman with short, tight curls, pushing a pair of round glasses up her hooked nose. Probably the librarian. "Sorry, I'll get going." I reach for the book and stop. Reeve said I couldn't take it home. He suggested I make copies before I leave.

I'll come back to finish. I scoop up my backpack and shut off the light. "Sorry, again."

The librarian only nods.

When I close the door, it seems I leave a part of myself behind.

CHAPTER FOURTEEN

THE NEXT MORNING, I walk into class moments before it starts. Professor Karina watches me sit down and my stomach tightens as she glances at me several times during the lecture, like she has something to say. Hopefully not that my essay was bad, or that she expected me earlier.

I slump back into the seat, trying to sink into it.

The AC whirs. Chalk scrapes against the chalkboard and I swear it gets louder as class goes on.

Then she dismisses everyone, and makes a beeline in my direction.

I wait, heart pumping.

She sits slowly at my side, her slim dress bending with her, layered long sleeves carefully folded back. She hands me my essay, and there's a yellow "C" on it. A hole carves itself into my stomach.

"What did you learn about King Henry VIII when you wrote this essay?" she asks.

I strain to remember. "He married a lot of women he didn't like and never had a son."

That should sum it up, except she peers at me with strange

intensity. Like I missed something.

"What were you trying to convey about King Henry when you wrote about him?"

"Well, he married Catherine of Aragon." I pause, trying to remember them in order. "Anne Boleyn, Jane Seymour, Anne of Cleves," my voice grows stronger, "Catherine Howard, and Katherine Parr." Too many people in England had the same names.

Professor Karina's voice is overly kind in her response. "But why does that matter?"

"Because…he was a jerk?"

The professor raises her eyebrows.

"Because nothing he had was ever enough," I add quickly.

"Exactly." She taps the paper. "Let me tell you a secret. Start with that statement, end with that statement, and organize your thoughts between. Your essay jumps around a lot. Be sure to make your points flow and transition coherently. You have a lot of interesting facts, but I know you have something to say about them. Don't be afraid to say it."

"I'll redo it," I say. "I can do better, if you'll let me."

"Good. I don't want you to get discouraged. People like you are often the most creative, hard-working students."

"Is that why you teach here?" I wince at my hidden question. Did she want to be an SEN teacher?

Her smile widens. "Part of it. I joined Burnley at the start of this year, so I haven't been here long." She brushes off her sleeves. "Good luck on your essay. I know you won't let me down."

When she leaves, her faith in me settles, thick and heavy, but there's hope, too.

I push the thoughts back as I walk out the classroom door.

"Briony?" comes Noelle's voice from down the hall. "Where've you been hiding?"

I jump, shake myself, and force a smile. Professor Karina doesn't seem to teach just special needs kids, so I tell Noelle the truth. "Professor Karina's history class."

"Oh, I love her—always giving that 'you're barely surviving life' look."

If Noelle is familiar with Professor Karina, does she know about my program, too? "She teaches the SEN class, right? Have you heard of that?"

Noelle waves her hand like she's brushing my question away. "Pssh, that's a joke. A journalist wrote an article on Professor Reeve's honorary student club, and the school got trashed online. The headmistress was furious, I heard. The SEN program was introduced to deflect attention and save face, in my opinion."

My neck heats, and I clear my throat. "Have you talked to your friend, Mika?"

Noelle glances down the hall. "Yes, but I have to run. There's some stuff I need to tell you, but later. Okay?"

"Okay." I shrug as she hurries off.

With several hours to kill before my next class, I head to the library. Papers rustle as I pass dusty shelves, the smell of old paper strong. I find the private room Reeve showed me and make a beeline to the book on the table. This time, I make the copies straightaway, and tuck them into my backpack. Then I linger in the doorway and stare out at the grounds outside, at the rain pattering on stained glass, the way the glass distorts the trees, even the overcast skies. Like smeared paint.

How different things look from here.

I leave the ancient book for a room with computers and chug a cup of coffee before starting on my homework. Within a half hour, I'm alive and focused.

The copied journals peek through an open zipper in my

backpack. I hesitate, then reach for it. Until the slap of a volume hitting the floor makes me turn. A book lies on the ground by the bookshelves. No one picks it up. Silence grins, and my skin tingles.

Forcing an exhale, I grab my backpack and pull it close. I'll read the letters at home. But the prickling at my neck doesn't fade.

I head for the bus stop, and glance over my shoulder. Reeve warned me about danger. This kind of danger? The faces of the people that stroll down the sidewalk behind me vary. Every time I look back, there are no shadows or odd shapes leaping behind buildings to escape notice.

I'm being paranoid again, the eerie impression clings to me as I take the bus to Birdie's Court.

I check behind me again before entering my dormitory and shut the door behind me. My hands shake as I sit at my desk. I bring out the copied journals but set them aside. Not right now. The light in my room yellows as the daylight fades. Still, I study. Until, finally, I allow myself to stuff my homework back into my backpack and slide out the letters to replace them.

The next letter in the pile, written in June of year 1603, bears the signature, *James Altham*. A ripple of unease twists down my back.

—1603—

I watched through the window as townsfolk gestured to my carriage, the gentle, steady clop of horses' hooves bringing me closer. Trees. Peasants. Lacey collars beneath plain faces.

Then the carriage lurched as it stopped. The smell of the local ale was so strong, I could almost taste it. We reached Cox Colne at last. The carriage doors creaked open, and my driver stepped aside. No flouncy dresses rose to greet me.

I grunted and my driver hurried to the alehouse door, pried it open. Someone played the flute inside. Grubby mugs littered the tile floors. There were wooden tables thrown together, antlers hanging from the walls. The magistrate's son lounged in the corner alone, greasy strings of hair slapped across his face. Along the windows, a few locals chatted, their faces turned away.

A maiden danced between tables. She made her way to me as the sun's dim rays streamed from the window. Dust stirred like glitter. She twirled into my chest, her breath hot and stale. I pulled her in for a kiss, requested a drink. She left with money clenched in her hand.

Behind the dancer, a woman with a low neckline watched, hair bright as blood. Her eyes lit up as I sat at her side, close enough to smell her perfume, a splash of nutmeg. She had to be at least twenty years my junior.

She introduced herself as Jane Southworth. I have heard of her on my travels to Samlesbury, for she is the wife of John Southworth.

Her unparalleled beauty would cause any man to risk disownment. John's family—all devout Catholics—contested his marriage to a Protestant. This was the gossip only six years previous, but Jane looked young. The kind of young that has yet to think of marriage.

She didn't like my questions about her age,

however, and instead asked if I had seen a young boy with yellow eyes.

Though I knew little of whom she spoke, I had heard much of her loveliness. Many speak of it. She said she knew of me as well and felt I could be very useful, for she could be the wife of James Altham, Serjeant-at-law if I wished it.

"Only heaven attempts to record the count-less marriages that have been consummated over the ages," she said. "We both know that neither of us will end our lives in heaven, seeing as thou hast three wives thus far."

No one knew this, not even my wives. I traveled so far, so often; I doubted any of them would ever discover this.

She might have slapped me. Indeed, it would have been better if she had. I demanded to know where she heard this blasphemy.

"I know much of thee, Altham," she said. "I

would not mind becoming the fourth wife, so
long as all thine fortunes are imparted to me
upon thy death."

The server brought my ale, and I guzzled
the drink. I could have used a few more.

She said man's life is fleeting, and that I
should die like all the rest. Her own husband
does not have long to live, and he is younger
than me.

At this, I stood, so fast my breeches tore.

I demanded to know if she intended to
threaten me, her superior before God and our
king, but she gave no answer. Instead, she
asked if I was afraid of death.

She trailed a finger down my arm. Her eyes
flickered red, and her cheekbones hollowed.
All the musculature and skin wasted away
until only rows of white teeth grinned.

Laughter broke through the hellish

hallucination as two girls walked together outside the window, arm in arm in humble dresses. One's loveliness surpassed even Jane. I needed to speak to them, to get their attention in any way I could. So, I pushed Jane aside and met them outside the door. They turned when I called.

I bowed to them, teetering a little on unsteady legs, and asked to be an escort.

A woman with a patched skirt and dark ringlets escaping from a bun curtsied. She wore a silver necklace around her neck with a tree pendant—too elegant for her homespun dress.

She gave me her name—Alice Grey.

I went to her side and whispered the directions to my residence, bade her meet me there tonight. With her attentions, I would have no need for Jane. So, I turned to the alehouse where Jane waited, paused, and made *for my carriage instead.*

—Sir James Altham

I recoil at his predatory thoughts. But Alice finally gets a mention—a relief after sifting through so many documents and journals. I was starting to worry she wouldn't be.

The tree necklace Altham mentioned is curiously similar to the one Reeve took. Maybe he made the same connection, and that's why he's studying it. He distracted me before when I asked for it back, but he won't again.

The letters continue with another entry from the same man.

—1603—

My sheets lay smooth and cold, an absence
of bare feet to warm the furs and thick rugs.
The oval mirrors reflect no curves. Winking
stars mock me from the window.

The girl at the alehouse, the one with dark
curls and pale skin, never came. Alice Grey.

Miserable folk trudge down the street below.

She is not among them. Even in Pendle, the women won't have me.

I will not allow this embarrassment to sway me. I am not at the end of my career. Alice will give herself to me, and youth and beauty will be mine. There is a way.

—Sir James Altham, Barrowford

I sit back in my seat, eyes aching from reading. Altham's thoughts make me uneasy—and fascinated—and I have to force myself to consider the historical context without wanting to hurl.

A woman called Jane who was either very ambitious or very desperate. A judge with issues. And a meeting that never happened that may have pushed Alice into the witch trials. She must have survived. Otherwise, I wouldn't have been born.

As I reach to turn the page, a knock sounds, and I crack the door open. "Hello?"

It's Noelle.

Her eyebrows rise. "Aren't you going to let me in?"

I open the door a little wider. "Yes, sorry."

Noelle glances at the papers on the desk. "What's that?"

"Homework." I bundle the papers and stack them beneath my textbook. She doesn't need to know about this part of my life. "What's up?"

"What'd you get on Karina's assignment?"

"An A." The lie comes so easily.

"Me, too," she says.

I want to be happy for her, but when I open my mouth to offer congratulations, no words come.

Noelle sits on my bed like she did the first day we met. "I tried calling you, but you don't answer your phone anymore. You spend way too much time studying these days. So, when I saw the light on in your room, I figured you're still awake. I have our group hangout all planned. Talked to my friend about it. It's tomorrow night."

The copied pages stick out from beneath my textbook, the darker edges of old paper shown in layers of black ink. There are more to read, but I still have homework to do. I spent hours on my essay to impress Professor Karina.

"Julian's coming," Noelle adds.

I look up. Her eyes are glittering—half dare, half triumph. As much as it bothers me, I'm not inclined to prove her wrong.

"I'll make it work."

CHAPTER FIFTEEN

YOGURT FROM HOURS ago wreaks havoc in my stomach as I walk down the hall to Noelle's dormitory for her arranged hangout. I knock on Noelle's door and reapply my lip balm, but my hand shakes, and I'm glad the balm isn't colored.

The door swings open, engulfing me in a woody, sweet vanilla perfume. I do a double take at Noelle's gold earrings, choker, and black dress. What really throws me is the reflection of my face in her dilated pupils, like giant black ice ponds spreading cold down to my toes.

I shake the feeling off. Maybe it's the dark. My pupils dilate indoors, too.

Behind Noelle, a perfect lineup of shoes is racked inside a small closet, with dresses that dangle in an ordered rainbow. The bed is made with a quilt tucked at the sides. A heart-shaped frame on the bedside table displays a fluffy puppy.

"Come on." Noelle leads me across the hall to a small bathroom where even the makeup is organized with plastic shelving, and then there's a flatiron perched on a stool. "Sit."

I do as she says. "Thanks for doing this."

"You'll look so good when I'm done." Noelle's voice is light and airy as she reaches for a black pencil and pulls my eyelid down.

Noelle outlines both eyes, and I dig my fingers into the stool to keep from fidgeting. "Did you get all these products at Mystic?"

I pick up a jar of coverup and sniff it. Lavender with a bit of lemon. Dang, it smells good.

The whole display at the cosmetics store was probably a joke meant to scare me. The store wouldn't be so popular if spider legs were actually in their soaps.

Somewhere, Ellen is laughing.

"Not all of them," Noelle answers. "Their products are expensive, and I've spent too much on them already." Noelle pauses. "Try not to blind anyone with all this beauty."

Noelle has added powder to my face, blush to my cheeks, and dark eyeliner that borders my gray eyes. The coverup goes on butter smooth. "I can't believe you don't wear mascara. I literally can't leave my room without it."

A smile steals over the reflection of my face in the mirror. "I like it."

Noelle's phone buzzes. "It's Mika!" Her mouth splits into a grin. She mutters something under her breath as she types her answer, and then looks up. "I want you to know I'm okay with you dating Julian. It's a bit awkward, maybe, but that's fine. Just wait till you meet his friend, Eser."

"Oh…okay."

Noelle pulls on her fingers. "Anyway, let's get going. Mika's waiting. She's the only one who can drive."

"You should try the products at the cosmetics store," Noelle says as we descend the stairs.

"Sure. Thanks again for the help."

We cross the courtyard and start down the road where the

tallest tower of the library emerges over the trees as the road turns. A girl on the front steps rises to her toes, waves, and rushes toward us.

I fidget as she approaches. She's Julian's friend, after all, and meeting new people is never as easy as it should be.

"Noelle!" The girl with long, black hair hugs Noelle and embraces me as well. She wears jeans and a wool coat, a gold-clasped leather bag on her arm. The type of girl I can picture walking down Oxford Street in heels.

"Hey, Mika." Noelle grins. "I've missed your beautiful face. That outfit—why do you always make the rest of us look bad?"

Mika's dark, almond eyes wrinkle at the sides. "I'll try to dim my radiance. Later, though." Her voice is sweet, the accent noticeable against ours. "Don't think we've had the pleasure, have we?"

Not sure if they shake hands in England, but I offer. "I'm Briony."

She takes my outstretched fingers.

"Not only does Mika have a beautiful face, she's a good cook, too," Noelle says. "She's making us snacks to take."

Mika only shrugs, like she gets this compliment daily.

Noelle checks her phone. "We'll have plenty of time to talk at the boys' dormitory. Let's get going."

Mika beckons. "Car's this way. Got the tickets, I hope?"

"And made dinner reservations."

My stomach churns as I imagine myself scrambling for words around a dinner table, and Noelle squeezes my arm.

"Where're we going?" I ask.

We round a curve in the sidewalk, where rows of cars fill parking spaces. Mika rummages for keys in her pocket. "Fishing. Thought the boys would like the idea. And I clearly forgot the water part when I put on these shoes." She puts her foot out to show off her loafers. "I'll mostly be watching anyway."

A Peugeot flashes from a few feet away as Mika unlocks it. "That's me. Hope you don't mind if it's a little messy—"

A whistle comes from behind, cutting Mika off. "Noelle, I've missed our conversations," calls a male voice.

We all turn to face a group of students covering their mouths, snickering. They're wearing all black. Black turtlenecks, black cloaks. Vests with Burnley Boarding School's emblem—a book, torch, quill, and lion. But slightly altered. Instead of the traditional gold, it's white. And it flashes a silvery blue when the boys move. When this happens, the lion looks almost skeletal.

The boy at the front looks me up and down and winks. "You look fit, my dear."

I turn away in disgust.

Their raucous laughter fades as Noelle drops into the passenger seat and slams the door shut. I sink into the backseat, letting the smell of new leather mask my racing thoughts. Mika starts the car, which is so clean, I couldn't find a crumb if I wanted to. So much for being messy.

"Reeve's students," Mika mutters under her breath. "They think they're so much better than everyone else."

Noelle's lips are pale, and she bounces a leg on the seat.

"Are you okay?" I ask.

She brushes her hair over her shoulder but doesn't smile. "I'm fine."

"Are you su—" Mika starts to say.

"Yes," Noelle snaps, and Mika pinches her lips shut.

I change the subject. "How do you know Noelle and Julian, Mika?"

"Oh, Julian and I have known each other a long time. I never had brothers, so he, Eser and even Robbie are as close as I'll ever get. Noelle and I have classes together."

"We saw Julian at the greenhouse," Noelle says in a flat tone.

Mika turns the wheel and backs out of her parking stall. "He goes there sometimes." She maneuvers the car out onto the road, makes a few turns between streets. Past buildings with stone cloisters, towering courtyards, and marble busts of historical figures. Then she pulls into another parking lot where she lets the engine die. The car's so quiet, the lack of a rumbling engine is hardly noticeable.

"Cliviger Fishponds is one of my favorite places. I'm excited for you to see it, Briony," Mika says.

"Me, too," I say.

Discovering more of England is always welcome, even if it separates me a little more from home.

Mika parks in front of a beige brick building that's more modern-traditional with twin gable fronts. The second floor has a little deck with stairs leading up to it. We follow Mika, her shoes clanking up the steps.

The sound of classical piano music wafts from one of the rooms, but we pass this door to one a few doors away. It sounds like an action flick on the other side. "Get out of there. It's going to blow," comes one voice, then a series of muffled gunshots. "Where's the bomb?" someone else asks. "Other side. Go, go, go!"

My dad would disapprove of how thin these doors are.

Mika scrunches up her face as she knocks. "I'll never understand the gaming appeal."

The action scene on the other side of the door quiets.

Noelle taps her toes on the floor.

"Eser, go get the door," a muffled voice says.

Another boy's voice comes loud and clear, just on the other side of the thin wood. "Why is it always me? You're closer. Or why not

Julian?"

The floor creaks, and the door squeals open.

I pull at my shirt again, but there are no wrinkles to smooth.

A young man with an aquiline nose and fitted sweater looks down at me. Shag carpet stretches wall-to-wall beneath his feet. Velvet brown couches and a coffee table with water rings marking the wood, oak bookshelves with school books and lego spaceships, and exposed beams overhead.

A guy with mussed, sandy hair reclines on a La-Z-Boy on the far side of the room, a controller in his hands.

Sweater guy at the door eyes Noelle and me with a scowl that borders on disapproving. "Hiya, Mika. See you've brought friends." His dark hair swoops into a stiff peak, and his black, pointed shoes gleam.

I wave. "I'm Briony."

"Eser." He gives me a flinty smile.

Eser—the friend of Julian's that Noelle mentioned. Welcoming guy.

Julian appears in a doorway on the other side of the room, and flutters multiply inside me. "I've got it ready for you, love," he says to Mika. He sweeps a hand behind him. "The kitchen is yours to command."

I guess "love" is an expression I should get used to. I force a smile.

Mika claps and squeezes past Eser. When she reaches Julian, he steps aside and follows her into what, I assume, is the kitchen.

Now I'm with Noelle and two guys I don't know, which wouldn't be half bad if Noelle wasn't gazing at Eser like he's the eighth wonder of the world.

Eser steps out of the way and I follow Mika with slow footsteps until I'm in no-man's-land, close to the kitchen, but still in the main room, uncommitted to either space.

I stare at my feet as Noelle starts a conversation with Eser, the open kitchen doorway casting me into shadow. Mika and Julian chat in front of the oven, but they don't notice me standing like a misplaced statue. Or don't seem to.

The minutes lengthen. I've stood at the edge of the kitchen too long. If they do notice me, they'll feel bad, and I'll feel worse.

I should walk into the kitchen like I own the place. Instead, I cling to Noelle, the only person I know.

Noelle bats her long lashes. "How's the season going, Eser? Any wins?" She uses a lower voice than I'm used to hearing, and it makes me cringe inside.

Eser's lips quirk. "A few."

She leans toward him, as if to close the gap between their bodies. "What teams?"

The tension in Eser's face and shoulders reveals an emotional chasm the size of the Great Barrier Reef. I examine again the polish of his shoes and the careful style of his hair. The slight flourish in the way he speaks—the occasional curlicue. Maybe Noelle hasn't noticed.

"A few," Eser repeats, his eyes focused on the TV instead of Noelle.

Noelle touches Eser's arm. "You said that before."

Eser flinches and steps back, smoothing his sweater.

"I'd love to be invited to one of your games," Noelle adds.

I feel like I should warn Noelle, but I'm not sure how. Rather than watch this exchange unfold, I opt for a cozy spot on the couch near the guy in the recliner. I still haven't been introduced to him. He smells like soap and something sharp, maybe peppermint.

He grips his remote, facing an enormous screen with roaming zombies and rags that whip in an eerie, virtual wind. He's too invested to spare me a word, and I'm grateful for it.

Watching him play recalls the nostalgia of sitting with my brothers. It's almost comforting, until gamer boy takes his socks off, and the whole room fills with the smell of sweaty feet. I do my best not to wrinkle my nose, but I can't stay. Instead, I flee the room to the kitchen, whether Julian and Mika want me there or not.

The room has dark cabinets with tiny carved details near the handles, black composite countertops, and a fridge half the width of one from the States, but just as tall. Piled in the kitchen sink, a mountain of dishes threatens a landslide. Despite the mess, it smells like flour and butter, and home.

"They assigned me the Virgin Queen," Mika is saying, "Too Posh to Party, and Head Girl Energy awards. Pretty sure they're insulting me."

"Take them as compliments," Julian says.

"Course you'd say that," says Mika, "You're too nice to say I deserve them."

There's a soft grinding noise and a wave of heat as Mika opens the oven and checks inside.

"I didn't ruin them, did I?" Julian asks.

"No, no, they're just as I left them." Mika looks over her shoulder. "Oh, there you are, Briony. You two've met already, right?"

He looks up. "I have. Lovely to see you again."

My cheeks heat and I give Julian what I hope isn't a shy smile.

"You look beautiful. Always do."

Before I can stop myself, I touch my powder-coated cheeks. I hope it's not overly overt.

"I like your apartment," I say, mouth dry. "Is there a reason you live off campus?"

He fiddles with the slender chain of his necklace, the crucifix hidden beneath flannel. "Can't say I'm fond of the others in my program," he glances at Mika. "Not to sound prudish, but I managed to find somewhere quieter. Got a few mates to do the same. Is there anything more I can do, Mika?"

"Just enjoy yourself."

Julian does a little bow.

"What're you making?" I ask.

Mika kneads a chunk of dough into a log. "Steamed dumplings."

"Looks good."

Julian watches me the same way he observes classrooms. Like he's trying to expose every corner and all he's finding are fluffy compliments. "I'd love to make them at home," I say. "If you'll give me the recipe. I'll need all your tips, so I don't mess them up."

"Just buy pre-made dumplings and save yourself the trouble," a voice interjects.

I turn as the gamer guy sidles in through the kitchen door, Eser and Noelle close behind, their eyes scanning the kitchen.

"Pre-made? Pre-made?!" Mika wrinkles her nose. "That's twice the cost with half the flavor."

"I don't mind pre-made," I start to say. "But—"

Gamer Guy talks over me. "It makes twice as much with half the conversation. I'll never understand why you put so much effort into making your food pretty. Reckon it's a positive affirmation thing. It tastes the same either way." He grabs milk out of the fridge and pours himself a cup, raises it like a glass of champagne, and chugs it.

I exhale silently.

Mika rolls her eyes. "I'd be offended by that, except I know you'd eat cow dung if it meant you never had to get off the couch, Robbie."

Mika rolls the dough on a cutting board, cuts the dough up, spaces them evenly apart and loads them into a steamer.

Noelle watches Mika close the lid. "I'm surprised you don't measure the ingredients," she says. "Maybe that's why the dough looks so flat? Did you not use enough yeast?"

"I don't measure because I don't need to," Mika says. "The consistency's fine."

Noelle raises a shoulder. "My parents say the best way to cook is to manage someone else who does it — and I think I'm doing a good job." Her tone's serious, but I'm sure there's a laugh lurking in the corner of her mouth, even if I can't find it.

Mika doesn't look up as she grabs a basket. "You certainly are."

"I don't cook," Eser says, "but I tip well—isn't that the American thing?"

"I bet you do," Noelle says with a wink.

Mika glances at me, and I rush to fill the silence.

"Speaking of tipping, uh—are we going punting, too? Do you tip the person who rows? I saw it in a movie once. Looked... relaxing. It was a romance, I think." I avoid looking at Julian and blurt the first thing that might undo the word *romance*. "Anyway, it's been years since my dad took me fishing. I'm excited."

Eser chuckles. "Punting's fine. But I'll sit it out if it's going to start reminding people of a romance movie."

Sweat gathers on my forehead, and I take a deep breath, imagining Sadie beside me. "Well, you're a bore." But I freeze as soon as the words leave my mouth.

Robbie elbows Eser. "Think this girl can stick around, eh?"

Eser actually smiles. Julian leans against the countertop, arms folded, content.

Noelle glances between us. "I don't think you're a bore," she says.

And Eser's smile fades.

Mika checks the dumplings in the steamer. "We'd understand if you chose not to come, Eser," she says. "We all know Julian and Robbie are not your type, mostly since Robbie is no one's type. Burnley football players are far too fit for the likes of us."

Noelle's brows draw together.

"I'm happy to come if you'll have me," Julian says. "I happen to enjoy the company of everyone here, and dumplings, too."

Noelle glances at Julian, and I struggle to read her expression. She hasn't said much to Julian before now, or even looked at him.

A timer rings, and Mika shuts it off. "Well, my lovelies, they're ready, and it looks like Julian's the only one who'll get one."

Noelle frowns. "What about me?"

"Don't worry," Mika says. "I only tease."

Noelle's frown stays as Mika puts the dumplings in a basket and ushers us out of the kitchen and into the hall. "I can drive four," she says.

Robbie pulls mismatched socks over his toes. "I've got a car. And it's much nicer than yours."

Mika jiggles her keys at him. "Your car is a complete mess, much like the boy who drives it. But let's remind you that you're still a baby, and you don't have a driver's license. You've got another full year."

Robbie gives her a dirty look. "You don't have room for all of us in your car, and it's not like we're driving far." He stuffs his keys into his pocket anyway.

Julian and Eser both shrug and follow him, apparently deciding they'd rather drive with an underage driver than get ferried by girls.

I got my license before I left, but I can't imagine driving on these backward streets. Even picturing it brings to mind head-on collisions and ambulances.

"Are you wearing those socks by themselves?" Noelle points to Robbie's feet as we descend the stairs. "What about shoes?"

He looks down in mock surprise. "Do you not like them? But they add a pop of color, don't you think?" He swaggers to the parking lot, ignoring Noelle's scoff.

Before I can follow, Mika pulls me to the side. "Can I talk to you for a second?"

Noelle looks over her shoulder, and Mika motions her on.

"Meet us by the car," Mika says. "Will you?"

Noelle's mouth pinches, but she shrugs and continues across the parking lot.

Leaning toward me, Mika speaks in a low voice. "Did something happen with Noelle?"

"What do you mean?" There are physical changes I noticed before, but I haven't known Noelle long enough to say if anything else has changed.

Mika's eyes flick toward Noelle and back to me. "Is it that boy who teased her?"

There's nothing else I can think of. Except Julian's cold shoulder at the Botanic Gardens or the general creepiness of Mystic Cosmetics. I raise my shoulders in response.

CHAPTER SIXTEEN

W E PILE INTO MIKA'S and Robbie's cars and follow
Burnley Road until it lifts onto a flat-topped ridge, the
rock beneath us banded with ripple-like formations. Trees crowd
the crease where the hills fold inward. Overhead, the sun peeks
through a drift of soft clouds, hovering high but already on its slow
descent.

I shove the car door open and scramble out, Noelle and Mika
already ahead, waiting by the street crossing.

Noelle checks her phone. "We're right on schedule. After this,
it's dinner on Mill Road and a quick side trip to my favorite store
on the way."

Her plans yank me from my happy thoughts.

The cosmetics store?

"I thought we weren't taking Julian to Mystic Cosmetics," I say.

"What store?" Mika asks.

Noelle smiles, and her fresh lipstick gleams like polished plastic. "The new one that just opened. There's something I need to
pick up if that's all right. Come with me? We could go as a group?"

Mika steps over a jagged rock and I nearly trip on it.

"Whatever you need," says Mika.

"I don't want to go there," I say.

Noelle stares straight ahead. "Thanks, Mika. You're a good friend."

"Why are you ignoring me?" I demand. Did I upset her?

"Can you give me a legitimate reason not to go there?"

She waits, and my tongue knots up. I don't know what to tell her. Maybe I shouldn't have brought it up. I don't want to go. Isn't that enough?

She stalks off.

Mika blinks several times before following. She probably doesn't understand why either of us care.

I hurry to keep up as we pass a wooden fence, sheep drifting lazily behind it. Farther down the road, a low stone wall leads us to a door made from rough timber posts. Steps cut into the hillside descend to a narrow walking path below.

As we walk, I kick at the dirt, sending little clouds of dust into the air. It's immature, but whatever.

The path takes us to the edge of a large pond, bordered by lush, overhanging trees. It's mud and moss, with the occasional plop of jumping fish. A platform or dock juts out over the water, and dumped across it, a pile of fishing poles. Julian crouches beside the poles, attaching bait to the line.

He stands, sturdy and confident, head tilted to the side like he hears us coming, and I stop for no definable reason. Noelle runs into me, and I stumble forward.

"Really?" she snaps. "Watch where you're going."

I stare, dumbfounded, as she walks off.

This is the same girl who welcomed me to Burnley, right?

We spread out a blanket on the grass near the shoreline, and I sit down just as Eser steps off the dock into a pile of mud. His shoes make a squelching sound similar to what I envision a bad French kiss sounds like. Everyone laughs at Eser's horrified expression.

Julian hunkers down on the picnic blanket, Robbie beside him. He did bring shoes (rain boots), but the stripes on his socks peek over the top.

"A penny for your thoughts," Julian says.

His hair is the perfect storm of messy and perfect. Warm and so soft I could run my hands through it. I can picture us sitting side by side, our feet dangling over the river I often see outside my window. He'd put a rose through my ponytail.

I try to picture Teddy in the same place, but I…can't.

"I didn't mean to put you on the spot. You don't have to say," he says quickly.

My brain is a ship I must steer from this onslaught of images.

"Just happy to be here."

His eyes crinkle. "We have Noelle to thank for that."

Noelle sits across from me, beside Eser, and she lights up at being mentioned.

Eser's smile strains, polite on the surface but cracking underneath. He and Noelle could make a cute couple, except, he doesn't look at Noelle at all.

I find myself grimacing, too. With one hand resting against the grass, I play with the individual blades, Mika at my side.

The silence on the picnic blanket perches thick and unnavigable. No one moves or seems inclined to break it.

Julian reclines against a tree trunk, his head resting against the bark. I wish I could warn him of Noelle's plan to take him to the cosmetics store, but he might want to meet Ellen as much as everyone else. Especially once he sees her.

Noelle shreds a leaf between her fingers.

As falcons flit between branches, the leaves grumble at the disruption. Mink scurry from bush to bush, and Eser points with animation when a deer peers from behind a tree trunk.

Robbie starts fishing and accidentally splashes us as he flings his line into the water. Droplets rain onto Julian, one falling from Julian's hair and slipping into his shirt, where the shape of a cross sits against his skin. He shifts to one side, and his eyes meet mine.

Did he ask me something? I can't remember.

I jolt upright, cheeks warm. "The trees are very pretty."

He grins. "Couldn't agree more."

Too late to say something interesting. I press my lips together.

"I know you've been waiting for these," Mika says, pulling out the basket of biscuits. "Be sure to save room for dinner."

I start with one and follow it with another. Within minutes, I've devoured my share. "Makes me miss my garden," I say as I finish the last bite. "Ginger and cilantro?"

"Yeah."

"Home grown?"

"Nah, I'm rubbish at growing things. Tried cilantro once and killed it."

I nod. Sadie struggled with cilantro, too. "Thank you, Mika. These are amazing."

Julian takes the last dumpling without apology, and Mika beams.

"You three know each other?" Julian gestures to Mika and me with his dumpling. His eyes linger on Noelle for a half-second longer.

"Met Mika through Noelle," I say. "Noelle befriended me on my first day." She's usually a lot more friendly, I want to say.

Mika leans back on her hands. "Noelle and I met on one of Professor Reeve's field trips."

Reeve never mentioned field trips. Guess he didn't say anything outside of "leave now," really.

Julian swallows his food and gives Mika a strange look. "You've been on one of those?"

"Reeve's field trips? Of course. Lots of students go, even students not in his program. Haven't you?"

Julian shakes his head. "He invited me once, but not since. I think our lovely professor may not have the best opinion of me."

I can't imagine anyone disliking Julian, not even Reeve, though Noelle might.

"Aren't you part of his honors program?" Noelle asks, her tone a bit patronizing. "I doubt Reeve invites people he doesn't like to be part of his club."

A dark cloud passes over Julian's features.

"I don't know why he wouldn't invite you," I say.

He glances up, and I avert my gaze.

Robbie hands Eser his fishing pole and offers Julian's, but Julian shakes his head, instead folding his arms behind his head, so his cross presses against the fabric of his shirt.

"Where'd you get that cross from?" I ask. "It looks vintage."

"My nanny gave it to me, I think," he says.

"Your nanny?"

"Mum wasn't around much," Julian says.

"Oh."

Mika, Robbie, and Eser have all gone quiet. Eser watches Julian's face, not even attempting to hide his interest. Maybe talking about Julian's childhood is off-limits, and I'm prying too much.

I grab handfuls of blanket in my fists.

Julian holds out a hand, palm up.

I glance between his hand and his face, trying to understand. He chuckles and drops a chain on my palm. "Take a look."

The weight surprises me, and I almost drop it. I can't believe Julian carries this around his neck all day without falling over. The details of the cross are faded, the edges worn smooth. It was likely once intricate, but now looks rather plain.

"Cool," is all I manage to say as I return it.

Julian slips the chain over his head and stands.

"Look." He points toward the lake, where fresh ripples spread in widening circles. "See that?"

He strides to the platform, grabs a pole, and settles beside Robbie and Eser.

I push myself up, and Mika and Noelle follow. Mika sits at the edge, feet skimming the water, safely away from any fishing lines. I curl up beside her, arms around my knees, while Noelle takes Robbie's pole.

Julian holds his pole aloft. "Would either of you like to try?"

I eye the pole. My idea of fishing has always been reading a book while my brothers put barbs through unsuspecting mouths. Surely, I'd find some way to humiliate myself if I were to try.

Even if fishing allowed me to stand closer to Julian. Maybe I should try?

Mika shakes her head, and I find myself refusing along with her. "No, thanks," I say.

Julian hooks another piece of bait, and tosses the line out. Maybe if I didn't have to touch the fish…but I already refused.

I focus on the scenery instead.

The water on the lake reflects the green of the trees on either side of the river. The green here is a different green than the darker pines at home. It almost looks unnatural. Oversaturated.

The sun deepens in the sky. Colors creep into the clouds, captured by the water, like the world is pausing to breathe.

We pack up our gear. Robbie offers me his hand as I leap off the platform, taking care to miss the mud. As I land, I grip his fingers, and Robbie steadies my wobble. I open my mouth to thank him, but Julian pulls me from the puddle's edge.

His hand is warm—stronger than I expect—and when our eyes meet, the rest of the dock blurs.

My fingertips tingle beneath the light pressure of his hands, a spark running up my arm, until Robbie wedges between us. "I'm not interrupting a moment, am I?" He grins as he helps Mika, Eser, and Noelle off the dock.

Julian doesn't even blink. He reaches for my hand again, and my pulse stumbles. While I'm busy trying to remember how to breathe, his thumb brushes the inside of my wrist, right where the scars run pale.

"What are those?" he asks.

I jerk away. "Vein problem. I've always had it."

Julian's lips part, like he's about to say something, but then he closes his mouth again.

"I booked Indian food," Noelle says from behind. "There's a place on Mill Road I'd like to try."

I wince, and the words to warn Julian jumble in my mouth.

"I like Indian food well enough," Mika says. "So long as the chef's decent."

Julian's brows pull together.

"I'm gonna get going," Eser says, a bit too loudly. Several steps down the footpath, he straightens his sweater and waves, a guilty grimace on his face. "Thanks for the invite, but I had something come up."

Robbie waves him off. "See ya."

Mika and Julian just nod, though their silence feels uneasy. I'm just on the fringe—I only think I know why Eser's leaving.

Noelle gapes at Eser's back as he strolls down the path to the road. "What?"

"He's probably meeting some people," I say quickly.

Noelle's cheeks color. "Fine, let's go to dinner then. Just need to stop by one store on the way before it closes. Park next to us on the corner where the new cosmetics store is. We can walk to the restaurant from there."

Julian follows Robbie up to the road with only one glance my way. There goes my chance to warn him. Trees sway from short gusts of wind as the boys file into Robbie's car, and Robbie starts the engine.

I let Noelle and Mika walk ahead as we cross the street to Mika's car. I might not be able to avoid a visit to Mystic Cosmetics, but I don't have to see Julian's face when he walks in.

Mika's car engine hums to life as I get in, and we pull into traffic. Fading rays of sunlight blaze through the window. Noelle lowers her visor. Robbie follows in his car, close behind.

"Uh, Noelle," Mika says, clearing her throat. "Eser's a bit full of himself. It happens to the best of us—especially being the top player on the team. He's witty and clever, and great fun at dinner parties. But, um…he's not into girls. Thought you might not have clocked it."

"Not into me, you mean?" Noelle asks.

"No, I mean—I thought about him once, too," Mika rushes on. "Didn't take long to realize that would never work."

"I see."

The car falls into silence.

A familiar purple awning appears around the buildings as we drive into town, and Mika parks. We get out. Car lights flash once and go out, and Noelle's still frowning.

The crowd outside the store has dwindled to only a few men conversing at the building's corner. Inside, Ellen waits at a cash register, dried bundles of sage and lavender brushing against her hair as she counts bills.

Robbie's voice carries from across the street. "We'll meet you at the restaurant and save you seats."

If Julian doesn't come, I've stressed about nothing.

Noelle's lips purse into a red line. "No, it'll only be a second. Just come with us." She rounds on Mika. "Get them to come."

Mika's look is black. "Why? They won't want to."

Of course, they wouldn't.

Noelle watches as Robbie and Julian stride further down the sidewalk. "They're going to have to get over themselves."

"Noelle," I say, "this is ridiculous."

Her eyes narrow. "Why is this such a big deal to you people? It's a cosmetics store. Not a porn shop."

She's better than this, and a significant reason I stayed in England when Reeve demanded I leave.

Mika gives Noelle a long look, sighs and calls out, "Robbie! Julian! Will you join us? It'll only take a second. I'd prefer we stay together."

Robbie stops. His lips move, and Julian gives a single nod before crossing the street. Together, their eyes rise to the window where Ellen arranges dried flowers on the other side of the glass, her hair tumbling over her shoulders.

A weight drops in my chest.

Bells chime as Noelle lets herself into the store. They chime again for Mika and me, and then Julian and Robbie, too. Julian stands at the threshold, glances at me, and steps inside. He'll never think of me again.

This is like a horrible motorcycle accident. I can't turn away.

They face the store counter, Julian shifting just enough to keep everyone in view the way he always does in crowded buildings.

Robbie stills. "Clearly I've been missing out on women's make-up. You seeing this?"

Julian stares at the clock and the bird perched above it. "The three-eyed crow? Or is it a raven? Can't remember the difference."

"No, mate. Behind the counter there."

"Her? What of her?"

Robbie gives Julian an incredulous look. "I might not be the most appreciative person of perfection, but she's as close as I've seen."

Julian studies Ellen. "Is that so?"

Ellen glances up from the register. "How may I help you?" Her tone is mild, verging on polite, but her gaze lingers a beat too long on Julian's hair. Then locks in on Noelle. "Oh," she says. "It's you."

The curtains ruffle, and a woman with red hair elbows through, a bundle of fresh herbs in her arms. A small, sharp face and green eyes. This is the woman who came to Professor Reeve's office. "El-len, are you being nice to our customers?"

"Yes," Ellen snaps.

"I could hear your tone from the back room. Sorry, boys, what do you need?" The woman winks. "Welcome back, my sweet."

Noelle flashes a smile brighter than any I've seen tonight. "Jane, so glad you're here. I came for the discount you promised."

"Oh?" Jane drops her herbs onto the counter in a loose pile and sorts them. She stirs the pile, and the lemon smell rushes up my nose before I'm ready for it.

"I brought Julian. You wanted to see him?"

Julian, still watching the crow, jerks to attention. His eyes snap to Jane, then to me. He doesn't think I planned this, does he?

All for a discount.

Robbie slaps Julian on the back. "The ladies call for you now, eh?"

Julian's face is unreadable.

"Julian." Ellen rolls the name on her tongue. "Julian Bristol. I've been looking for you." She pushes Noelle aside, reaches for Julian's neck, and tugs out the chain he wears. The crucifix catches on his shirt, then swings free.

I step forward, hand clenched at my side, as Ellen watches the crucifix twirl and lets it drop.

"Who are you?" Julian asks. A nervous edge catches his voice.

"I'm Ellen." She smiles with blood-red lips. "I own this shop with my two sisters."

"Do we know each other?"

"I've wanted to meet you, that's all." Her eyes rove his hair again. "You look just as I thought you would. It's been too long."

"What has?"

"Since I first heard about you. And I've heard so much about you, Julian."

"From whom?"

"Professor Reeve. He's known you a long time, hasn't he?"

"He has." He blinks as Ellen steps back.

"You're welcome to come in anytime you like," Ellen says. "I'll make something special for you, and I'll give you a better discount than Noelle gets on the days I like her most. And we do more than just hair products. I can get you anything you need. Anything at all."

I'm not sure what I expected Ellen to do when we brought Julian, but I didn't expect her to act like an ominous schoolgirl with a crush. It makes her seem almost human. Perhaps I should appreciate my levels of awkwardness more. I could be so much worse.

Jane touches Ellen on the shoulder and shakes her head. Ellen bites her lip, hands Julian something small, and withdraws. "I'm here. Don't forget me, Julian. I haven't forgotten you."

Julian stares at his hand, at an origami cat resting on his palm.

Didn't the journals mention a paper cat? The second witch in the journals went by Jane, too, but that's common enough.

Julian stuffs the paper cat in his pocket and retreats to the door.

"Did you get her number, mate?" Robbie asks as he hurries after Julian.

Only Noelle remains to pick out her discounted products. The door tinkles to a close as Mika follows me out.

Mika scrunches her nose. "What was that?"

Julian's face is pale, but everyone looks at me.

I heave a deep sigh. "Ellen bribed Noelle with a discount to bring Julian here." I can't feign ignorance. "But Noelle promised she wouldn't do this."

Mika laughs. "Why?"

"Don't know."

"How much is Noelle buying?" Mika glances over her shoulder at the store windows. "Enough to make up for all this nonsense, I hope."

"Not enough," I say. "It costs an arm and a leg."

Robbie peers over Julian's shoulder at the little paper cat. "Is it her number?" he asks again.

"No," Julian says flatly.

Robbie's face falls. "Go on then—what is it?"

"Just a cat. That's all."

"Rubbish. I don't believe you." Robbie snatches for it, but Julian pulls it just out of reach. Then, without a word, he unfolds it and holds it up. Smooth. Blank. Black.

CHAPTER SEVENTEEN

J ULIAN STIRS HIS CHICKEN sauce and stares through the fogged window toward the weather-stained sign. "Crown Curry," it says, in curling gold script. Noelle, on the other hand, shines like sunlight off a car mirror. She opens her gift bag and shows us wrapped bundles of handmade soaps and shampoos in thin cardboard and colored bows.

"Can we talk about how perfect this wrapping is?" she says.

Julian doesn't bother to look.

We're sitting at mahogany tables with maroon table runners, brass lanterns flickering above us, casting a low, contemplative light. Jars of spices and candles dot the table and the air hums with the low clatter of cutlery, mingled with cumin, clove, and cardamom.

The waitress refills our drinks, skips Julian's untouched water, and tops off mine.

Robbie finishes the last bite off his plate and eyes Julian's chicken. "You plan to finish that?"

Julian startles, like he forgot Robbie existed. It's my job to tune out, not Julian's.

The spice-heavy air turns thick, like it's pressing on my throat.

"No," he says.

"Well then…" Robbie pours the contents of Julian's dish into his own bowl, joining the rest of his rice and spicy tomato sauce. "Cheers, mate."

Julian's face goes a little green.

"Are you okay?" I ask.

"Yes." He enunciates the word very clearly, arms folded, not for warmth—more like he's bracing for something.

"Are you sure?"

He scans the room.

At least he isn't drooling like Robbie, but him shutting down like this is almost worse. "Look, I'm sorry about the cosmetics store—"

He opens his palm again, and there's the black origami paper. "I've seen this cat before." He touches the folded edges. "But never with my eyes open."

Cold pricks down my arms as images of stone walls and suffocating flames come flooding back.

"I'd rather forget about it," he says.

I stir my curry, pretending not to watch him, but my eyes keep drifting to his hand lingering over the black paper.

"Siamese cats make excellent house pets, especially the black ones. I'll top Ellen and get you a few of those."

Julian tosses the black paper onto the carpet. "Please, don't."

The waiter distributes checks, but Julian swipes mine before I can reach for it.

"My treat." He slides his card to the waiter.

Heat rises up my neck, and I murmur, "Thank you."

Our headlights reflect off the windows of old buildings and compact cars parked along the streets. Water pools in the road, and a gentle drizzle blurs our window, making the darkness ahead nearly opaque. And still, I'm warm all over.

Did Julian consider tonight a date? Did he want it to be?

I want to ask Mika and Noelle, but Noelle leans against her seat and clutches her bag, as if already planning what to do with her Mystic products. At home, Noelle would be on the driver's side, but here it's Mika. The shift still feels strange.

Mika glances at Noelle as she turns toward a grassy field. Then brings the car to a screeching stop.

"Can't they let one more car through?"

A construction crew sets up cones around a bold "road closed" sign.

Flashing lights burn my eyes and just beyond them, teenagers slump on the pavement, hands behind their backs. Several officers stand guard over them.

Noelle sits up straight. "Just take the other road. It's only a few minutes longer. Bet that's a drug bust."

Mika flips the car around and turns left.

The full moon emerges from the clouds. Trees flash by, their lines broken by a bridge with balustrades.

Suddenly, a sickening stench slaps me, coming from nowhere and all around me. It lingers on my tongue, like fermented blood.

I clutch my abdomen. "I think I'm gonna throw up."

"What?" Noelle turns and her eyes widen. "Mika, pull over. I think she's serious."

Mika slows, and as soon as the car stops, I push my door open, stumble out, and rush to the bridge's edge. The cool concrete eases my stomach while I puke into the blackness below.

"Did you have something off at dinner?" Mika asks at my side.

Noelle puts a hand on my shoulder.

My fingertips dig into the rough cement, quivering in protest. "I don't know." Only minutes ago, I felt so light. "We should go."

Noelle lurches forward and snatches at the empty air as a tiny light drops over the edge and goes out. "My phone!" She leans over, and her hair tumbles around her face. "We have to get it."

I step back. "No." I'm breathing quickly, lungs collapsing with the weight of the air.

"It could be halfway down the river," Mika says. "Might not even work anymore."

"It's waterproof, and I need it. Besides, we don't know if it fell in the river. It might have landed on some pebbles." Noelle strides to the end of the structure, where cement meets grass, and calls over her shoulder, "Are you coming?"

They don't need me. There's no reason for me to go.

Mika starts ahead, but glances back. "Briony?"

My feet have solidified into the pavement. A knife at my feet, edge dull and bloodied, my face reflecting off it, except with hair that is dark, and curly.

Fire flares from the thick trees, smoke curling over the bridge. It fills my lungs.

"Briony?"

The blood clears, quick as a breath of air, and gone like a gust of wind.

My eyes water, and I clear my throat. My brothers used to make fun of me for being overly jumpy, but I'm not afraid of the dark.

I force my voice steady. "Can't we come back in the morning?"

"You can stay if you need to," Mika says.

And be alone?

I force my feet forward, and catch up to Mika and Noelle.

Noelle presses on down the riverbank. Frogs croak somewhere nearby, low and hollow. Mika and I follow, though my courage frays more with each step. A sigh of arctic wind rattles gnarled branches with a light patter of rain. Brambles shelter the water's edge. Trees sway, tall specters trooped in a dark netherworld, while chilly air prickles my skin, damp and smelling of leaves and mud.

I scan bushes. My feet drag, but do I dare turn back to the car?

Mika's voice carries as she yells, "Can't you try calling it?"

"Can you? I'd do it myself, but as you see, I don't have a phone," Noelle says in a clipped tone.

Mika holds her phone as she dials and continues through the reeds. "All I see is a load of marsh." Mika yanks leaves back, and water shimmers in the moonlight. "I don't think we'll find your mobile, Noelle. Not with so many bushes and only our phones for torches."

Noelle rubs her arms. "I swear I saw it land by some rocks, but maybe you're right. I can't see anything either. We can come back first thing in the morning."

That's permission enough to leave. I make a beeline for the road.

The sounds of Mika and Noelle stomping through grass follow close behind. My feet move faster as I will the car closer. I swerve around a willow tree, but the end of a torn trash bag makes me stop. To the right, a limp foot sticks out of the brush. I've always carried cold places inside me, but this—this is a plunge into some-place glacial.

"What's that you found?" Mika's hesitant voice comes from

behind.

I hold out a hand to stop her, mouth dry. "You won't want to see it."

My chest struggles to expand.

"Is it my phone?" Noelle splits the weeds, and I'm too far away to stop her.

Her scream slices the air. Mika yanks me toward Noelle, and I stumble, limbs numb.

Noelle gapes downward over the split grass, moonlight highlighting a face in the water with black, curly hair that drifts and caresses her cheeks. Empty holes glare from gouged out eye sockets. Then there's an exposed throat, hands upturned, with deep slashes. Fresh blood trails from the wounds and darkens the water. A faint unnatural scent—crushed belladonna. And the sheen of oils and plant sap over her skin.

I close my eyes to squeeze out the image.

Mika's voice rises. "Oh my gosh, oh my gosh. What happened to her face? You don't think the murderer is still here, do you?"

I force my eyes open again and scan the darkness. Nothing moves but trees and whispering wind. I bend over and touch the dead woman's cheek.

Warm.

Mika coughs, followed by a splash. She wipes her mouth, sways, then straightens. "We need to call someone," she rasps.

"Let's do that in the car. We have to leave." I search the trees, their trunks, and the darkening spaces between them. Where anyone could be lurking. Then I inject more urgency into my words, "We need to go now."

Noelle stares at the murky water. Mika rubs her lips. Neither of them seem to have heard, so I take hold of their elbows. They don't resist. We move like zombies. I pull harder to spur us into a run, and Noelle and Mika snap into their senses, running faster than I do.

We crest the hill. Inside the car, I lock the doors behind us and rest my forehead in my hands. "Call the police," I say.

Mika fumbles for her phone, dials a number, and presses the device to her cheek. "Hello? Hello? My name's Mika Song. There's a body here. We've found a body on the river. Where? Behind…" Mika stops and looks around. "I'm sorry, we're on a bridge." Her voice quavers. "Wait here? But—yes, I understand." She cups the mouthpiece. "They want us to stay on the line until they arrive."

I shut my eyes.

An eyeless face with a noose around her neck stares back from behind my eyelids.

This can't be happening. It can't be real.

"Sure," Noelle says, voice distant.

The hum of crickets fills the car. A buzz that echoes as Mika puts her phone on speaker.

"Yes, I'm still here," Mika says.

Lights flash, everything blue, and cars arrive. Someone raps on the window. Mika rolls it down, and the person on the other side considers me with bloodless lips and empty pits for eyes. What happened to the eyes?

"Briony, he's talking to you." Mika's looking at me from the driver's seat.

I blink, and the demon face dissolves into a man with a concerned smile, dressed in an officer's uniform.

"They want a statement from each of us," Mika says.

I feel myself nod. "Fine." If I stay sane long enough.

An ambulance, a fire truck, and an SUV park on the bridge. Officers accompany medics while one man pushes a stretcher with a blue bag. Blue and white tape wreathes the bridge. They'll alert the girl's family soon. Someone's daughter will never come home.

"They want us to get out of the vehicle for a moment," Mika says.

The officer watches me open the door. Boots. Vest. One hand on the radio at his belt.

My legs wobble as I press my back to the car's cool metal. He asks questions. Answers slide out of my mouth and float away.

Another officer kneels to pass me a card, and I realize I've slumped over, an undefinable weight dragging me downward. "This is our department psychiatrist," he says. "Don't be ashamed of seeking any help you might need."

"Do you have flatmates? Anyone you can stay with?" the first officer asks.

Mika's voice reaches from somewhere on my left. "She can stay with me."

I won't be alone.

The officer stands. "Good. You'll want the support tonight."

An officer drives us to Mika's dormitory while another follows in Mika's car. The officer parks, and Mika leads us to a flat in a quiet corner of a corridor on the second floor, separated from the rest of the flats by a set of worn stairs. "Flatmates are out. It'll be just us tonight."

We enter a low-ceilinged room, radiator-heated, and a narrow but friendly kitchen smelling faintly of toast. The common room has sagging armchairs, a mismatched couch, and corkboards peppered with posters. An award: "Too Posh to Party." The Beatles. Elton John. When I blink, bloodied eyeballs populate the frames instead.

I spread blankets and pillows on the floor while Mika turns on a movie and lets it play. Then Noelle and Mika disappear into the kitchen.

As soon as they're out of earshot, I dial Sadie's number.

"Hello?" comes the sleepy answer. "Bree, it's early here."

"Sadie?" My voice wavers.

"Is everything okay?" The drowsiness in her voice dies.

I blink back tears. "Just missing you."

"What happened?"

An explanation hovers on my tongue, but I reel it in. She'll tell our mom, who would demand I come home. Reeve would win. I might as well escort myself to the airport, and I don't know yet if I want to leave. I've tried so hard in my classes.

Tell me I'm supposed to be here. Tell me I did the right thing in coming.

Sadie's voice sharpens. "What are you not telling me?"

"School is hard, and I'm tired of studying, and the people on the river outside are too loud, and I keep finding spiders on my window, and—"

"Oh, Bree. I want you home, but you can handle a few spiders. What's going on, really? Is that special education program giving you tutors?"

If I went home, I wouldn't have to spend hours every night writing essays. I'd never see that bridge again, never have to bear the dry stir of wind or see bloodied pits that were once eyes. I could return to work where thorns are the most frightening things I would deal with.

Mika and Noelle appear in the doorway, worry in their eyes.

"I have a teacher who helps a lot," I say into the phone. "I just wanted to hear your voice."

I hear her yawn through the receiver.

"I'm always here for you, Bree, you know that."

"I do."

"Sure you're okay?"

I pause. "Thanks for listening. Get back to bed."

"Love you a million chocolate strawberries," she says.

"Love you, too. Bye, Sadie." I end the call and stare at the red telephone icon.

"We didn't mean to eavesdrop," Mika says.

Noelle chews her lip.

"It's fine." I set the phone down and bundle up with blankets.

Mika and Noelle do the same and turn their faces from the running T.V. series. A comedy featuring a group of friends. After a few episodes, Mika drops off to sleep. Then Noelle. I keep watching, staring, eyes heavy but unable to close. Until the figures on the screen blur and blend together.

I'm walking along a bridge. Water saturates the ground for miles on either side. The road curves, dusty and full of loose rocks. Trees spring from a swamp, their branches growing shadows as the sun sinks.

"Alice," a small voice calls.

The water drains to a boggy marsh. Mists rise and fall like white serpents. Then a boy emerges, holds out a rose, its petals dim beneath his smiling eyes. The flower withers and the boy's smile fades with it.

Tears spill down his cheeks. "I didn't mean to," he cries. And vanishes, leaving nothing but the outline of the trees in the encroaching twilight.

I wake up, and the TV is off, Noelle's and Mika's forms a few feet away. I grasp the blanket Mika left for me and roll to my side.

Just a dream.

CHAPTER EIGHTEEN

"WAKE UP. MIKA'S making us breakfast." Noelle's brisk voice pierces my sleepy fog.

Something solid prods my shoulder, and fuzzy cream blurs into textured carpet. I force myself upright and wait for my eyes to focus.

"I've got eggs," Mika calls from the kitchen.

The world tilts as I stand, so I grab the couch and shuffle to a circular drop leaf table.

Mika's kitchen smells faintly of burnt toast and soap. Peeling wallpaper curls from the corners, and a shelf of orphaned mugs leans above an old radiator.

"Thanks." The milk jug feels heavier than it should as I pour myself a glass.

"It's all over the news." Noelle scans Mika's phone screen. "Her name was Ava Lange. Dead fifteen minutes before we found her, with missing eyes and toes. Ew. They said she had traces of hallucinogens in her system, but nothing else. No one knew she was missing. Her friends said she walked home from a party on Mill Road and insisted on being alone."

Mika sets down a gold-trimmed platter of eggs. "Poor girl," she murmurs.

"We're in here, look," Noelle says. "'Three students found her body at approximately 8:00 p.m. last night and called the police. Police officers arrived on the scene only minutes afterward as several of the officers wrapped up a drug arrest only a block away. The detectives on the case have yet to say whether these two incidents are related, but they found no traces of the confiscated illegal drugs in Ava's blood or on her body. The hallucinogens above mentioned were not among the drugs confiscated, nor does Ava Lange have any prior history of drug use. Police are now searching the river for the bodies of two more students who have been missing for several weeks in case the disappearances are connected. More information to follow—'"

Noelle looks up. "How soon do you think people will hear about this?"

"I don't know, but I can't believe there've been others," I say. "How have I not heard about this?" I vaguely remember a "missing persons" sign on Mill Road, but no one talked about students vanishing. That should be a hot topic.

Mika raises her shoulders. "I heard about it, but no one suspected they might be dead until now. I think one of the missing students was thought to have run off."

"What do you think the school will do?" Noelle asks. "This happened on the edge of school grounds. All the students and parents will find out."

I grip my mug so tight my knuckles ache.

Mika picks up a steaming mug of coffee on the counter, stirs it and leans against the laminate. "I think they'll tell us to be careful and not go walking at night alone. The police will handle it. It's not like it happened inside a school building."

Noelle pours a mug as I sip from my cup, the taste like acid on my tongue. But I drink anyway.

Mika's phone buzzes, and she answers. "Hello, yes, good morning, love." She pauses. "As well as can be expected, I suppose. Briony? Right here. I'll put her on." She passes me the phone. "It's Julian."

I don't want to revisit that river, even if it's just in words, but I take the phone anyway. "Hello?"

Julian's voice comes through like the distant roll of waves. "Mika told me what happened, and I saw it in the news. Can I do anything for you?"

"I really appreciate it," I say, "but I have a mountain of homework. Rain check?"

"You'll not take a break?" Julian sounds surprised.

"No, but thanks again." I hand Mika her phone back.

Mika chats with Julian for a minute before hanging up, and then stabs her food with a fork. She keeps her plate by the kitchen sink, as if prepared to abandon it at any moment.

"I think I'm just going to buy myself a new phone," Noelle says.

Mika half-smiles. "Might be a good idea."

I stand, and my plate clinks as I set it in the sink, avoiding Mika's gaze as I pass. "I've got homework, so I'll get going. Thanks for letting me stay the night."

Noelle's eyes widen. "It's Saturday."

"I know," I say.

Mika considers me and says only, "we're here if you need us."

"Thanks."

I step outside my cocoon of friends, out of Mika's flat, out of her building. Raindrops seep into my shirt as rain patters over the cobblestones and fans the ground in tiny ripples. Cars drive by, splashing water. Two students huddle beneath their umbrellas by a roadside bench. I keep walking.

Bleeding eye sockets. Dark, swaying trees. Slow-moving water, black as tar.

A walkway leads me through a line of trees. The clouds hold their breath. No voices weave through the foliage. No students appear. No backpacks. No breeze to stir the hair on my neck.

The students likely heard about the girl's death. Had I been alone on Mill Road only an hour earlier, I might be the one floating down the river with no eyes.

My stomach curdles.

I wait at the bus stop, ride to my dormitory, and make my way to my room. At my desk, I sit and write. The sun blares through the window. Students call out to each other below, and I cover my ears with headphones.

I toss aside paper after paper. The wastebasket fills with my failed attempts. Daylight wanes, and I flip on the tungsten lights.

I have a few weeks to write this paper, but it will take several drafts. I need this paper to be flawless. I need it to be full of hope for a better future and not the mark of a bitter end.

CHAPTER NINETEEN

"ARE YOU OKAY?" students ask.

The news leaks—my connection to it too—and spreads like wildfire through the school. Faculty members watch me with concern as I trudge down the halls, and I know what they're thinking.

No cuts. No bruises. I'm not the one who ended up in the river.

"Was she as bad as they say?" a girl in a plaid skirt and butterfly glasses asks.

I ignore her and head to my dorm, ready to hole up for as long as it takes.

Instead of returning to *Northanger Abbey*, I reach for something lighter. Back home, I used to lose myself in books on bad days, but not even Eliza's wit or Darcy's aloofness can bury the image of the girl in the river. Her pale face and hollowed eyes burn at the edges of every page.

I need something else. So I pull out the journals Professor Reeve gave me and sink into their impossible puzzle.

—June of 1603—

I tied Dantes outside the alehouse, dusk creeping across the horizon, cool air on my cheeks. After a quick pat for him, I rounded the corner—and collided with a pair of skirts.

Someone gasped as I stumbled.

I gathered myself, muttered an apology, and helped a laughing lady to her feet. Her coat was well made, her boots less worn than her friend's. The other woman steadied her arm—dark hair, gentle eyes, layered skirts weathered by travel. Both were a breath of clean air after months of smog.

The dark-haired one asked my plans.

I told her I was travelling, staying the night, and searching for a haunted lake with a ghost bound by a sword.

"I have heard naught of the kind. Good

fortune attend your journey," she said.

She promised to pray for my safety, inclined her head, and the two passed on. I might have turned to the alehouse for more information, yet the girl with the necklace carried an aura unlike any I'd known.

The sunset faded to ash-grey. It was late for ladies to be abroad, so I offered to see them home.

The fair-haired one gave her name as Katherine; the other, Alice.

Alice's smile was shy, but something lingered in her expression——like a locked chapel room, or a buried sorrow.

I told them my name was Guido. When they asked my surname, I lied and said I had none.

They exchanged a glance.

*"We shall call thee Master Guido, then,"
said Katherine.*

*I led them to Dantes. Alice stroked his nose
as he tossed his mane. She said her brother
would love him—he'd only ever known
his father's horse. A faint rose touched her
cheeks when Katherine's eyes flicked toward
her.*

*I helped them mount, and Katherine sug-
gested we ride to West Close to meet a
woman named Chattox—she said it might
be "advantageous" to hear my fortune.*

*Alice smiled faintly but shook her head.
She'd sooner give up her garden than go near
Chattox. They settled on Foulridge instead.*

*We rode beneath yew trees ancient as Scrip-
ture, their bark twisted and dark. The owl's
call echoed through the gathering dusk, and
Dantes's hooves drummed a steady rhythm
on the road.*

Alice looked down at me. "Where will you travel on the morrow?"

"I seek a witch bound beneath a lake. Have you heard the tale?"

"Have you some quarrel with witches?"

"Perhaps," I said. "They creep like vines through the cracks of our government—or coil like serpents round it."

She fell silent, thoughtful. Then, softly, "If you could go anywhere, where would you go?"

I told her, "Flanders." True enough. I'd fled there from childhood and persecution both, found the Knights, and with them, purpose. And God.

Perhaps I shouldn't have said so much, but Alice's quiet interest disarmed me. Soldiers rarely speak their hearts.

Katherine told stories of local lakes—bog-garts, portals, restless spirits. Alice listened, detached but not dismissive. She remarked that Pendle could use men like me rather than its current serjeant-at-law.

A serjeant, here? Perhaps God had laid the answer before me.

I asked to meet him. Katherine protested—it wasn't proper—but Alice watched me, eyes steady. "If it is your desire," she said, "I shall take thee. Propriety concerns me not."

She had only a brother at home, she said, and could protect herself. I accepted, though I wondered if I had made an error asking this of her.

We left Katherine at her home. When I mounted behind Alice, she stiffened. I took the reins and her tension lingered half the ride—unease, not fear.

The forest closed around us, trees leaning close, their bark green as moss in daylight, black as pitch by night.

"I'll take you home once I've spoken to the serjeant," I promised.

"He is arrogant," she said. "He believes he is owed whatever he desires."

"But perhaps he'll understand my urgency."

She warned he lured the desperate with titles and fine dresses, though were she to bear a wart on her nose, she'd find no place in Pendle.

"So small a blemish could hardly spoil your beauty," I said.

Her answering smile was slight.

Dantes carried us to a grand mahogany door carved with a stag and a ring between wolves' teeth. Moonlight glinted off the *pewter handle.*

I dismounted and raised my hand to knock, but Alice drew back.

"He cannot know I am here."

"Take Dantes, then. I'll find you again."

She gave directions to her cottage on the forest's edge and begged me remember them—no villager would guide me. Then she vanished into the dark.

I had barely lifted the knocker when the door creaked open.

—Guido

Likeable as Guido is, I doubt Altham will care—but I've read too long anyway. I need an A on this next quiz. That, at least, is something I can control.

So I study all day. All night. All morning. When laughter drifts through the hallway, I clean my room and stack chocolate bars on my desk. Then the wrappers pile up. My leg bounces. I trim my nails. Still, the restlessness grows.

I open the window. Outside, the air bites with the faint chill of rain. Students' voices float up from the riverbank, light, and careless.

Wish I could be.

I grab my bag, slam the door, and take the stairs two at a time to the first floor of Birdie's Court. Shoving my hands into my pockets, I walk faster, the rhythm of my boots filling the silence.

Vending machines line the wall by the administration offices beside portraits of professors—Professor Reeve, Headmistress Chelsea Craig in her pressed blouse, head tilted as though she's weighing every word. Light from the high windows stretches thin across the floor, catching the dust like drifting ash.

Most students are at lunch. Perfect. No awkward conversations. No corpses.

I scan the vending machine for caffeine. Mom calls it my "downward slope." Maybe she's right—I need caffeine to focus.

Nothing. Either the UK has stricter health rules for minors or they're just out of stock.

I stoop to pick up trash, ready to hurl it into the bin—then straighten as the office door creaks open, its sound sharp in the empty corridor. My pulse leaps. Reeve steps out, the light glancing off his gold watch, Jane from Mystic Cosmetics a step behind him, her heels clicking with practiced confidence.

I press against the vending machine, holding my breath.

He'd seemed afraid of her before. Now, his smile is boyish.

"I ought to thank you," Jane says, the door clicking shut. "I hoped you'd come through for me, but I didn't expect—"

"Shhh."

I peek out as Reeve presses a finger to her lips.

"There are other ways to show appreciation." His tone is teasing; my stomach twists.

Jane tilts her head, perfume sharp and floral, an expensive contrast to the stale corridor air. "Is that so? You do realize we're in the middle of your school. One of your pupils could appear at any moment."

He sighs, shoes clattering softly. "You're quite right," he says, and kisses her anyway. "But that does add to the thrill, doesn't it?"

Jane laughs, light and sharp. "I only kiss men I want to play with. And playtime's long since over, my sweet."

She walks away, red hair catching the light as Reeve follows. The sound of their laughter echoes after they turn the corner, thin and hollow. My skin crawls. The corridor is suddenly too bright, too exposed, every light humming loud as a wasp.

I flee back to Birdie's Court, and hope I never have to witness Reeve's flirtations ever again.

In my room, I pace. Then I head to the library. Even tucked behind the copy machine, daylight drains too fast to hold.

Tomorrow, I'll find caffeine, even if I have to walk to London.

Until then, I open the next journal—Altham's.

CHAPTER TWENTY

Late into the night, a knock echoed through my halls. She arrived at the last possible moment.

In a previous fit of temper, I reduced my extravagant bedchamber to something approaching chaos. Tapestries hung askew, gold threads loose and frayed. The hearth had long gone cold, ash pooling like snow around the grate.

I bustled about rectifying the mess, shoving

bottles and garments into any convenient
crevice while I fancied the finest woman
ever invited to my rooms. I know faces—
every one of them—and hers outshone them
all. Naturally.

But Alice slunk off, skulking behind a horse
as she led it by the reins. In her stead stood
a tall, broad-shouldered fellow with long
brownish-red hair and a pointed beard
and moustache. His thick leather boots and
gentleman's coat were travel-stained; the
feather in his cap drooped and straightened
with the breeze. Mud spattered his cuffs, and
the scent of horse and rain clung to him.

He bowed with manners that were, frankly,
almost comically fastidious and introduced
himself as Guido of Spain. He apologised
for the hour and asked whether he might
find the serjeant-at-law here, for he carried
urgent news.

My years sat heavier upon me than my

priciest coat. The fellow was young, strong—the very sort of man Alice would favour.

I suggested, with a cordiality as cold as good crystal, that we should speak on the morrow. He replied that he would be in Lancaster ere the sun rose—apparently Heaven itself had dictated his arrival this night.

So I invited him in. Each step he took left a dark print on the marble, like ink stains creeping toward me.

He announced that my lord the king stood in peril, that rebels plotted the monarch's death within the year. To his credit, the revelation staggered me. I nearly dropped the goblet of wine clutched in my hands.

Did I believe him? Partly — the king had betrayed and persecuted the Papists; retaliation might be expected. Yet how came Guido by such knowledge? Why plot at all?

Guido supplied an answer: he and his companions opposed the king's measures. Not only that, but they believed the "wicked" have infiltrated the higher ranks of government. When I asked whether his friends were Papists, he hesitated before admitting they were Catholics. He preferred the gentler name. How quaint.

When pressed as to his own creed, he conceded I was correct. A rebel, then. The king would doubtless see their heads, and Guido intended to desert them, leaving their fates to his God. Too many men entrusted their fortunes to nameless deities; I stand by a different theology—my god is a profitable one.

Their scheme, he said, aimed to restore a Catholic crown by placing the king's daughter upon the throne — treason, in plain terms. He argued treason was a matter of perspective; he served God, not man. He claimed the pope, not the king, was the head of the true church. Fine abstractions. What mattered to me was how I might exploit the intelligence.

He confessed he had hoped for open war and had sought Spain's aid; with the Armada's failure, that hope had died. Now their plot imperilled innocents in the House of Lords — some even sympathetic to the Catholics. He favoured a fair fight with trained soldiers and would not consign innocents to God's providence.

Their plan, he said, used rooms beneath the House of Lords, stores filled with barrels of gunpowder disguised as provisions, poised to blow. I knew those rooms — I owned some of them. The thought of my stores reduced to matchwood made me sweat.

They had considered Guido fit to ignite the powder: once a veteran, they presumed him a murderer by trade. He refused and was instead searching for alternative ways to fight.

He expected a meeting at the Duck and Drake on the Strand in May; there they would assign him the task of lighting the fuse. If he did so, he and his allies, and countless innocents, would perish. If he refused, they would hunt him down. He would either be their instrument or their victim.

Guido declared he would not attend the meeting; he intended to flee England if he found no alternatives and begged me to inform the king's guard. How thoughtful — that I might receive the credit for saving the sovereign. Or perhaps it was a trap. What would he gain? I weighed both possibilities.

He said he must fetch his horse from the woman he had lent it to. Few know where Alice lives; her father keeps the cottage's location secret and has not told a soul, save to the magistrate and myself. Perhaps Alice had entrusted Guido with that secret. Fool-ish of her.

Guido possessed strength and experience in combat. I possessed influence, connections, and an appetite for advantage. If Alice would not be mine, I would see that she had no other. I intended to exercise every advantage at my disposal against Guido and demonstrate which arts were, in truth, deadliest.

—Sir James Altham

If, after reading these journals, I'm to conclude that I'm a descendant of Altham, I'll never forgive Professor Reeve.

—1603—

The magistrate arrived bearing alarming tidings. His son slipped away, time and again, into Trawden Forest; whispers and complaints traced back to Demdike and her association with the Bierley sisters of Samlesbury. More disquieting still, the magistrate had found bodies in the wood—eyes, fingernails and toes cruelly absent. The villagers were aflutter; some demanded action. It fell, naturally, to me to sift fact from fiction. There was truth tangled among the tales, of that I had no doubt. And, with all that had transpired concerning Alice, the world presented me with precisely the sort of opening only the ambitious know how to exploit.

—Sir James Altham

I stop reading.

Missing eyes and fingernails…The dead girl in the river.

I pace the room, pause before the table, and sit down again.

Perhaps this is the real danger Reeve spoke of. Something happened at Burnley before I came. He should have told me, instead of leading me down a blind ancestry hole.

I open my laptop, connect to the library's Wi-Fi, and search the web for "Mystic Cosmetics." Nothing pulls up. No website. I'd look up last names, but I don't know them.

Instead, I stack the copied letters and stuff them into my bag, then leave the library the same way I came, threading a path through the trees toward Sharona dormitory. Mist curls low, coiling around my ankles like smoke as I move. It clings to the bark, the bright leaves fading to a deep evergreen. Dew slicks the roots, and the air hums with insects. Behind me, a branch cracks, and my hands ball into fists as I spin to face my intruder.

I won't be the next girl floating in a river.

The woods swallow the path behind me. Only the sound of rain—then a footstep. Professor Reeve emerges from the trees. He stops a few paces away, his fedora askew, rain droplets rolling to the brim.

"Saw you from my window."

Perspiration drips down the back of my neck.

Does he know I saw him with Jane? Does he care?

"I wanted to ask if you've read any of the journals since I showed them to you?" His right foot taps against the pavement.

"I have."

His mouth curves upward, but the smile doesn't reach his eyes. The motion of his foot is too even, too rehearsed—like a teacher marking time before a reprimand.

"I think it might help for you to experience the place where the witch trials happened. I'm taking a tour group to Lancaster on the second of October. There's limited space, but I could accommodate you if you'd like. Would you want to come?"

He either doesn't know, or he's pretending not to, and I don't have a good enough reason to bring it up.

"October second?" I ask. "Next week?"

Not much notice.

"If you'd like to attend, be at the car park outside my building at 6 a.m.," he says. "We'll take the bus." The professor adjusts the suede computer bag over his shoulder, which still carries that strong new leather scent. "Read the journals. The sites won't mean much if you haven't."

"I've read a bunch already."

He nods several times. "Of course you have." He shifts his weight. "You've done well since you started here. I checked in with your old school and saw your report card. Thought you'd struggle here, but you haven't failed—not yet. That's not to say you won't. I still plan to find a way to get you home. Some of my methods may not be pleasant."

"Uh, thanks?"

Professor Reeve inclines his head and turns to leave, but I call after him. "Bryan?"

He stops and turns. Maybe using his first name was too much, but I need him to be upfront with me. "Are witches the danger you meant me to see?"

He purses his lips. "Keep reading."

He turns, and his footsteps fade. Leaves rustle, though no wind moves them.

CHAPTER TWENTY-ONE

A FTER REEVE EXTENDS his invite, I call Noelle to join me for dinner, but her phone goes to voicemail. "Noelle, here! Leave a message and I'll get back as soon as I'm done shopping."

So I eat alone, the hum of the radiator my only company.

When I return to my room, chocolate wrappers are scattered across my desk. There are a few crumpled on the floor too, one even with a dirty footprint, but I leave them and lie on the bed.

Reeve thinks I've done better than expected. I close my eyes, let those words sink in, and keep sinking until there's only a river, and a girl's mutilated face.

There's a danger lurking at Burnley School, and I need to uncover it.

It's in the river, in the trees. On Mill Road.

I force my eyes open again, count the individual cracks in my ceiling. But dusk settles, and I'm not in my room anymore.

There's rough stones beneath my fingertips. My fingers find the familiar shapes of an "H," followed by a "U." A name. Hugh.

Somewhere, a low hum builds—like the air itself is breathing.

The wall dissolves and I'm in the thick of a deep forest, the slow trickle of a river nearby, the smell of moss and wet dirt. A cold emptiness that thrives between tree trunks and a pair of yellow irises that blink and vanish.

My eyes fly open. A thin wash of light filters through the window, the clock's neon glow marking six in the morning.

Just another dream. Mystic Cosmetics, on the other hand, is real.

I rush through breakfast, cram in homework, make every class, then bolt for the first bus to Mill Road. Across from Mystic Cosmetics, I find a coffee shop. The wooden chair by the window digs into my legs. Coffee beans burn faintly in the air, the bitter scent clinging to my hair. From here I have a perfect view of the store's purple awning.

I set my history book on the table, pretending to study while I wait—though for what, I'm not entirely sure. Outside, bikes and cars blur past. A line snakes from the cosmetics store down the sidewalk, shrinking bit by bit. The words in my textbook fade into shadow until a barista finally flips on the light. I order another drink, hoping it makes my lingering less suspicious.

Ellen chases a group of men out the door. The men scatter, and Ellen glances up and down the street with a forlorn expression, then goes back inside.

I doubt she remembers me, but I pretend to be busy by scribbling some notes in my notebook.

A waitress sprays the table beside mine, sprinkling my face with dewy drops of vinegar.

"Excuse me." I point to Mystic Cosmetics. "Have you noticed anything odd about that store over there?"

The waitress chews an overly large wad of gum. Sporting goth boots and tights, she looks me up and down. "Such as?"

"Such as oversized garbage bags?" Body-shaped garbage bags?

"Or lights upstairs and unusual crowds at night?" Rituals?

She tucks her rag into her belt. "Nope." Gives the table one last spray, and wanders to the back room without wiping it up.

When the last customer leaves, I sit alone. Just me and the grumpy waitress.

Daylight disappears, the buildings' silhouettes, when a recognizable figure with long, dark hair and fading acne rounds the corner and hurries into the cosmetics store.

Noelle.

The line has died down. Noelle quickly reappears with two bags full of product that only a large stash of extra cash can explain.

I shove my books into my bag and run after her.

My footfalls resound against the pavement, and she turns bags swinging at her hips.

She's smiling. Grinning, even. Maybe me following her is unfair and overbearing. But Mystic Cosmetics is a creep fest. Doesn't she see that?

"Briony, what're you doing here?" she asks.

"I'd ask you the same question."

Noelle opens her bags and shows the contents. "Bought more hair dye and a few soaps and shampoo. Told them I'd be a testimonial if they ever needed one. Oh, and I bought lessons."

"Lessons?"

"Soap-making lessons." Her face glows. "So I can make them myself. They're not about protecting trade secrets. It's a community."

"A community for what?"

A community for the chronically unmoisturized?

"It's like this group where everyone actually gets to be who they want, you know? Like, finally belong."

Am I so terrible a friend that Noelle needed to replace me?

"A support group?"

Noelle considers. "More like joining a sorority. There are initiation rituals, that's all."

"You don't think that's weird?"

Noelle's expression becomes petulant. Maybe I overstepped.

"Why would it be?" she demands.

"Because their hair is perfect all the time, they sell potions with spiders in them, and they have crows and cats. The name of the store is Mystic Cosmetics."

"And?" Her hand finds her hip.

I try a different angle. "Look, we found a girl with her eyes cut out very close to here. And you're walking around alone at night. Doesn't that bother you?"

"Doesn't seem to bother you."

I exhale. "Can we go home together?"

Noelle's tone toes the line of friendly. "Sure."

On the bus, she won't look at me. Lips pressed thin, body angled toward the window, she fixes her gaze on the passing rows of brown-brick buildings. The guy next to me keeps tapping his heel, a steady grind that crawls under my skin.

"I'll walk myself, thanks," she snaps when we step off. She hurries ahead, as if distance alone could erase me. I let her go, trailing behind.

Back in my room, I slide the letters from my backpack. The top page slips to the floor—it's the first journal Professor Reeve ever gave me. I pick it up and skim the cramped handwriting. Danger...and a place called Moorhill Cemetery.

I run a quick search on my laptop, and my browser depicts moss-covered gravestones and maps of York. The initial search item displays, "Find a grave." I type, "Marguerite Dye," the author of the letter. No results.

I examine the letter again and try two other names. "Alice Grey" brings no results. Not even "Gray," the Americanized version. Marguerite's hurried signature at the bottom, however, shows, "M. Dye." I search that, and one result remains.

"I don't believe it," I mutter, though no one's around to hear. An obscure name—M. Dye—turns up at Moorhill Cemetery.

I jot the directions to the graveyard on a scrap of paper and slip it into my pocket. Maybe there's an inscription on the headstone. If not, at least I'll know Marguerite Dye was real.

The next morning, I climb the stairs to class and debate how I'll get to Moorhill Cemetery. I can go Saturday and take a train. I've already mapped the route. Not sure how safe it is for me to travel so far alone, but—

I trip over the top step and drop my bag.

"I do that all the time." Julian's behind me, smiling in his wool coat and scarf.

He had to see that.

I rub the back of my neck. "Lies, but thanks all the same."

He waits for me, one arm out as per usual. I nudge him with my elbow rather than take it, and he lowers his arm to his side.

"Busy Saturday?" he asks.

I planned for my trip to Moorhill Cemetery Saturday, but… "No, I'm not busy."

"Good. I'm heading down to London. Fancy coming along?"

"What's in London?"

"Mostly errands for my dad. Though I've got a few other cities to hit."

"York?"

He glances at me out of the corner of his eye. "Yeah, actually. I go to York quite a bit."

That'd save me the train ride. "Care to swap London for York instead?"

He blinks, a bit thrown, then shrugs. "Sure."

"I'd love to." I pause. "Mind if I stop at one place while we're there? I've been meaning to do some family history stuff, but never got around to it."

"Ah. Where's that?"

I force back a grimace. "A graveyard."

Julian's brows knit together.

"Research," I add quickly, like that explains everything.

"If that's what you want," he says.

"I'll make it short, promise."

"Take all the time you need. I'll pick you up at six in the morning. We'll have to leave early to make a full day of it."

"Works for me." I'll down some cold water to wake up.

"Right. Let's get to class, then."

For the full hour, I sneak glances at Julian. He takes no notes and scans the room more than he looks at the slides. His pencil taps against the table, veins popping against his knuckles. A line of sweat forms around his temple, just below his hairline. And when a girl drops her pen, he twitches.

Toward the end of class, he picks at his nails. If I didn't know better, I'd say his hands are trembling—just slightly. I want to take his fingers, wind mine through them, steady him. But he doesn't know me well enough for that.

When the lecture ends, he turns to me with that familiar sparkle, as if nothing at all is amiss. "See you Saturday." He dips his chin and walks off, a book tucked under his arm. Not a Bible or ancient volume from the library, but a "History of Ancient Legal Codes." Likely for Professor Reeve's honorary program.

"Julian," I call out.

He stops and turns.

"You plan to study law, then? Is that why you're here?" I ask.

It's none of my business, but law doesn't seem like his thing. It just feels… off. If he really does want to become a lawyer, well— this is the place to do it.

He holds my gaze a beat too long. "Yes," he says finally. "And no. I just want to be done with this place." He looks down at the book under his arm. "And then from here—maybe find something that actually makes sense." His jaw tenses. "Something that feels right, for once."

He shakes his head. "Never mind."

My heart drops.

Outside, the chapel bell tolls once—low and distant. Julian tears his gaze from me to the window.

CHAPTER TWENTY-TWO

On Saturday, I tug my raincoat tight across my chest, the cold seeping through every layer and down to my bones. Colorado snow is dry and crisp—nothing like this bitter rain that soaks my jeans with each splash. A late-70s Mercedes, old, brown, and in need of a new paint job, glides to a stop, back window rolling down.

"Got the heat on." Julian sits in the back seat of the car. His waxed cotton coat and wool trousers, cuffed above the ankle, carry no signs of water. Unlike my skirt. At least I'm not wearing dress pants.

A man I don't know sits in the driver's seat wearing a suit.

Struggling paint job and a suited-up driver? I can't reconcile the two.

My laugh is a nervous chuckle as I climb into the back passenger side, toss my turned-out umbrella onto the floor, and inspect the car. The tan ceiling is slightly discolored, and the whole car smells of damp upholstery and coffee grounds. "I thought—"

"You thought my car would be nicer?"

"Kind of."

The driver pulls into traffic, lifting a lidded paper cup to his lips—probably the coffee I'm smelling.

"Sorry to disappoint," Julian says.

"No, no disappointment. It's better this way. I don't have to worry about ruining it."

Amusement flickers in his smile. "With a wet umbrella?"

"Maybe. Or I might spill hot chocolate all over your seats. I've done it before."

He grabs hold of his driver's headrest. "Silas, can we make a quick stop?"

The driver turns off the road, parks, and Julian disappears into a corner coffee shop. I crane my head for a glimpse of what he's doing, then drum my fingers against the car door. Silas simply sips his drink and says nothing. About fifteen minutes later, Julian reappears with three drinks. "Spill as much as you like," he says as he hands one to me and the other to Silas, rain dripping from his hair onto the seat cushions.

I take a sip, smiling over the brim as hot cocoa warms my throat.

"Ready for a bit of a drive?"

"It's not too long, is it? An hour's nothing."

"Right." He makes a quote sign with two fingers. "Close to California."

I only smile.

The driver starts the car again as Julian slides on wide-frame aviator sunglasses, wavy hair tumbling around them. "Just ring me as soon as we've dropped you, yeah? I'll nip back after I've said hi to a few people and grabbed what I need. Trust me, you don't want to meet this lot anyway."

"I hope this isn't too much of an inconvenience."

His smile is reassuring. "My dad'll thank you."

"What does your dad do?"

Especially to merit sending Julian on social calls between class-es?

"Parliament."

He says it as if it's a job title all on its own and needs no other explanation.

"Your mom?"

"Mum's a lawyer. Like Reeve." His fingers twitch over his knee.

"Huh…" My voice fades as I take another sip of hot cocoa. Then I clear my throat.

"How long've you known Mika, Robbie, and Eser?"

At this question, Julian relaxes against his seat, loose hairs brushing the ceiling above his head. "My whole life. They're the closest I have to siblings."

"I have too many siblings."

"How many?"

"Five."

His brows go up over the brim of his sunglasses. "Five?"

"Yep." Most people respond that way when I tell them.

Our driver merges onto the highway, and several cars pass. I want to tell Julian about my garden at home, the reason I came here, and what happened with Professor Reeve. He might not mind that I'm not as stylish as Mika, as friendly as Noelle, as funny as Robbie, or as athletic as Eser.

"What're you thinking about?" Julian asks.

I blink. "What do you mean?"

"You're somewhere else."

I can't help but grin. "I was thinking you have such different experiences than me."

"Oh, love — if you're thinking about *me*, that's already some-thing we've got in common."

I laugh and he laughs with me. When we finally stop, he rests his hand over his kneecap, inches from mine, his fingers perfectly still.

Forget Moorhill Cemetery. I'd rather spend the rest of the day at his side. Except…

"Do you—" Julian hesitates. "Do you ever think about what life would have been like to grow up here?"

"All the time," I say.

If Reeve had adopted me, everything would be different.

Before I can ask what he means, he clears his throat, like he's unsure whether he should keep going. "This might sound a bit mad, but… do you ever hear things about someone who's not here anymore and the stories about them feel familiar? Or incorrect?"

It's usually me who dives out of the clouds to say something random.

"I—I'm not sure," I stutter.

"Have you heard of the Gunpowder Plot?"

"The what?"

Julian's shoulders curve inward, as if he's just remembered that I come with a different accent, and an even more different background. "It's a historical event, but never mind."

I touch his arm. "Tell me."

He looks out the window, expression glazed, but then his eyes snap to the road signs. "This exit, Silas."

Silas swerves. A car honks and I clutch the sides of my seat.

"So sorry," Julian says as our driver continues on without a change in his expression. "I wasn't paying attention."

"But you're always paying attention," I say with a laugh.

The only time I've seen him space out was when he was given an origami cat, but no to bringing that up.

"It might not be appropriate to blame a passenger, but it's

entirely your fault."

"My fault?"

"You are a lovely distraction, Briony."

I squirm. "Guess I should come with a warning label."

We chat about Mexican food and the books we love to read, and Julian tells the driver to pull up near a quiet pub tucked into the heart of York. In the distance, a colossal building rises against the sky—all grand columns draped in scaffolding like bones with bandages.

Cumulus clouds drift lazily overhead, and for a moment, the building is caught in a shaft of light, pale and golden, as if conjured from a dream. The air still carries the scent of rain.

I feel oddly at ease. The kind of settling calm that's like reading a book by the fire. Nothing is urgent, and the world, just briefly, is waiting with you.

"Welcome to York." Julian steps out, opens my door, and extends his elbow. "Walk with me?"

The first few times he did this, I thought it was just a joke. Now, I'm not so sure. So I slip my arm through his and let out a mock sigh.

"If I must."

He only looks at me, arm loose, like he's waiting for me to pull away. Instead, I draw him closer. And then he holds me properly, his other hand finding its place like it's always belonged there.

CHAPTER TWENTY-THREE

W E DRIFT THROUGH the cathedral, and my mind spins. Stone pillars rise like sentinels, frescoes and stained-glass bleed color into the silence, and every staircase curves like it's hiding a secret.

Outside, a crowd gathers around an artist selling their work from a street-side stand. I half-consider asking for an autograph, in case they're someone famous. Julian pulls me gently onward before I can follow through.

We turn down a crooked little street called Shambles, lined with timber-framed buildings so old they seem to sag under the weight of their own stories. It's like walking through a Grimm's fairytale. When Julian takes my photo, I'm comically large beside the child-sized doors and leaning windows behind me.

Later, we trace the curve of the city's ancient walls, still standing from Roman times. I try to take it in: all this history, untouched by time, layered beneath my feet. I imagine processions of soldiers, their banners snapping in the wind, and queens in gowns so heavy they'd make my backpack feel like a feather.

York doesn't bury history in old tomes beneath stone floors. It wears it.

I catch Julian watching me, and he looks away with a satisfied smile.

Locals play soccer by a lake on the edge of town as we make our way back to the road, double-deckers squealing past pedestrians. I take cheesy pictures, and Julian humors me with one in a telephone booth, his smile more of a grimace.

As the sun quickly loses warmth, we linger on the grass overlooking Clifford's Tower, a squat chess piece perched on a hill. Rain drizzles and Julian passes me his jacket to cover the goosebumps marching up my arms.

We rejoin the crowds on the sidewalk and pass tourists absorbing scenery from behind glass lenses. Julian passes them by.

We stop beneath an overhanging tree, and I press close to his warmth, wind trying to rip the beret from my head.

Julian buries his chin in my hair. "Thought you might like this place. It's twenty acres of gardens and a shop with rare plants."

"Will you take me?"

"Aren't you off to a graveyard? I called for Silas. He's on his way."

I press closer and sigh. "Is it too late to visit your father's friends?"

He squeezes me, a bit too tight. "No such thing as too late. Some evils don't bother sleeping."

No laugh comes, and I study his face, unsure how far to press. "You don't like your parents?" I ask.

"Didn't say that." He releases me and sits in the grass. I start to settle beside him, but he tugs me closer, until I'm half on his lap, his arms wrapped around me, the two of us facing the tower. "Why go to school in England? If you don't mind me asking."

Do I tell him about Teddy?

Julian's arms tighten around me.

Coming here wasn't about Teddy. Not really.

"My parents wanted me to get a better education. They were worried I wasn't doing well. Professor Reeve got me into," I clear my throat, "well, he got me in. Or the headmistress got me in, or something like that."

He lifts an eyebrow. "And he didn't get you into his honors program?" He puts a hand to his chest, mock offended. "Right, let's make a deal. You take my place in honors, and I'll join the 'unremarkables.' Be a bloody relief, honestly—the lot in my program are a bit…" He trails off, like he's said more than he meant to.

"Creepy?" I offer. "Like goth reflections of the rest of us."

He huffs a laugh.

Silas pulls up in his Mercedes, engine idling. Julian helps me to my feet and brushes off his coat. He glances between me and the car, his eyes shining more intensely in the twilight. He looks so good in brown. It makes his hair richer, somehow. But not like he's had one of Noelle's treatments.

"Briony?"

I blink, scrambling to catch what I missed. "What?"

He laughs. "Are you ready?"

"No."

He gestures to the parked car. "Thought you wanted to go to your graveyard."

"I did. I do." I cough into my hand and stride past him.

He laughs again and follows.

"Which graveyard?" Silas asks as we climb in, clutching what must be his third or fourth coffee.

"Moorhill Cemetery. Do you know where that is?" I ask.

"I do."

I have a lifetime of curiosity tied up in the graveyard, but I'd rather not be there after dark. Not after what happened on Mill Road.

Julian's driver drops me off at a gate flanked by two grim columns and a rally of spindly trees. Someone stacked carved pumpkins by the entrance, the scary faces already starting to wilt and rot. I wave goodbye before turning my back on the road.

I may be at a graveyard, but this isn't Mill Road. No need to worry about "disappearing."

Still, my heart pounds as I pass crypts with stone guardians. Most protect the graves of notable authors and poets. M. Dye's tombstone wouldn't be with those graves, so I move on to a grove of trees. These gravestones have black weather stains and faded carving, and crisp leaves that huddle in corners and crevices.

Across the grounds, the gravestones shrink and grow less distinct, like soldiers in broken formation, tilted from the shifted soil. Over the curved tops lies a tombstone so small it could be a rock.

I stroll toward the smallest stone, to where half-naked trees cast long shadows.

Beside it, a woman stands alone, head bowed, a wide-brimmed hat shading her eyes and tight coils of hair. I stand behind her for several long, uncomfortable minutes, but she doesn't sniffle. Her cheeks are dry, and she's not reading labels or looking up names on her phone. So I step around her and crouch by the smallest gravestone.

Someone inscribed a list of names into the face, faint and hardly legible.

M. Dye & J. Burbidge

A larger stone beside the first bears another inscription that's so faint, another gust of wind might erase it entirely.

Some stories don't end.

And then, *"you're being watched."*

I turn around and check behind me. Just trees. Even the woman with the hat is gone. I didn't hear her go, hardly glimpsed her face. Then again, I was fully focused on the gravestone.

I take out the old letter I brought from Professor Reeve and confirm the name matches. Marguerite Dye was a real person, and, somehow, I found Marguerite among thousands of crypts and gravestones without direction.

I suppress the urge to wrap my arms around myself, still wearing Julian's coat. Then the hairs on my neck rise. I whip around to check behind me just as something lands with a heavy thump at my feet.

Resting on the stumpy blades of grass, a richly dyed leather book flattens everything beneath it. As if someone dropped it from the trees, not realizing how much it weighed. Except there's no one in the branches.

Curiosity wins, and I reach for it.

Inscribed into a complex lock, there's a tree matching the one on my necklace. The cover warms under my fingertips—an energy or awareness. The texture is supple, velvety like stretched skin. But a plum purple.

I tuck the book under my arm and turn around, half expecting the owner to be standing behind me, but there are only trees. And blades of grass losing their color to the dark.

I should put the book back, but my fingers wrap around it. Someone might have left it for me, so, obviously, I have to keep it.

Right?

CHAPTER TWENTY-FOUR

JULIAN'S WAITING OUTSIDE his car, Silas leaning out the driver's side window with a cigarette. Silas flicks the end, scattering ashes as I approach, and then closes the window.

Julian's holding a hand-thrown ceramic pot with a worn label at the top in some strange language, moss with a rare ghost orchid growing inside.

My mouth drops open. "Where'd you get that?"

He opens my door, his eyes snapping to the leather book sticking out from beneath my arm. It's not like a book of this size, or this strange plum color, could slide in beside my schoolbooks.

"Could ask the same for you," he says.

I get in the car, keeping the book tucked firmly at my side. "Found it."

"In the graveyard?"

"Just lying on the ground."

Out the window, the trees in the graveyard sway, and a few leaves flutter to rest in the grass.

He gets in after me, sits at my side, and surveys my face. "You all right?"

I eye the plant rather than answer his question. "What's the orchid for?"

He passes it over, and I'm forced to set the book down so I can hold the orchid instead. "Thought you might like it. One of the people I visited is a botanist. Most of their plants aren't much to look at, but I remember you looking at one just like that is at the gardens. Thought you'd like it."

"Thank you."

He looks at me with an expression I can't quite read. "I like watching your eyes light up like they did at the gardens. It's what drives you, isn't it? Your connection, you said. The moss even looks a little greener when you hold it."

I only clutch the plant closer.

"Want me to hold it? You've got your hands full." He holds out a hand and I pry my fingers from the pot before passing it back.

The car slides away from the graveyard and I take a deep breath as the pumpkins and gate recede. My hands find their way back to the book and he's right; it takes up most of my lap.

"How was work?" I ask.

"Shook a few hands, planned a few things, dropped some packages off. It's Reeve's favorite way to make me useful."

"Wait..." I frown, piecing together what he said earlier. "Didn't you come for your dad?"

"I came for you. My dad's a side thing."

"But you said Reeve?"

He shrugs. "They're a package deal. Close friends. Have known each other for years. Years and years. That kind of thing. When I do something for one, it has dual application."

"I see. And you...like your dad, right?" He did say that didn't he?

"There are perks to having a dad in Parliament. I got invited to a party next week. It's a Halloween dance of sorts. Care to join?"

A date?

I study the gold flecks in his eyes, the sincere turn of his full lips. How he relaxes against the leather seat without even the tiniest twitch of his thumb.

An image of Julian in a suit comes to mind. Cufflinks. Maybe a vest and rolled-up sleeves. "I'd love to. If you don't mind bringing someone with zero rhythm."

Silas turns up a street and accelerates, gravity forcing my back flat against the seat.

"Not to worry. I'm decent enough," Julian says. "There won't be anyone you know, but there'll be food and wine. And dancing if you're into that."

"You sure you want me to go?"

"Course I do." He winds his fingers through mine. "You can just sway about if you like."

I lean against his shoulder, and his lips brush the top of my hat. Silas glances into his rearview mirror and looks quickly forward. My cheeks warm, but I can't stop smiling.

When we reach Burnley, stars glitter, and streetlights burn dim, casting sepia shadows on rain-slicked cobblestones. The car slows and I reach for my book, prepared to get out, but Julian's gaze fixes on the lock with the tree.

He's been so kind that it seems like a betrayal not to open some of my pages, and I want him to understand.

I run my thumb over the book's deckled edges. "You said you feel sometimes like you don't recognize your own life, like there are stories you recognize better, and you're searching for your passion."

"Didn't use that exact wording, but…"

"I feel like a piece of me is gone." My voice trembles, and I have to force the next words out. "There's a hole and I'm scared to fill it."

"Scared?"

"What if—" My voice loses strength. What if I fill that hole and they tell me to leave? To go home?

I try not to picture Reeve's face, but it sneaks in anyway.

"What if I'm not good enough?" I don't look at him but attempt to open my book, despite the lock. The mechanisms don't budge, so I set it back down. "I've been trying to track down my ancestry. This book was at the gravestone I visited. Not sure I'll even be able to open it, but I hoped, maybe, it would have something useful."

Silas opens the window again, and puffs on another cigarette, glancing only once into his rearview mirror.

"Who're you trying to find?" Julian asks.

"Honestly, I don't really know. Someone."

I consider telling him about the journals and my suspicions with the cosmetics store, but he'd think I'm crazy. And it would require bringing up what happened on Mill Road. Instead, I reach for the car door handle.

"I'll get it." Julian hurries to climb out, taking my potted orchid with him. He opens my door, still holding the potted plant. Then he holds it out but doesn't give it to me. "Only if you promise I'll get to see you again," he says. "And you update me on your search."

"I promise."

"Want me to carry it to your room for you?"

"I've got it."

He passes over the potted orchid and bows a little. "Right then, have a lovely evening. Thanks for making my monthly trip far more tolerable."

I hold my book close with one arm and clutch the potted plant with the other. Tires hiss and slip on wet stones as they drive off, and two red lights disappear in the night.

I head to my room, close and lock the door, and set the book I found on the desk. The tree engraved on the cover has an eye at the bottom. Branches intertwine and a star crowns the top. It's too close to the shape of my necklace to be coincidence. All along, my necklace was a key.

CHAPTER TWENTY-FIVE

THREE DAYS LATER, I lurch out of bed in the morning and rub my eyes. The scheduled buses for Reeve's field trip leave at six o'clock in the morning, and my clock shows twenty minutes till. I throw on clothes, wash my face, and brush my teeth in record time. Then I rush out the door and cross the grounds to where two buses wait in the parking lot by Professor Reeve's office.

As I board, I scan the rows of seats. No recognizable faces smile back, not even Mika. Just the backs of people's heads and a few empty chocolate bar wrappers, lonely and crumpled on the ground.

I sit in the back and rest my head against the seat.

The bus door opens again, and a small group enters. They're all dressed in black—black ties, black boots, high-neck shirts with black lace, velvet blazers. In front strides Professor Reeve in an Italian wool overcoat. His eyes fix on me, and he inclines his head, but his expression burns cold.

Eser and Julian step out from behind him, and my stomach gets queasy. Julian's looking at the nearest open seat by the door. Until Eser nudges him. Julian pauses, listening, while Eser nods in my direction.

My heart skips as Julian's eyes lock on me. What if he pretends not to see me? That's not likely. He's not that kind of person. He's not Teddy.

But he said he's never been on one of these tours.

Eser gives him a two-fingered salute, and then sits down by another group of boys.

I sit up straighter, though part of me wants to scatter like petals, as Julian makes his way toward me. Then he sits at my side and stuffs his backpack under the seat.

I want to reach for him, to curl up at his side. Instead, I say, "I thought Reeve didn't like you?"

"Nice to see you, too. And yeah, he doesn't. But Mika goes on about these field trips, so I thought I'd give one a go. Made my parents call. He actually told them 'no' at first, but my dad can be quite persuasive. Seems like you were invited."

Guess I never explained Reeve to him, or how we're connected, but our relationship is nothing to brag about. Sure, Reeve doesn't hate me—or I hope not, but he doesn't want me around either.

"I was, yes, but I'm not sure why he would invite me and not you, unless he feels obligated."

"Why would he feel obligated? I very much doubt Professor Reeve has ever felt obligated, not in his life."

"He found me as a kid and adopted me out," I say. "Maybe he feels responsible."

Julian stares, the shock in his expression making me shift in my chair.

"What?"

"You mentioned a hole and I wondered about it—figured you'd elaborate if you wanted to. But you weren't just adopted, you were found?"

"Yes." Not sure if that's a big deal. "Why?"

He leans forward. "So was I."

My brain blanks. That can't be possible.

Now it's my turn to gape, and the amazement lingers longer than his. I don't know what to say, except that I never expected this, not ever.

Professor Reeve doesn't strike me as the type of do-gooder who searches streets for abandoned children. Surely, he doesn't adopt out kids in his free time.

Julian winds his fingers together. "I was abandoned, and Professor Reeve discovered me. My father is a friend of his."

"When?" I ask.

He scrunches his face. "What?"

"When did this happen? When were you adopted? And where?"

His face clears. "August twentieth. Old Street."

My blood crystalizes. August twentieth is my birthday, or the birthday my parents assigned me, though they only ever said Reeve found me in London.

If Professor Reeve found two discarded babies and not one, Julian might be my brother. I study his face. He has green eyes, not gray. My mousy hair doesn't have an ounce of his auburn red. I'm small and scrawny, while Julian stands tall and broad shouldered.

Julian chuckles. "Looks like you're as surprised as I am."

Julian claims Professor Reeve likes me better, but it was me that Reeve sent to strangers across the ocean, not Julian. Somehow, it's a new form of rejection.

"And you want to know who your real parents are," Julian says, voice hesitant.

My parentage has always felt like a scale, oscillating between fairytale and tragedy. "Do you know who yours are?"

"No." Julian pauses, like he wants to say more, but the bus lurches, and Julian's eyes flick to the front of the bus where Professor Reeve sits, and then back to me.

"Professor Reeve says I have family from Lancaster." If Alice Grey is family. "That's why I'm here."

"Then this trip will mean more to you than to me."

So, he doesn't have family there. Good.

Reeve's deep voice resonates over the commotion of students. "I think that's everyone, then."

The engine starts, and the bus lurches, rounds a sharp corner and sends Julian sliding into me. "Really sorry."

I blush as he rights himself, his jacket brushing against my fingertips.

He slings one ankle over his knee, settling back into his chair, while I'm stiff as a ruler stuck in the snow. Though a drop of hot cocoa from our date still stains my shabby canvas purse.

"Glad you're here, Briony," he says. "I hoped you might be."

He doesn't put his arm around me—I wish he would, but his smile is all warmth, and I relax against my seat. It's nice to be the one he wants to be with, rather than the one he ignores.

Outside the windows, stacked stones make fences to contain wandering sheep, like fuzzy balls on a grass blanket. The road curves toward a purple plateau, crowned with a gathering of clouds. The grass glows too green for a place built on bones.

The bus rocks as it moves from paved roadways to dirt paths, back to paved roads, and then to cobblestones. Until the bus halts at the top of a hill.

Professor Reeve stands. "Attention students—what you see there is Gallows Hill." Just a grassy rise overlooking fields of green. Worn bare by sheep and dog walkers. "I've done a lot of excavation in this area, especially regarding the famous Pendle Witch Trials in

1612. It was yours truly who was first to find the possible remains of Malkin Tower using old land ownership documents. That's what this tour concerns.

"Now, back in 1612, Pendle was nothing much to speak of. Remote, rough about the edges, and full of uneducated folk. A handful were Catholic, most Protestant, and naturally that stirred up all sorts of squabbles. Religion, politics, money, inheritance—you name it, they found a reason to quarrel.

"And then, as these things always do, it all boiled over with one unlucky incident. A young girl passing along the road, an old man drops dead of a stroke, and—well—she hadn't the faintest clue how to help him. Instead of common sense, they decided she must have cursed him. Witchcraft, of course.

"Well, the village went into uproar, and the magistrate at the time—Roger Nowell, Senior—he wasn't slow to spot an opportunity. Before long, the so-called witches were rounded up. And right here, on this very hill, they were carted in to face their punishment. Hanged until they were barely breathing, dragged through the muck behind a cart, and finally hacked to pieces. Alive till the very last gasp. Grim business, but quite the story, eh?"

I shiver at the imagery, but in the back of my mind, a little voice whispers, "but Alice Grey survived."

"Malkin Tower," Professor Reeve continues, "was where the witch meetings allegedly took place. It was said the witches met and plotted against the more righteous villagers to capture their wealth and kill them off. After the hanging, Malkin Tower was burned. I studied land ownership records and have reason to believe that before the tower was burned, it was located at Black Moss Reservoir, which is where we're headed."

The bus shudders as it rolls over bumps in the road.

Small villages lie nestled against the landscape with pitched slate roofs in varying shades of gray and red. If Alice Grey lived in the valley beneath the plateau, her descendants could still be there. I may have aunts, uncles, and cousins minutes away.

The bus drives down a road that winds between old Victorian homes, with flower boxes in the windows. We even pass a sign with a witch riding her broomstick, hanging over an inn. The driver pulls in by a picnic area, and Professor Reeve beckons. "Come along." He tips his hat to the driver as he steps past and descends the stairs, then waits outside for us to disembark.

As soon as my shoes touch the wild earth, he's off, leading everyone past a café, across grass, and then a bridge, before turning down Barley Lane.

It's a short walk from there to the reservoir, which reflects Pendle Hill in lovely green and blue hues.

"This way." Professor Reeve gestures to the woods. "It's a bit off the beaten path."

He leads us into the trees, which start out sparse, with the occasional tree carved into an elaborate sculpture, cylinders stacked on top of each other, trees creating metal and wood arches, and people with blank eyes.

We pass them all by, the trees growing more numerous.

No paths or signs mark the direction, so our only choice is to follow Reeve between knotted trunks, the branches outstretched like blackened fingers. We climb uphill, and my breathing quickens as the ground sucks in my boots, thick with rotting leaves and the smell of stagnant water.

I peek over my shoulder at Julian. He's close, only a couple feet behind me. Near enough to reach for his hand. Instead, I take a deep breath and search for signs of Professor Reeve.

Surely he won't take us any farther? He must be ahead because the other students plod along, chatting easily with each other, not a word about feeling lost or small. Maybe forests like these are as normal to them as thousand-year-old cathedrals.

Dense trees squeeze out the light. I squish between two of them and stumble into a clearing filled with broken brambles, strangled grass, and half-walls of crumbling stones. The cool wind dies, and a stale stench settles, like road kill. Crows caw in the distance. A twig snaps and I flinch. It's an emptiness that feels too full.

Julian bows his head.

"This is the spot." Professor Reeve's discordant voice echoes. "See the rocks here?" Black scorches streak the stones. "Now, what do you think? Do you believe in witches?"

Eser, standing at the front of a group of students, casts Professor Reeve a withering look. "You brought us here to look at rocks?"

"These rocks are the only remaining evidence of where Malkin Tower once stood." The professor's voice is smug. Light, even. But his eyes are somber.

Someone might've made a campfire, but that doesn't explain the uncontained circle of dead grass. The lack of firewood. Or how the stones look familiar, like I saw them on a camping trip in Colorado. They also feel wrong.

No new growth has replaced the circle of dead grass. Perhaps the earth hasn't forgotten what transpired here. Or the very ground is cursed.

I've never believed in curses. Or I thought I didn't.

I shiver, despite there being no wind, and lift my arm, wrist turned up. The scars on my skin glare back and start to bleed.

All around me, the blackened stones grow into brick walls that block out the sun, tongues of flame reaching skyward. Heat licks my skin. Wood crackles beneath my heels. I stagger, catching myself on a stump before I fall.

Just hallucinations, that's all.

Reeve's face swims into focus. "It's what happens to people who get tangled in witchcraft, Briony."

My brain spins. In reference to Alice Grey? The cosmetics store?

I scan the students in the clearing, but the others keep chatting, unaware.

Reeve faces the group. "Let's eat lunch by the bus, and then we'll head to our next destination. Stay with me, please. I don't want you to get lost."

"You alright?" Julian asks, watching me closely.

"I dunno."

Just can't shake the feeling that I'm intruding here.

I wobble past him, but he stops me with a touch.

"There are roots everywhere, and you look like you're going to be sick." Again, he offers his arm and I take it.

Light floods back, and suddenly my feet are planted, the air sharp with rain and earth.

As we walk, the trees thin, and Julian glances at my face every time I stumble. When the bus appears between the leaves, I exhale. I hadn't thought I was hungry, but maybe that's all this is—low blood sugar. We had to have walked a mile, at least.

There are brown paper bags piled in a plastic bin on the ground. I snatch one, take out the contents, and perch on a rock, hunched over my sandwich.

Julian sits beside me, holding a bagged lunch, but not bothering to eat it. "Why're you so quiet?"

I've always scared easy, but this is a new low. My hands won't stop shaking.

They were rocks, that's all. Like Eser said.

Except I can still smell lingering smoke.

Julian leans back. "You know, Reeve got so much notoriety from his research here—I thought there'd be more to see."

I bite into my orange, and cough out the bitter peel.

Julian stifles a laugh. "Sorry, I've never seen someone try to eat an orange like an apple."

Of course, he noticed.

I strip the rest of the peel and eat the orange slices the way a normal person does, but the mirth doesn't fade from Julian's eyes.

Professor Reeve's voice rises over the group. "Let's go. We don't have a lot of time."

CHAPTER TWENTY-SIX

I BOARD BEHIND Julian, and we drive another hour until the spiked tips of a medieval fortress surface over the treetops.

My stomach's still a knot from the woods, and Julian's quiet beside me.

The bus stops across the road from a row of rough-hewn buildings streaked with weather stains, and apartments with white lattice windows. A cobblestone road weaves to the fortress, its columns welcoming us like smiling teeth on rotten gums.

Shadows cling to the stone facades, damp and heavy.

Reeve ushers us beneath the arched entrance and I wipe my sweaty palms on the folds of my skirt.

"This is another favorite spot of mine. I can tell you many stories about this place. You've heard of the Pendle witches, but have you heard of the Samlesbury witches? Both groups of witches were tried here in the Lancaster Assizes.

"The Samlesbury witches were three of many witches tried here. The magistrate released them after they convinced the jury they'd been the target of a Catholic plot. A clever bunch. The other women accused did not prove so lucky. The jury moved the condemned witches from here to the gallows on the moors above the town, where they were hanged for all to see.

"We'll tour the jails, so you can see for yourselves just how dismal they are. This was where they held the witches before trial. One accused witch you never hear about was Alice Grey. It's generally said she was acquitted, but I have reason to believe she was imprisoned here for seven years."

I don't have to look at him to know he's speaking to me, and I know I should be excited to see where Alice stayed, but my legs stiffen as we approach. Like there's an invisible wall my body doesn't want to cross.

He continues. "After seeing her jail cell, you might comprehend, just a little, how terrible such a sentence must have been. Nowadays, Lancaster Castle is still used as a prison and courtroom, but also for much lighter affairs. There's a museum, and a lovely café, and sometimes they hold music festivals, marathons, and Christmas fairs."

Christmas wreaths and prisons.

I turn to Julian. "This your kind of place?"

The corners of Julian's mouth tick up. "I see places like this all the time, but I'm glad you're enjoying it."

He says it lightly, like castles and tragedies are his weekend routine.

As we enter, paid actors gallivant in knights' uniforms across the castle courtyard, overseen by spectators in raincoats. No one is looking at me, but I'm on a stage, and it feels like the spotlights have found me.

I shake myself. It doesn't make sense. No one here cares about little old me.

Julian watches the knights with interest, a sparkle in his eyes. "The knights are funny," he says. "But they're hitting swords, not targets. In a real fight, you end things quickly. They're just dragging this out."

I force myself to focus on his words. "End things quickly?" If I joke, maybe the violence will feel less like it's closing in. "Have I missed your recent fencing matches? Or are you a serial killer on the weekends? The Broadsword Butcher?"

"Only on Saturdays. Sundays are for tea. And hot chocolate."

I laugh, despite the tightness in my chest.

Julian walks close beside me as we cross the courtyard and enter the castle through a dim corridor, bowing our heads for the low ceilings.

The professor pauses and slides a key into a door lock. He turns it with an audible click. Hinges groan, and the wood swings inward, letting loose a puff of musty air.

Sweat slides down my forehead.

"These are prison cells," Reeve says. "See the marks?"

I step inside and run a finger over the scratches marring the stones' gray surface, where prisoners tallied their anguish and unfounded hopes into days. Some marks cut deeper than others.

I turn my hand, palm up, so the thin, white lines show, and jump at Reeve's sudden voice.

"Next room." He directs the other students to another cell down the hall, much like the first. Except—

A rock drops to the bottom of my abdomen.

"Not many are permitted in these rooms," Reeve says, "so don't touch anything, please. I don't want my privileges revoked."

I stop in the doorway. Not even an avalanche could have moved me.

Someone gouged, "Hugh," into the wall.

The name steals my breath. It's a name that lingers beneath my skin, like something I've dreamed but can't remember.

Hugh.

The walls of the prison press in from all sides. I reach forward and touch each of those carved letters, letting my finger curl over the rough corners. I'm drowning in a pool of skeletal dreams.

Then pain lances through my right forearm.

"Briony?" Julian's urgent voice is faint. "We're not supposed to touch…"

This is the same room, the same low ceiling, the same smooth stones. The complete absence of light and windows. Unlike my dreams, there are no scorch marks. Just carvings. Someone wrote a scriptural reference by Hugh's name. "Vengeance is mine. I will repay, saith the Lord." Scrapes, like trenches made by nails, deepen the words into the rock.

Putting one hand against the wall, I try to steady myself, but my fingers leave streaks of red.

I stare at my wrist, ears ringing. For a second I don't even register it's mine until the blood hits the floor.

Black shining shoes tap the stones at my feet. I look up into Professor Reeve's full black eyes and heat flashes through me, wild and hot. I want to seize his neck and wring the life from it. Watch the skin gray and the eyes pop from their sockets.

I wrap my arms around myself, try to hold these emotions in.

My eyes burn. Faces blur all around me.

Julian's expression is full of concern. He reaches out, touches my elbow. "Briony?"

He thinks I'm crazy.

I bolt—down the hall, out the doors, across the courtyard, until I find a bathroom. I crouch in the corner with the stall door closed. My teeth chatter, and cold sweat drips down my neck. I clench my hands to keep from shaking, and my arm continues to bleed.

"Briony?" Julian's voice carries from outside the bathroom. "Can I help?"

I take a shaky breath. "Just sick."

"Shall I fetch a doctor?"

A doctor is the last thing I need. I rub at the tears and push myself up, knees wobbling as I open the stall door. "No. Coming." I keep my head down as I leave the bathroom, face away from the spectators in the courtyard. This is one form of entertainment they didn't pay for.

"What've you done to your arm?" he demands.

I don't even know. It feels like someone else's skin.

"I feel awful."

"Stay here." He disappears into the bathroom, then reappears with a wad of toilet paper, and presses it to my bleeding skin. His hands are steady, like he's done this before.

"Thanks," I mumble.

We pass crowded tables in the courtyard, and my breathing escalates. I think I'm hyperventilating, but I can't stop. Eyes like dull pencils stab my back. Julian holds me like I might break as we board the bus, and I hate how nice it feels.

I curl up on my seat cushion and he hovers over me.

Now that I'm away from that cell, it's almost like I imagined it. The pain. That name carved into the wall. Is it all in my head?

"Do you feel well enough to keep going?" I haven't left him any room. "There might be another stop planned."

"I don't know."

If he stops talking, I can close my eyes and forget.

"Maybe Reeve can send a bus back early. It's worth asking."

I rest my forehead against the cool metal panels as Julian sits across the aisle. In any other circumstance, I would want him to sit beside me. Now, I want to be alone.

Julian's voice rises over my tremors. "I get it, you know." He lowers his voice. "I've always loved cathedrals. Time slows. The quiet echoes. I love to look through the stained glass depictions of Mary and Jesus, especially when it's raining. When I was a kid, my parents took me to Parliament, and I wandered into Westminster Abbey. Don't know what it is about that place, but…"

Other students board, their feet shaking the bus, clomping against the floor.

I shut my eyes, and there's hollowed eye sockets. This time with fire and scorched stones.

"I went into the women's toilet to get paper for you," Julian says. "I hope you remember that. I wouldn't do that for anyone else."

My sickness recedes, and I almost smile.

Professor Reeve's voice rises over the chatter. "Students, we'll cut this tour short. We're returning to school." His feet move down the aisle until he stands over me. "I'm sorry," he says in a low voice, "but I wanted you to see it, to remember. If you've read the journals, you know this place. It's not just a story. Go home, Briony."

For the first time, I almost want to.

He casts Julian a look of pure loathing before he moves on.

Another threat, warning, demand, whatever he wants to call it, but a name from a nightmare won't make me leave any more than a dead body can.

The buzz of chatting students grows louder as more students board.

"What's that about?" Julian asks.

I sit up and rub my forehead. I wish I could explain. I wish I could state the reason Professor Reeve works so hard to scare me away. "I don't know."

The rest of the drive passes in a blur, with me spending most of the time with my face pressed to the metal siding on the wall, coated in greasy fingerprints. As we leave the prison behind and then the flat-topped mountain, my breathing quiets and my hands stop shaking, but the dizziness lingers.

When the bus rocks to a stop in the parking lot, I wait until all the students have left before I follow them out, dragging myself like a zombie with Julian hovering behind.

"She looks well, doesn't she?" Eser says to Julian in his usual dry sarcasm.

"Leave her be."

My head clears as I step off the bus—familiar spires and oak doors with black iron hinges just ahead.

Julian supports my elbow as we enter Birdie's Court and climb the stairs, hands careful. My balance is coming back—I don't need help anymore—but I let him hold me. Let his eyes track me to the door. "Ring if you need someone to talk to," he says.

"I will."

He just looks at me with those stupidly pretty eyes, all concern. "Sure you'll be all right?"

I press a hand against his jacket and Julian grabs my other hand, too, holds them with both of his. He runs a finger down the back of my hand, along my palm and then over my wrist and scars. I shiver and his jaw tenses.

"I hope you feel you can talk to me," he says.

I want him to stay. I want him gone. I want him to hold me but not see me.

"I'll text you," I say.

Because that's easier than talking.

He backs away, dropping my hands, and I listen as his shoes thud down the hallway until even the scent of him fades. Then I ease the door shut and drag myself to bed.

My head throbs, but curiosity beats louder than fear.

The sheets look comforting, like a hug, but instead of falling into it, I lift the mattress to expose the purple book beneath. The eye on the lock stares back.

Hugh is important. The feeling resounds in my bones, even if I don't know why.

I slip the book beneath the mattress again, and the intensity of the eye bores through the sheets. It prickles my skin. If the journals don't mention Hugh, this purple book might.

Reeve's right about one thing—I need to finish the journals. But I need my necklace, too.

CHAPTER TWENTY-SEVEN

THE LETTERS ON THE pages run together into one muddy pool. I squeeze my eyes shut and open them again, scanning for Hugh's name. It must exist somewhere in these journals, or I don't know where else to look.

I read from where I left off, beginning with Guido as he departs from the judge's house to meet Alice.

—*1603*—

I followed Alice's directions to her home and arrived at daybreak the following morning. I had planned to depart as soon as I arrived, but Dantes had gained a slight limp, and I had few leads as to where I might search for the sword.

Alice claimed I looked worn. I may have been delirious.

Ellen had been following me, and she caught up to me on the path to the parish church, insisting that I visit her. I cannot blame her for my horse's limp, but I wondered whether she was capable of stranding me here.

I also made the acquaintance of Alice's younger brother, Hugh. She doted upon him as if he were her son.

However, the resemblances between sister and brother were difficult to trace. His eyes were an unnatural, livid yellow—the same colour Ellen had been searching for when we met in the woods. When he looked at me, his gaze bore straight through me.

Strange things occurred when he was near. He ran faster than I deemed possible. Once, he ran into a tree and leapt away unharmed. He picked a flower for his sister and wept as it withered in his hands. Alice would not permit Hugh to step outside the cottage without his boots for fear he should kill the grass beneath his feet.

Predators flocked to him. A wolf appeared amongst the trees with a rabbit in its mouth, and Hugh accepted the gift and sent the beast away. Dantes neighed fearfully when the boy came too near.

Alice did not allow Hugh to leave the meadow surrounding the cottage, nor did he have acquaintances, save for a young girl I saw slip into the garden to play—though I never spoke of her to Alice.

I admit, I am wary of Hugh, but his uniqueness does not seem to be caused by necromancy or witchcraft. Or at least, I have yet to see him employ magic in any purposeful way.

After weeks of staying in the village nearby,

we became familiar. Whilst loved tenderly by his sister, the boy lived without a father.

I still searched local lakes, rivers, and marshes for any whisper of relevant legends, but I also visited Alice's cottage to tend to Dantes, who remained there. With every day that passed without finding any tales or signs of the sword, I grew anxious that I had come to the wrong shire.

Still, I continued searching, though time diminished. I must find the sword before the Duck and Drake, or discover another weapon designed to end immortals.

As Dantes's health improved, I took him on gentle walks each evening before the sun went down. One night I glanced back at the cottage. A hooded visitor slunk to the doorstep. Then the door opened to admit the stranger, only to shut quickly behind him.

Alice did not mention a stranger coming,

and whilst Alice's affairs are her own, I felt uneasy about it.

I waited for the stranger to depart, and he did not stay long. When the door opened again, the hooded figure stooped over Hugh's bent head, then hurried towards town.

When I asked Alice about him the next day, she seemed both surprised and distressed that I had seen the stranger, but readily identified him as her father.

What manner of father visits his children in the dead of night?

—Guido

I clutch the paper in my hands. Hugh isn't a fabrication of my mind. Not only does Guido mention him, but he describes him as someone important to Alice.

My chair squeaks in my rush to pick up the next letter.

—1603—

A wild man in rags watched the house from amongst the trees. I warned Alice, but she assured me all was well.

She clutched the silver branches of a tree pendant she wore about her neck and said, "This necklace is protection. Iduna gave it to me."

I did not know who Iduna was, but Alice checked her neck often, perhaps to reassure herself the necklace remained there. Though I did not wish to give Alice the disservice, I worried she placed her hopes in fairytales.

Today I spotted another stranger in the woods, a woman I had glimpsed at the alehouse. She had long, fiery red hair and bright eyes, but the sight of her turned my blood cold. I ran to the trees, but she had vanished. Whilst saplings and giant oaks fortified the cottage on all sides, we were exposed.

Alice tried to conceal her anxiety from me, but she lived in constant dread of a threat she would not reveal. Hugh played in happy ignorance, hunted rabbits for sport, wrestled with wolves, and, occasionally, ran into the woods with a little girl who came to find him.

Dantes's leg improved, and he was fit for travel, but I could not leave. Not yet. Even if I found the sword, I could not leave Alice here alone. Though Alice commanded me to depart before dark each day, I returned at dawn.

—Guido

Guido mentions an all-too-familiar necklace, and the journals note the names of the women in the cosmetics store. They're common names though, so that can't mean anything. Even if the woman with red hair in the trees sounds an awful lot like the Jane I know.

The journals also mentioned Alice's necklace being a form of protection. If Alice's necklace and my necklace are the same, that would explain Reeve's desire to study it. But if he's worried about my welfare, he should have wanted me to keep it.

Two sharp knocks make me jump. I set the journals aside and rise to answer it.

Reeve stands in the doorway, raking his fingers through his slick hair so many times it stands on end. Around his neck, my necklace glimmers silver. Does he mean to torment me?

"What're you doing here?" I demand.

I need to invest in a peephole. Unless…he means to check on me?

"I'm fine, really," I say. "You didn't need to come—"

"Have you read the journals?"

I stare at him.

"I saw who you were with yesterday," Reeve continues. "Has anything happened between you and Julian?"

Guess I was wrong to think he cares.

Being told to leave the second I showed up was crazy enough, but this?

"Answer the question." His frightening tone makes me tremble. No professor should be allowed to ask such personal questions, not even one who claims to be connected with me.

"Give me my necklace." My voice shakes but I keep my chin up.

Reeve buttons the topmost button on his shirt, hiding the necklace beneath the fabric. "Stay away from Julian," he says.

My hands tremble. "Unlike you, he's been nothing but kind to me."

"Of course, he has."

"And what about Jane from Mystic Cosmetics?" I demand.

"You think she's good for you? You were terrified of her when she came to see you."

He crosses his arms. "What do you mean?""I saw you two together."

He gives me a death stare sharp enough to cut steel. "It's how I keep tabs on them, and it's none of your business."

"Exactly." I shut the door in his face and lock it.

It feels so good.

All morning, I search "Hugh Grey" online and find nothing while Professor Reeve's words and the characters in the journals clash for space in my brain.

I heft my backpack after a long afternoon of classes and hurry down the hall, students parting around me.

"Did you hear about the girl that disappeared on Mill Road? They found her in a river," says a voice that savors the poetry of someone else's misfortune.

"That's why you don't go out walking at night alone. She was asking for something to happen," says another student in an immaculate uniform, her nails a poisonous shade of mauve.

I shove past them.

My phone buzzes in my pocket. No one calls, except my mom and Sadie, and I don't have time for a long chat right now. I reach for the device and check the tiny neon screen on front as Julian's name flashes. I fumble as I flip the phone open. "Hello?"

"Briony?"

My stomach flips at the smooth rumble of his voice. "Hey, Julian."

"That Halloween dance I mentioned—it's tonight. Black tie.

Shall I collect you at four?"

I squeeze my phone. "I'd love to."

"Brilliant. Do you have something suitable to wear?"

In my closet of dress pants and school-girl skirts? "I'm sure I can find something."

"Anything you have should be lovely." His voice drops slightly at the last word, and warmth crawls up my neck.

Black isn't a color I wear often. But I do have black dress pants. "What time did you say?"

"Four. It's in York, so we'll need to leave straightaway."

"Will Mika and Robbie be there? Or Eser?"

He hesitates. "No. Rather elite crowd, this one. My dad wanted me to make an appearance, but I'd rather not go alone. You don't mind, terribly? There'll be cocktails and dancing."

I love dancing more than I'll ever admit, but my chest tightens.

"Your dad's going to be there?"

"He's keen to meet the one person who can tolerate me for longer than an hour."

I laugh, even though I'm still uncertain about the idea of meeting his parents. It can't be so bad with him beside me though.

"Four o'clock," I say. "Don't be late."

"Wouldn't dream of it."

I snap my phone shut and walk through the door to class. I'll see Julian's infectious smile in only a couple of hours, and there's nothing Reeve can do to prevent it.

CHAPTER TWENTY-EIGHT

Julian and Silas, his driver, pick me up at the street corner right on time. He opens the door for me and takes my pack. His hand brushes my arm as I climb in—barely a touch, but my pulse jumps anyway. I breathe in the smells of coffee and old leather and clasp my hands in my lap.

After I've settled, he sets my pack next to me and puts on his seat belt. Then raises both brows. "Lovely dress pants."

"They're black." I survey his tailored corduroy trousers. And the aviator sunglasses he wore last time we were in this car. "Don't think you got the memo."

Julian laughs. "My dad's bringing my suit." He draws a simple white mask out of a shopping bag, and another with pressed leaves and tarnished gold, ivy veining along the cheekbones.

"It's—wow—I've never seen anything like it." I take the mask carefully and fit it over my face. The weight settles comfortably across the bridge of my nose. "Did you make this?"

"Found it at an antique store. It looked like you."

Something about the way he says it—quiet, like a secret—steals the air from my lungs.

"Thanks," I say.

He just smiles. "If my mask were a bit bigger, I'd draw a mustache. With a bit on the chin, too."

I nudge him in the ribs. "How about not? Where's this party?"

His smile turns roguish. "It's not at Burnley Boarding School, if that's what you're asking. You can't run off to do homework tonight. You're stuck with me." He checks his watch. "The party starts now, and we have a two-hour drive, so we've got to hurry."

"That doesn't answer my question," I say.

His response is simple. "You'll see."

As we drive, the streets thin into a hush of forgotten roads and crumbling walls. Then the road widens again to overgrown gardens. A half-collapsed barn and tall, narrow apartments. Julian's driver parks on the side of the road before a dimly lit store, its windows clouded by age and rain. Gowns with lace sleeves and faded silks hang from manikins on display.

Julian helps me out of the car. Cold, wet wind tears through my sweatshirt, and I pull it tighter.

A few of the dresses are Halloween themed with bats, stars, monsters, and jewels.

Julian glances at me and then at the window. "Want one? We can make a quick stop."

I shake my head, blushing. He doesn't need to buy my clothes. "No, I'm good."

"Sure?"

"Yeah." I step quickly away from the store's front door.

Julian leads me further down the road, pressing a hand against the small of my back. His palm is warm even through the fabric, a quiet anchor I shouldn't want as much as I do. He's inches away; I catch the scent of old paper, like he's been reading the Bible again.

Julian slows before a pale stone tower, its black glass windows catching what little light breaks through the clouds.

He takes my hand and kisses my fingers. "Don't be nervous."

I don't trust myself to speak.

The sliding doors sweep open to admit us, along with a wave of artificial heat.

We step into an elevator that carries us up several flights and keeps going.

"It's just a small party," Julian says as the elevator dings. "Bigger parties are usually at someone's country manor, like Blenheim."

"What's Blenheim?"

Julian just smiles again. "Wait here for me." He leaves for the bathroom and reemerges wearing a turtleneck beneath a black suit. The suit hugs his broad shoulders and trim form, while still being a slightly relaxed tweed.

I might as well be wearing last-year's tent.

"You look like an old soul," I say.

"I am an old soul." He holds out his elbow.

I stare at his outstretched arm, at the individual fibers of his suit, the complex pattern they make, and down at the wrinkles in my dress pants. "Give me a minute." I pull away, prepared to rush to the bathroom, but Julian winds a hand around my waist and presses his lips to my forehead.

My heart skips, stumbles, then stills. The kiss isn't romantic, not exactly—just steady, careful—but it unravels me more than anything else he's done.

I take a deep breath and the lightheadedness recedes.

"You'll be okay," he murmurs.

A door down the hall swings wide. "Julian, there you are." A wiry man in his early sixties strides toward us, also in a black suit and cloak. He stands so straight; his back must be made of oak.

"Father," Julian says.

Julian's dad clasps my hands with weathered fingers. "Briony." He gives me a shallow, formal bow. Even without heels, he's barely taller than me.

"Your steps echo soft, but the old wind knows your name. I'm delighted to meet you."

Strange introduction, but it is Halloween.

"Nice to meet you, too."

"You're from America?"

"Colorado."

His forehead creases. "And you're at Burnley School. Are you an honor student as well?"

As in, am I in Reeve's accelerated program?

I open my mouth, but my answer lodges in my throat.

Julian squeezes my hand. "Not to worry. She's as bright as they come."

My cheeks flush.

Lord Bristol bobs his head in satisfaction. "Join the party. Your arrival is highly anticipated. Just steer clear of the darker shadows. The skulls—you know?"

I search Julian's face for an explanation, but he doesn't look at me. Probably just Lord Bristol's odd sense of humor.

Lord Bristol ushers us into a glass sports bar with black leather seating. The air smells of spiced wine and candle wax, and something faintly metallic beneath it all—like autumn rain on old iron.

Suits and a plethora of elegant black dresses whirl around the polished floor, with pearl or feathered masks. One even looks made of snakeskin. Champagne glasses clink. A piano composition of the Phantom's "Masquerade" drifts from hidden speakers, and York's city lights wink through wall-sized windows, the outline of a river barely visible beyond the balcony.

So modern and normal, if not for the haunted look in each

person's face. How the age range spans teen and adult but only a few looks related.

Eyes turn. Conversations fade to low murmurs.

I scan my pants and sweater for a rip or stray thread but there's nothing but wrinkles. Maybe I should've bought an iron.

We hover on the outskirts of the dance floor while Lord Bristol makes his way toward the bar and returns with two sodas and lime. He offers one to me. A black olive on a stick pokes over the top, carved like a mini pumpkin to have deep-set eyes and a wide grin.

It's not a Halloween party without creepy décor, of course.

Julian accepts his and eyes the crowd over the top of his glass. Then Lord Bristol pulls me into a circle of people and introduces me to an older woman wearing a black diamond bracelet and matching necklace.

"Miss Downey, this is Julian's new friend, Briony."

"Pleasure." Except she doesn't smile. Not even a little.

He introduces me to several more circles of people, and I beam until my cheeks hurt. Lord Bristol seems to know everyone, and the partygoers survey me with a little too much interest.

After several more introductions, Julian stops his dad with a hand on his shoulder. "Give us a minute," he says.

Lord Bristol steps aside and bows, arm out. "Introduce your guest to your mother. She's on the balcony." He raises his cocktail. "It's been a pleasure. May your gravestone never crack." And he joins another group deep in conversation.

I stare after him.

"He really gets into Halloween character, doesn't he?"

"You could say that." Again, he doesn't look at me.

"He wasn't serious, right?"

Julian just presses my knuckles to his lips. "You promised a dance."

Julian leads me to the floor, where dancers twirl with open-backed dresses, or dresses with deep V-necks. Some have porcelain skin or unblemished, dark skin that shimmers like someone rubbed oil into it. As if they all made trips to Mystic Cosmetics and found Goth Fairy Godmother.

Julian takes my hand and sets it on his shoulder. I touch his waist and we sway from side-to-side. "You have gray in your eyes," he says.

"You thought they were blue?"

"Kind of."

"Sorry to disappoint."

He laughs. "Hardly a disappointment."

The song changes to an organ with a bass accompaniment. I study his feet for a pattern to follow, but stumble over his shoes instead. Probably scuffed them.

Julian steadies me with one hand. I don't know if he notices, but I lean into the touch a heartbeat too long before stepping back.

"Do you know any steps?" he asks.

"Don't think so."

I left my collection of dance videos in my closet to rot.

He spins me to face him again, grasps my left hand, and sweeps me into fluid steps, moving me with him.

It's not so bad. I stumble a time or two but manage to keep up.

When the song fades, he doesn't release me, but holds me close, waiting for the music to start again. His breath brushes my hair. The world's turning too fast.

When the music swells, he adds a bend. I fall into his movements, sliding as he slides, twisting, twirling, touching only to pull away and draw close again. Holding his gaze and following his lead.

The melody ends, and another begins. I'm all sweat and movement. Spinning and whirling, while the heat of Julian's hand keeps me grounded. Until Julian lets go and takes a step back.

A small crowd of people have made a circle around us.

Julian runs a hand through his hair. "I'll get you a drink. Wait for me." He pushes through a wall of dresses.

I find a chair on the side of the dance floor to sit and wait. And breathe.

"Excuse me?" a high voice asks. "Where'd you get those trousers from? The clearance bin?"

I twist to look at the speaker—a girl about my age in black lipstick, an inky dress with silver thread, bright like the moon, full hair, and a narrow face. The type of star who can stand beside Ellen and not dim.

Beside her, a curvier girl with a belt of bones around her waist giggles.

"Same place you bought your personality," I say.

The girl's lip hitches upward. "Think you're clever, don't you? That's sweet. But I know you've never been to one of these before. So how well do you know Julian?"

"Enough, why?"

"Curious, is all." She dissolves into the dancers like a black ghost, the girl with the belt following.

Julian returns with more soda, his smile bright and unassuming.

"Who's that?" I point in the direction the girl went.

He follows my gaze. "A girl in my program. Why?"

I sip my soda. "Past girlfriend?"

He shrugs. "For like a week, maybe."

Everyone has a history, even me. "She came to say hi."

"That's nice of her." Julian sits beside me, leans back in his chair. "I'm not sure I've properly enjoyed one of these before. Should have found you years ago."

I elbow him. "So why didn't you? Colorado isn't far."

"Says the person who considers a twelve-hour drive 'not far.'"

He turns to the balcony and the partygoers outside. "Want to meet my mum?"

"If she's as welcoming as your dad."

"To mum, there's no obligation to be welcoming. So if she is, you'll know she likes you. Dad's harder to read."

"Oh."

He guides me out onto the balcony, overlooking dark, rippling water, with a softly playing background song that's like velvet on my ears. Julian's dad follows us out and stands at the railing, looking down at the river with his hands clasped behind his back. "The night always smells like something dying and something beautiful," he murmurs, like it's the most normal comment in the world.

Couples chat at rounded tables, aside from two elegant women beside a pillar, close to the glass railing. One is all soft curls and gentle smiles, smelling faintly of myrrh. The kind of scent that clings to mourning veils and midnight vigils. The other is as tall as a shadow at dusk, dark skinned and dark-haired. The kind of woman death itself might follow home.

Julian stops beside the first woman and squeezes my arm. "Mum, this is Briony, the girl I told you about."

"It's a pleasure. I'm Raven." Her voice moves with a slow, lyrical cadence, each word drawn out. She holds out a hand, palm down, and I'm not sure what to do with it, so I squeeze her fingers and give them a little shake.

"Nice to meet you, too."

"You two met at Burnley? In the honor program, of course. I

was in that program as well when I was in school." Her lips spread outward without a curve, as if her smile is on a platter, waiting until a box is checked before she'll confirm delivery.

"No, mum," Julian says, pulling me toward him. "But she goes to Burnley and she's sharp as anything."

His mom tilts her head, expression going a few degrees colder.

Rather than correct Julian, I press my lips shut.

My heart has become a pancake, flattened at the bottom of my chest. If Julian's mom knew I'm in the program created to avoid bad press, she'd escort me out the door.

Julian leads me through the doors again, to the dance floor, and turns to me. "One more dance? Will you give me the pleasure?"

I hesitate but take his hand.

Julian searches my face. "Are you all right?"

I nod, but don't meet his eyes.

"Reeve's program isn't a big deal," he says.

I nod again.

He touches my chin and forces me to meet his gaze.

"I'm fine." I pull away and attempt to put on happiness the way I put on my clothes, simply taking off the negativity and shrugging on a smile. Easy.

"Do you want to leave?" he asks. "We can get gelato."

"Please."

We walk to the elevator and I look for patterns in the wallpaper opposite me as the doors slide shut, my stomach jostling as we drop.

As soon as the elevator doors open, I hurry out. Julian's driver starts the car as we exit out front, and I clamber inside. The air's thin even in here.

Julian's looking at me.

I take a deep breath and recompose my face.

The car rumbles to life, and takes us along winding roads, deeper into town, where roads twist and apartments tower, squished together like passengers on an uncomfortable train. If that train had old leather seats.

Silas turns music on.

"Tired?" Julian asks.

"I'm sorry," I say.

"You don't have to apologize. You don't owe anyone that."

A lump forms in my throat.

The driver slows in front of a mint-green gelato shop, with a brass door handle, a pink sign, and heaping mounds of ice cream behind the glass windows. We park along the road, and cars fly by as Julian closes my car door.

I follow him into the shop, which smells like sugar and cream, sweet and cold. With shelves of pastel candy and wallpaper that matches the mint exterior.

The moment we stop in front of the display, an associate addresses me in an accent so thick I can only stare back.

"Which flavor?" Julian prods.

"Oh."

I point and the associate scoops the ice cream up and ushers us to the register.

"I can cover this one," I say, but Julian raises a hand.

"Thank you," I murmur.

"Course."

We sit down at a round table and I stab my ice cream with the tiny spoon. Then stir the melting cream into a lump at the bottom.

Julian sips from a cup of water, watching me over the top of his glass. "You like gelato, right?"

"I love gelato," I say.

"That's... an interesting way to show love."

I look up. "What?"

He leans back against his plastic chair. "You're a lovely dancer, you know…you never said you could move like that."

"Liar."

"You are."

"Thanks," I say.

He feels bad for me and knows it's what I want to hear.

"Did you notice my dad's friend wore my dad's face as a mask? He teases my dad for being too soft, and wanted to poke fun at him. He was talking like my dad all night. But my dad will get him back. Always does."

"I didn't notice, no," I say. My smile comes a little easier.

"I was surprised at his bravery. Most everyone's terrified of my dad."

"Why? He seemed nicer than your mom."

"Oh, he's very good at being nice. That doesn't mean he's kind."

Julian takes our bowls and tosses them. "Let's go. I think we danced the muscles off our feet. I'm sure you're feeling it."

We leave the gelato shop, drive to my dormitory, and Julian walks me to the door.

I fumble for my keys in my purse, Julian's presence inching closer, until he's practically breathing me in.

My legs stiffen; my fingers tremble as he reaches for my face, drags his knuckles down my cheek.

For a second, I think he might kiss me. Or I might let him. Then the moment slips, too fragile to hold, and my heart jumps into my throat.

My fingers curl around my key and I shove it into the lock. "Thanks for taking me. Bye." Averting my gaze, I close the door behind me.

Definitely screwed that up.

I drag my feet to my bed, shoulders heavy, and stare out the window. The river is too dark to see. Stars flicker dully in the sky, like they're about out of battery.

Julian's mom's underwhelmed face follows me, like a weight dragging at my waist. I imagined this dance being so much more magical. But it was magical, wasn't it? Just not in the way I expected. Every look, every almost—everything I could ruin if I think on it too hard.

Rather than dwell on my disasters, I open my computer to a blank document and start my project for Professor Karina. Then start over. Rewrite and write again. I delete five pages of single-spaced words and let the frustrating black line of my cursor flash on the screen.

It taunts me as it flashes.

And flashes.

And flashes.

CHAPTER TWENTY-NINE

TWO DAYS LATER, my phone pings, but I ignore it. The sun's been up and down again, and tomorrow's another round of lectures I'm nowhere near ready for.

I massage my temples and close my eyes.

I've torn through everything on King Arthur—*Idylls of the King, The Arthurian Legends,* every dusty article I can find. I've written my thesis and am writing circles around it, but everything I write is clunky and awkward and boring.

Were King Arthur's attempts to create a perfect kingdom a failure? Why or why not?

He failed because he didn't create the perfect kingdom. His round table buckled under the Holy Grail, and he lost everything. Simple answer. So why do I feel that's not sufficient?

I drag a finger over the dry pages, the ink starting to smear where I've stared too long. When I blink, the letters just get fuzzier.

The ink isn't smudging. It's just me.

This is useless. So I pack up, run to the closest store, and buy a set of potted plants. Mint to keep me alert. Rosemary for focus.

Then I return to decorate my room. As I shelve lemon balm, I call Sadie, but she doesn't answer.

Fine, then. I'll find something else.

I toss my phone onto my bed and empty my trash. Maybe I'll think on my essay and clean my room at the same time.

On second thought, a tub of ice cream sounds nice.

A light knock sounds on my door.

It's probably Noelle coming to check on me because that's the kind of person Noelle is, even if her recent behavior suggests otherwise. But right now, I'm not in the mood to hear Noelle's essay results.

I'm still careful as I pry the door open, after all my mishaps with Reeve.

But it's not Noelle or Reeve.

Julian tucks his hands into his pockets. He looks out of place in the doorway—like he's stepped out of an old photograph, auburn hair catching the light, scarf hanging just so.

"Noelle said you haven't left this room in days, and no one's heard from you. Wanted to make sure you're okay. Can I come in?"

I'm wearing sweatpants, and I haven't brushed my hair in two days. I rake my fingers through the tangles to smooth them out and lean to cover the door opening so he can't see in.

A plate with a slice of bread sits on my desk alongside a devoured box of donuts. No magical mice have cleared away the papers that litter the floor.

There's nothing to do but step aside, so I do—hesitantly.

Julian brushes past, stepping around the junk to sit in my desk chair—the only thing not covered in mess. I stand awkwardly, torn between wanting him gone and wanting him to never leave.

"What're you working on?" he asks.

"My history essay."

He peers at the books on my bed. "Going well?"

I sigh aloud. "Not really. I'm the worst at writing essays. I'm sure you could sit and write one in an hour, no problem, and put mine to shame."

Maybe my brain's just wired wrong. Everyone else makes it look easy.

Julian grimaces. "Do you really think that?"

He spends most of his time in class watching the room. That's hardly listening.

He shakes his head at my silence. "You think you struggle alone. But sometimes people's struggles are just different. You probably haven't noticed, but…you steady me. Somehow."

His hands—the tiny tremor that goes almost unnoticed unless you're looking.

My throat tightens.

"Since I'm obviously an expert essayist," he continues, "though you haven't read a single essay I've written, might I offer to help?"

I bury my face in my hands. "I'm supposed to write about King Arthur and whether he botched creating utopia."

"What have you written?"

"A bunch of facts. And then a yes." That's pretty much it.

He pulls a book toward him. "Is this *The Arthurian Legends*? Ah, *Idylls of the King*." He flips through a few pages, runs a finger down the paragraphs, and points to one. "This is a favorite of mine."

He is all fault who hath no fault at all:

For who loves me must have a touch of earth.

"The low sun makes the color," he reads aloud.

His voice lingers in the air like light through stained glass, and for a moment the whole room feels warmer.

"Why's it your favorite?" I ask.

"Think about it."

I read the paragraph again, as well as the paragraphs before and after. It's what Guinevere says about King Arthur to explain why she doesn't love him.

If perfection is the goal, and it's the path to perfection where we live, perhaps King Arthur didn't fail. Not entirely, because reaching perfection wasn't the point.

There's color in imperfection, and the journey creates the color.

It's almost like his words have jarred something loose in my head.

I grab a notebook and scribble notes, hand twinging. Words tumble from my head, and I simply try to catch them.

"I see you're onto something. I'll leave you alone." Julian stands.

He hovers in the doorway, like he's reluctant to leave, his nod delayed. "Let me know if you need anything."

"I'm fine," I tell him. Or I will be soon.

I spend all night writing, eyes heavy as if they were made of lead, and pass my paper to Professor Karina the next morning in class. She takes it without comment, and I don't hear from her for several days until she pulls me into her office.

"Please, take a seat," she says.

I sit down and cross and uncross my legs. Is she happy? Disappointed? Please don't be disappointed. Nothing could be worse. Unless she thinks I plagiarized it.

Professor Karina picks up my paper. "Guinevere's admiration for the shifting light of sunset stands in quiet defiance of Arthur's rigid ideals, showing that beauty exists not in unchanging purity, but in transience—" she reads aloud. "In an imperfect state of becoming."

Her eyes shine. "Briony, this essay is leagues better. I'm impressed. You've really outdone yourself." She clears her throat and adjusts her sleeves. "Keep up the good work."

For the first time in weeks, the world doesn't feel so heavy.

She hands the paper back to me, and I smooth a crease in the corner.

"Thank you," I manage.

A small, quiet kind of victory, but it glows all the same.

To celebrate, I put on my nicest skirt and cardigan—and my beret, for good measure—just in case I run into Julian. At least this time, I'll look halfway put together instead of like a gremlin who lost a fight with her desk chair.

I catch the bus into town and fill a basket with glossy-wrapped European chocolate bars—the kind that snap cleanly in half and melt in my mouth.

I smuggle my loot to the library and slip into the little side room Professor Reeve lent me, the one that smells faintly of dust, to unwrap the first bar. At the table, I set my bag down, letting the light from the window warm my face.

Here, I hope to finish the journals undisturbed.

I bring out the copies I made, find the next letter in the series, and set it on the table, starting with one by Sir James Altham.

I had posted my watchers at the Duck and Drake, and naught was heard until the twentieth day of May, when the man I pursued — a Catholic sympathizer named John Wright — was at last espied.

When I entered the inn my contacts had spoken of, I found a circle of men arrayed in dark doublets edged with lace, high starched collars that nursed their chins, and broad-brimmed hats that cast their faces into theatrical shadow.

They gathered about a low table by a sputtering fire, sheltered beneath an iron hood. The wooden walls and benches offered a domestic warmth so innocent as to be almost indecent — a comfort altogether unsuited to the contrivances of stratagem and murder. I took my station in a crowded corner nearby, to observe and, as ever, not to be observed, and I listened.

One of the men spoke in a voice kept low;

the sides of his moustache trembled. Perhaps a sign of zeal rather than reason. He urged immediate action, for delay would be the death of any hope they possessed. John Wright replied that they must first build alliances, he said; wars are not won by handfuls but by armies. If they must root out their enemies in parliament, why not seek succour from other Catholic powers? King Philip remained their greatest sympathiser.

Another scoffed that King Philip would not offer aid, not after the Armada; if he could not be counted upon, who then would stand against England? A thick silence fell as the men considered one another. I could not help but notice the varying states of their garments — coats with differing degrees of mending, boots fastened with brass buckles. Brass — the very metal of pretence.

John demanded news of Guido, who was to come with a special sword without which their designs could not be accomplished. He asked if any had seen him. The answer slid between them like a cold draft: they had sought the sword for years and found it not; the weapon could not be relied upon. Robert — who claimed to have spoken to Guido in Brussels and again in York concerning an alternate scheme — alleged that Guido had stoutly opposed it, and that in York he departed in a pique, leaving no trace in Flanders. Robert judged that Guido had forsaken them.

Gravely they considered this; gravely, because Robert's alternative involved a quantity of gunpowder secreted beneath the House of Lords until the appointed hour. How to amass such stores without observation, and without Guido? Robert smiled the smile of a man who believes his answer simple: he had leased a cellar beneath the House of Lords and employed a servant to convey barrels thither. So far, his enterprise had run unimpeded.

"If Guido does not strike the match," John asked at last, "who shall?"

A troubled hush took the room. It was then that I rose. I smoothed my sleeve, and announced—without flourish and without false modesty—that I possessed the means to solve their difficulty.

—Sir James Altham

The sword itches a forgotten place in my brain. Guido explained earlier that it's supposed to end immortals and mentioned something about there being evil in the government. This group might be some religious secret society formed to end those evils. I'm sure the journals will explain more. So I turn the page.

—1604—

I continued my search for any lake or reservoir that might harbour even the faintest whisper of a ghost, or perhaps some small, undiscovered pool. Went to church and sat in the front seat, stayed after to pay my respects. Kept my cross in hand, always.

Between days of travel, I taught Hugh the rudiments of rabbiting and, when the moment was right, entrusted him with my knife—its serpent-hilt being the companion of many a journey and skirmish.

When I bade him throw the blade at an old oak, his first effort buried the hilt in the earth; with only a little direction he improved, became steadier of hand and truer of eye. I found, to my surprise, that I could be something like a father to the boy, and that the thought of watching Alice dance to the piano each evening warmed me more than any conquest. Should I recover the sword, staying could be possible. I pray every night that this be so.

When her father returns, I shall be on the doorstep to meet him.

—Guido

They seem happy, but something bad must have happened to Alice.

—1604—

I wrote a fine letter to warn Lord Monteagle, with a date and location that fast approaches. I signed Guido's correct name at the bottom corner with my left hand. No conspirator would be so imprudent as to admit to a scheme with his signature. Yet there are many fools in Parliament willing to believe. I need only one to credit me.

—Sir James Altham

—1604—

I know not what became of Alice.

Last night, dusk fell too soon upon the valley, as though heaven urged me away from her doorstep. Yet I lingered; I had seen that wild figure in the trees again, and I would not leave her unguarded.

We sat by the fire, Alice, Hugh and I, and I spoke of Spain, of laughter, heat, and sunlit battlements. She forgot to dismiss me, forgot to keep that careful distance she always held. A wind hissed through the resin-soaked linens at the windows, and the fire died as if commanded.

Alice flinched. "You should go," she murmured.

But I dallied. Her father had long neglected to call, and I intended to speak with him, to ask permission, declare my heart. She repeated her earlier words of warning, this time with urgency, and busied herself with the hearth and did not meet my eyes.

The door burst wide. A finely dressed youth with a tangle of brown hair shouldered past me, all urgency.

"They are coming," he said. "Right behind me."

Alice moved at once, gathering candles, herbs, salt. She knelt in the moonlight, drawing symbols with a shaking hand. Circles and angles. Patterns meant to invoke witchcraft.

Light flared beneath her skin. A star burned upon her wrist, stark and vile.

I stared, frozen, while my pulse turned to ice. Magic. Her magic. In the woman I—

I drew my knife.

Alice backed away, skirts brushing the scattered seeds into disarray.

Her father stood in the doorway. "Mercy," he pleaded, palms raised.

Alice's tears shone silver in the moonlight. Her lower lip trembled—the same lip I had caught myself admiring only nights before. I ached to pull her close, to shield her. But she had woven herself into my heart only to corrupt it. To blind me to my duty.

Every twirl by the fire, every touch, the midnight strolls in the woods...every minute of sparkle is dust.

All this time, I sought the sword. They told me purity and unwavering faith would reveal it. Perhaps she—her deceit—was why I failed.

My calling is to sever evil from this earth. To kill witches before their rot spreads.

She was reserved. Guarded. But I never suspected that she had buried every part of herself, even the nature of what she was.

This was my test.

I advanced, step by unwilling step. Every fibre strained against the command I forced upon myself. She stumbled into her table of dried flowers and vials. A jar smashed, the scent of rosemary rising like incense at a funeral.

"Please," she breathed, voice breaking.

I lifted my arm to strike.

Alice's hand shot outward, and the wooden floor shuddered. A crack surged between us. Vines, thick as rope, burst from the seeds and coiled round my ankles. I slashed them free, sap spraying like blood.

"Alice," I rasped, "cease this!"

She shook her head, backing deeper into moonlight.

I lunged and the vines surged again. One seized my wrist. The knife jerked. The blade kissed the soft place beneath her chin—just enough to draw a bead of scarlet.

We both froze. Her breath warmed my shaking hand.

God forgive me—I wanted to kiss her, not kill her.

"That's enough!" her father roared, and the roots tightened around my body.

But the door crashed wide again and Sir James Altham stormed in, followed by a magistrate and soldiers. Steel glinted. Boots stomped out her circle of salt.

My grip faltered. Relief and despair twisted within me.

If they had come for the witch, they could finish the duty God demanded of me.

Instead, rough hands seized my shoulders.

"Guy Fawkes," the magistrate barked. "You are under arrest."

My knife clattered to the floor. Alice choked a sob as the soldiers swarmed her, too. And I—fool that I am—felt only grief.

—Guido

My hands tremble.

The scene is too vivid, the tension between love and violence, too raw. But this can't be what happened. It's like reading the end of a story where the hero turns on the girl he's supposed to protect, and it leaves a bitter taste in my mouth.

Why does it feel like he's apologizing to me?

I pull forward Guido's next journal.

—November of 1605—

I awoke to the echo of footsteps—a sound I had not heard in some time. A tender ache pulsed behind my right temple as my eyes adjusted to the stone vault above me. Barrels, firewood, and heaps of coal hemmed me in on every side, the spacious chamber heavy with the scent of mildew and stubbornly resistant to warmth.

As I pushed myself upright, a crowd of armed men burst into the room. One prodded my leg with the muzzle of his musket.

"Who art thou?" he demanded.

"John Johnson," I told him — the lie leaving my mouth before reason could intervene. "A servant to Thomas Percy."

I sometimes think I should have let them shoot me. It might have been the kinder choice.

—*Guido*

It wasn't enough to accuse Guido in a letter. Altham wanted him found on site as well. I reach for the next journal, but my phone buzzes. The screen lights up with a message from Julian.

Stay put and check the news. They found another body.

I gawk at those words for several moments before lunging for my laptop, blood pounding in my ears as I search the web for local news articles. I click on one with an image of paramedics pushing a blurred body on a stretcher. Body found near Rowley Lake. Investigators connect finding to a recent murder at Burnley Boarding School. Police discovered a boy with missing hands and a slashed throat. The photo at the bottom displays two mismatched socks sticking out of a body bag, and then one of a smiling boy holding a retro game controller.

My mouth dries.

It's Julian's friend, Robbie.

I call Julian, and he doesn't answer.

Just days ago, I'd have sold my sleep for a better grade. Now my ambitions feel hollow, almost absurd. Whatever ache I feel, Julian's must be deeper.

I text him again. I'm here for you if you need me.

CHAPTER THIRTY

BARE FEET SINK into moss, earthy, damp, and faintly sweet with decay. Even the gnarled trees growing in all directions look like creatures between life and death. None shelter the yellow eyes I'm searching for.

I stumble and fall to my knees, my hands sinking into muck. It clings to me, no matter how hard I wrestle.

Then I jerk awake with a scream.

I'm alone in my room, wrapped tightly in my covers, like I accidentally rolled myself into them. My hands clutch bundles of fabric with a death grip, and I pry my fingers loose.

There are no trees, no swamps, and certainly no yellow eyes peering in from the window.

I take a deep breath and rub my eyes, though a sense of loss clings like a handwritten farewell note. My lips are cracking when I check my reflection in the cabinet mirror. A scaly, red-skinned, pimpled face stares back, my wrist swollen from the additional scratches I gave myself during the night. I can't go to class like this, but I can't not go either.

I wash my face and scaly skin peels onto my hands. Despite

my commitment never to buy anything from Mystic Cosmetics, a moisturizing cream wouldn't be unwelcome. Eye shadows are hidden beneath makeup. So I yank a hoodie over my cardigan, throw on the closest pair of pants—brown dress pants. And wrap my wrist.

The halls are clear of students, so I don't have to hide until I duck into class. Then I sit in the back corner with my hood tugged around my face. Julian's broad shoulders enter through the doorway, hands shoved into his pockets, his movements slower, more deliberate. His eyes don't sparkle like they usually do.

I should talk to him, comfort him somehow. But when he looks in my direction, I want to vanish.

This place didn't have monsters until I arrived.

He sits near another girl two rows ahead. She's in a sleeveless sweater, with big eyes and bigger hair. Her face brightens the moment she sees him, and her whole body leans instinctively in his direction.

Julian opens his backpack and glances over his shoulder. I should wave, draw his attention. Instead, I pull my hoodie down closer to my nose.

The professor passes the tests down the lines of students, and I hunch over mine. I forgot we had a test today, but I've studied for weeks and should be prepared.

After…I'll talk to Julian after.

Julian starts his assignment and doesn't look up, his pen held tight in his fist. I follow suit and scan the words in paragraph one. At first, they don't register. So I try again.

Julian stretches and I look up just as he starts writing again. He drums his thumb restlessly on his desk, but he's not done yet.

So I return to my paper. When I look up again, he's gone.

Students follow until there's only empty chairs left.

I finish filling out my paper, turn it in, and trudge across frost-stiffened grass. My breath trails in the air as I move from paved sidewalks to courtyards, then to Birdie's Court. I walk inside to find posters covering the walls.

Missing since Saturday. Has anyone seen me?

Robbie, with his mess of sandy hair, gives me a smug I-never-clean-my-room smile from each photo.

The edges of each flyer curl into themselves, the bottom right corner listing Julian as a contact. Guess he can take those down now. I'm half-tempted to do it myself, but that almost makes it worse.

I hurry down the halls of Birdie's Court to my room, and close my eyes as soon as I shut the door. Two breaths. Inhale. Exhale. At my desk, I move the journal pages I already read aside. My phone dances across the table, and the tiny screen lights up. I flip it open to a new message from Noelle.

I have exciting news about our favorite store. I need to tell you!

Probably about Mystic Cosmetics' newest shampoo. Clearly, she hasn't heard about Robbie, and I don't want to be the one to tell her.

I put my phone down and turn to the entry from James Altham.

—*1606*—

When last I confronted Alice, I set before her a single ultimatum. In the guttering candle

light she blinked—pupils wide, hair knotted,
her cheeks smeared with dirt—every sign
of a girl who knew full well why she stood
there yet would not bend to my terms.

Until she yields, she shall remain confined;
I have no mind to unmake the sentence I lay
down. Perhaps she harbours some strange
solace in stale air, stone walls, and the
narrow of a barred window—an affection
for constraint I cannot fathom. Could I be so
grotesque an alternative?

If she refuses to comply, she is condemned,
and her little brother may as well be dead.

—Sir James Altham

If Alice was sent to prison, this may explain how she evaded the witch trials.

—1606, Westminster Palace Yard—

No soul alive comprehended what was lost upon the guillotine that day—save I alone. I stood in Palace Yard at Westminster Hall as they carried out the sentence, the air thick with cloud and clamour, a forest of raised arms casting restless shadows upon the scaffold. When they pressed the pen to his hand, poor Guido could scarcely hold it. They dragged him forward—emaciated, diminished—and I beheld him at the end.

Behold, the first honest man ever to enter Parliament. And what has his honesty done for him?

—Sir James Altham

When I see another account signed by Altham, I'm tempted to skip it, but grit my teeth instead.

—1612—

Alice had tormented herself for

*months—scratching until her skin split,
opening ugly seams upon her arms and legs.
I had supposed such torment would at last
bend her, yet she made no sign of surren-
der; not even after seven years. When I
next sought her out, her skin was raw and
scabbed, her hair wild as peat; she muttered
to herself and started at the slightest noise.
Still, when I looked upon her, all I read was
refusal.*

*Perhaps, if I gave her a measure of freedom
—just long enough to taste the air and
soil — she might learn to see me otherwise.
Failing that, it would be the more expedient
course to make an end of it.*

*Releasing Alice Grey would be an act of
mercy made difficult by the world that
watches. The countryside bears a hunger
for explanation; at Pendle every misfortune
finds its scapegoat. When I confined Alice on
the pretext of witchcraft, some questioned my
judgement. In time, a tale took root: a witch*

who howled and tore at her flesh in the night. They dubbed her "Mouldskin."

The magistrate — her grandfather, and a man who values his repute more than any inconvenient truth — has no stomach to defend her. Accusations have multiplied like seed: Miss Preston, a foolish girl whose lover met a sudden, untimely death at a wedding — witch. A peddler fell dead in Colne accompanied by the granddaughter of the notorious healer Demdike — witch. Strange illnesses have claimed townsfolk; healers boast of forbidden arts; each week some villager disappears and is never seen again. Witches, they say.

To Magistrate Nowell, this is providence: a trial is a splendid stage. To condemn is to curry favour in Lancaster and at court.

The village looked to me to staunch the contagion of fear. I could do this: repair my standing in Lancaster and at court, and at

> *the same time rid myself of Alice. All would*
> *be laid, with perfect propriety, at her door*
> *—for she alone refused my counsel.*
>
> *—Sir James Altham*

When strange things started happening around town, James Altham took full advantage of it, but the prison part can't be a coincidence. Reeve said Alice Grey was imprisoned for seven years. I had a breakdown at the Lancaster prison, and now I dream of cells almost every night.

But the magistrate, the witches, and Altham lived centuries ago. I never knew them. I've never seen that cell before.

It's not real.

A sharp pain shoots through my arm where fresh scratches bloom red over old scars. I curl my fists tight to stop myself from doing it again and take a deep, shaky breath.

I'm not crazy.

I picture Sadie looking at me from across the table, one eyebrow raised.

"I'm not," I say aloud.

I twitch and scan my room, but I'm not in the library, and no one heard me talk to myself. I exhale and continue with a letter by Altham, dated the same year.

—*1612*—

*Word of witchcraft spread as far as Liver-
pool, carried by men of consequence; those
same gentlemen greeted our proposal for a
witch-trial with approving hands.*

*When tidings came of a village assembly,
Magistrate Nowell and I conferred at once.
Friends and kin of the accused hope to press
for the temporary release of those confined.
The hour has, therefore, arrived to dis-
charge Alice Grey — known to the vulgar
as "Mouldskin" — and I shall see that she
attends the meeting. None doubts her reputation; none could don the part with greater
ease.*

*This is her last opportunity to accept me.
Should the concession prove vain, I must
steel myself to allow her to perish in common
cause with the rest.*

—Sir James Altham

I can't think of anyone more deserving of a witch trial than Altham.

A woman called Widow Nutter writes the next letter.

—10th of April, 1612, Good Friday—

I found a young girl in the woods, wandering alone, calling out a name in desperate madness. I knew her at once—for I had seen her in happier years, when she was young, fair, and much sought after. Now her beauty is spent, her face drawn and wild; yet she is no more a witch than I.

The girl required aid, and I brought her before a gathering of the townsfolk. We met in a house of rough stone and timber, sagging with age and smelling of mildew; chairs scraped against the uneven boards as I told them of her misfortune.

My good neighbour, Mistress Isabel, was first to speak, and she rebuked me for bringing the girl at all, burdened as she was with so dark a name. I replied that such tales must be disproved, for witchcraft lives only in the fancies of frightened minds. Isabel would not be moved. She urged we appeal to the magistrate—that if we presented ourselves in number, he must heed us. The girl, she thought, should be sent away.

"I shall not remain another minute while this witch — this Mouldskin — stands among us," she said.

The candlelight wavered, throwing long shadows against the walls. The company stared at Alice: her threadbare rags clinging to her form, the dirt and withered leaves caught in the folds. Her hands shook; her lips pressed tight, as though speech itself might rend the world in two.

Then another at the table spoke, saying the magistrate would not listen—that he would hang us all for our insolence, and our kin besides.

At this, the youngest of the Device children rose beside her mother. Her thin face was lit by the candle's glow as she fixed her gaze upon Alice. She said we ought to strike back and blow the gaol to pieces. The magistrate may believe in magic, she said, but he does not fear it. We could use Alice to frighten them.

Alice turned as pale as chalk. I reached for her hand; she flinched, then met my eyes, and her trembling eased—though only by a little.

I told the youngest Device to take heart: her family had not yet been condemned to the gallows, though they sat in prison with the rest of our loved ones. If they truly feared magic, I said, they would burn half the countryside. We must show them their fears are false—that we are no witches. I pointed to Alice. "Alice Grey is as innocent as any here."

Alice took a step back toward the door.

The Device girl crossed her arms, defiant.

I entreated them once more. Alice's brother vanished into the woods seven years past; she knows not his fate. I begged them to listen for any word of him.

"Who is her brother?" Isabel asked.

"Hugh Grey," I told her.

Isabel's expression softened. She promised to watch for him.

I thanked them and led Alice out into the night.

We are to meet again in a week's time. Something must be done.

—Widow Nutter

Alice searched for her missing brother while Widow Nutter

hoped to protect her kin by disproving the witchcraft rumors. Instead, Widow Nutter would be hurt by association.

Only a few entries remain for Alice to find Hugh, and I'm afraid to keep going.

Still, I try another.

—*1612*—

We recaptured Alice Grey. She tasted freedom yet her resolve did not falter. At every turn I deemed myself victorious, only to find my cunning wanting. What manner of man must I become to sway even the lowliest of women?

Craving but one more chance, I sought the root of the reports concerning potions and charms, and there uncovered Jane Southworth at the heart of it—the same woman from Samlesbury who accosted me at the alehouse. I believe she and her sisters, Ellen and Jennet, trafficked in potions and wares through a network of village healers, among them our own Demdike and Chattox. Some brought affliction upon their foes; others bestowed comeliness and grace. I must learn by what means they work—and whether they work indeed.

I had purposed to journey to Samlesbury myself, to parley with these witches and draw forth their secrets, yet the magistrate discovered my intent and brought it before me. He dispatched word to the king seeking leave for another trial, but His Majesty received not our petition kindly. Perhaps he wearied of slaughtering his own subjects.

The king's wrath turned upon the magistrate and me alike, and he withdrew his favour from all witch trials throughout the realm, despite his late proclamations to the contrary. My title was forfeit, my coffers emptied, and the devotion of my wives proved frail as frost.

Thus my yearning for power grew not from vanity, but necessity. I could not live diminished, nor hope to move Alice's heart as a *man bereft of standing.*

If there be truth in magic, I shall be the first to master it.

—James Altham

The sisters, Jane and Ellen, sold wares to the villagers just as the Jane and Ellen I know sell cosmetics to students.

While the journals mention another sister called, "Jennet," I haven't heard her name among my peers. The entry also talks about recruiting more followers, and how Altham wants to become a witch himself.

The Jane and Ellen I know can't be the same Jane and Ellen, so maybe they're descendants, too.

Witches returned to the modern world. Is it too far-fetched?

The sisters must be causing students to disappear. They're the thread weaving through everything. So if this is what Reeve wanted me to realize, why hasn't he called the police?

I lift the mattress, pick up the book with the fancy tree, and run a thumb over the cover. The journals said my necklace is protection. I need it back, and not just to open the purple book. I have to know if my suspicion holds weight, and the only way to do this is to investigate the characters involved.

Or ask Reeve.

Shoving the book beneath the mattress, I snatch my purse and hurry out the door. I run across the grounds, down sidewalks, to the dark-paneled door with the gold plaque, raise a fist, and pound on the door.

My chest rises and falls as I struggle to pull in air.

The wood creaks open, and Professor Reeve stands in the opening with his fedora hat. Waves of sleek hair curl over his ears. His eyes widen. "Briony?"

"I finished the journals," I say.

He recovers quickly and folds his arms. "All of them?"

"We need to call the police. We need to give them a reason to investigate."

"What're you talking about?"

I hesitate for only a moment before plowing on. "The women at Mystic Cosmetics," I say. "The witches in the journals."

Reeve knits his brow. "Enough of this, Briony. Go home. It's not safe for you here."

"It's as safe for me as anyone else. People are dying. Those students can't know what kind of cult they're joining." If he doesn't care about the safety of his students, I misjudged him.

"They know," Professor Reeve says in a flat tone. "Go home and reread the journals. You've clearly missed something."

"You can't let this happen at your school."

"I can."

I gape. "Haven't you seen the flyers?"

"People disappear all the time."

"All the time, huh? I suppose you're right. You find someone in the river with their eyes cut out every night when you head home from the bar."

He only looks at me.

If he won't talk about the witches, he might answer other questions. "What happened to Hugh then?"

Reeve's brows pull together. "Who's Hugh?"

"He's in those journals."

His eyes are empty, his stare blank. This isn't funny.

"Alice's little brother," I add.

Professor Reeve's expression clears. "I've no idea what happened to Alice's brother, and that's the truth. You're wasting my time."

"But you do know she had a brother?"

"She did, yes." Reeve leans against the doorway and folds his arms. "But that's all I can tell you about him. He's never been the subject of my research."

Useless.

I leave him behind, stride down the hall, and dial the police. I don't need Professor Reeve to push these numbers for me. There will be no more posters on the wall.

This is how I help Julian.

"Lancashire Police," comes a no-nonsense voice on the other line. "What's your address?"

"No need for an address. I'm calling to report nefarious activities at the new cosmetics store on Mill Road—"

"Mystic Cosmetics?"

The store must already be on their radar. "Yes, I believe the owners are behind the recent disappearances and murders."

"What gives you reason to suspect this?"

I cup my hand over the phone so students passing in the hallway don't overhear. "They're a witch coven."

The officer's voice turns crisp. "I know it's Halloween, but this is not a number for jests, miss."

"It's no jest." How do I explain this? "I think they're the reason behind the kids disappearing at Burnley Boarding School. I have these journals—" Would my journals be proof of anything? Likely not. "They attract people to their store and charge people astronomical sums for cosmetics."

"That doesn't prove they're behind the disappearances. Do you have a specific reason to suspect them? Have you seen something?" Despite asking questions, the officer's tone is disinterested.

"No, I just know it's them. Their store is close to where the first girl disappeared."

"Lots of shops are close to Mill Road."

"That's true." I try to think of something tangible I can give them, but nothing comes to mind. "Will you at least take note of this call?"

"It's protocol."

"Oh, right." My arm droops as I clutch the phone. "Well, thanks anyway."

"Goodbye, miss. Thanks for calling."

The line goes dead, and I rub my face.

With her long, black hair swaying, Mika walks down the hall, squints, and claps her hands. "Briony, love."

I struggle to arrange my face, so my emotions won't burst through. "Mika, what're you doing here?"

"I'm glad I caught you." Her eyes shine. "Noelle's been trying to get hold of you. Remember that cosmetics store Noelle loved so much?"

A tightness coils in my stomach. "Yeah?"

"They offered her a job. She's ecstatic. I can't tell you how many times she listed off all their products. I know them so well, I feel like I could be a sales rep myself. Maybe I should be." Mika's expression turns thoughtful. "Don't give me that look, Briony. I have no real intention of applying." Mika grimaces. "Anyway, call and congratulate her. She's been applying for months."

The very store I hope to shut down. She's going to hate me.

"When did she start?" I ask.

"She started today. It was all rather quick. Are you okay, Briony? You look a bit peculiar."

"Fine."

Without proof, no one will listen—not the professor and not the police.

"I have to go," I say.

Mika looks taken aback. "Where?"

To the only place I can find proof. "To Mystic Cosmetics."

CHAPTER THIRTY-ONE

WITHOUT WASTING A moment, I go straight to the source of my concerns. The bus halts, and I step out onto a street blanketed in midnight. Darkness empties the doors and consumes the roads. Streetlight glints off metal verandas and white paneling like skeletons dug up by the moon.

The purple awning of Mystic Cosmetics pretends subtlety among the muted greens and browns, yet the dense, knotted vine crawling up the wall to the windows ensures it's impossible to miss.

I creep toward the front door, shut with a "closed" sign. Lights brighten the windows in a narrow upper level where a cracked opening lets smoke and whiffs of fresh lavender escape to spiral into the clouds. Murky shapes move behind the glass. I open my phone, press the record button, and stuff it in my pocket.

The vine is rough and fibrous as I pull myself up and jam my foot into the thickest branch. When I tug again, my chin rises above the door, level with the second-story window.

A circle of silhouettes surrounds a mixture of blankets and trinkets, chanting in some peculiar language. The air throbs with it.

I shift to get out of the notch in the vine, but waver as a shape is dragged into the room.

My muscles scream to climb down, but I'm frozen in place.

The silhouettes, or black robed figures, drop the shape on the ground, bundle a set of feet, and tie those feet to a stair post. Then they form a circle, more joining from the stairway.

As the circle expands, black robes draw closer to the window.

I drop lower, sliding down the vine so fast my phone slips out and clangs against the store's metal awning.

The chanting ceases. I stiffen, my heart roaring in my ears.

Someone cranks open the window. Silence—every passing moment a needle on my skin, a hold on my breath.

"Did you hear that?" says a voice.

"Must be the cat," says another.

The window cranks shut again and the muffled chanting resumes. Tension in my shoulders eases, but my heart is still pounding, fast as a bird's wings.

I scurry down the rest of the vine, legs trembling as I leap onto the pavement. Knees buckle. My phone is a tiny light behind the store's sign above my head. I can't reach it, but if I abandon it, my whole trip is for nothing. I need the incriminating footage.

I waver.

Then the store's front door chimes, and a dry voice speaks, "Excellent."

I turn to Jane standing on the doorstep, watching me. "Hello, sweet. Think I've seen you before."

And I've seen more than enough of her.

Ellen follows, a black cat balanced on her arm. She pats the feline's head. "I wondered if anyone would try to climb that vine."

The cat hisses.

My thoughts disperse, replaced by one primitive command. Run!

Before I can, two sets of nails grab me from behind and dig into my shoulder.

"You're not going anywhere," Jane snarls into my ear.

Jane and Ellen tow me into the store, knocking over a table covered in soaps. Spiders scatter. They shove me to the back of the room. Black curtains close and floorboards groan as they lug me up the stairs, wood scraping against my shins, to where incense is burning. Unnatural scents I've never smelled before.

We crest the top stair, and the two women hold fast to my arms. The room is bare, except for a circle of black-robed figures surrounding a pair of frayed blankets spread over the floor. Strange items are assembled in a star-shaped sequence, and, around the pattern, someone drew a second circle with chalk. Candles flicker from every flat surface around the room, casting shadows that dance.

A boy tied to a post has long blonde hair hanging in his face. And his wrist—sliced and smeared with fresh blood.

A scream rips the air. My mouth is open, my throat raw. Strong hands hold me in place, their grip so tight it's painful. I'm thrashing, kicking, and spitting.

"Shut the window, or they'll hear!"

"The walls and windows are warded—no one will hear a thing."

Hands let go. Ellen stoops in front of me and jabs me hard in the throat. My knees and elbows hit the ground and I claw at my neck, gasping for breath.

Someone touches my shoulder, and I bite until I taste blood. Until a slap sends me sprawling and Jane thrusts me into the staircase post.

"Enough!"

My cheek stings. My throat is on fire. Everything goes fuzzy around the edges.

Only a few feet away, the tied-up boy doesn't flinch, doesn't even move. The horror of it expands inside me, until it's all I can do to stay in one piece.

"Don't hurt her!" One of the robed figures throws back their hood and hurries toward me. I look up as recognition clicks into place. Dark-chocolate hair, and what's left of her acne now just scars—Noelle.

Jane glares. "Get back in the circle, sweet, unless you want to join her."

Noelle flinches, casts me a shameful glance, and melts back into the circle, leaving behind dread's cold shadow.

I stare after her, straining against the rope binding my hands, but it only cuts into my skin.

People in the circle sit in unison, legs crossed.

The chanting swells, at least fifteen contributing their voices. Ellen sets up more candles, and several almost flicker out when another black-robed figure ascends the stairs and saunters into the circle, obsidian hair flowing from their hood, the ends tinged purple. Several rings on each hand.

The figure kneels on a bed of tattered blankets, dragging sharp nails over a grim arrangement of teeth, knucklebones, an enormous crystal, and a pile of feathers. Beside them, a wooden stump bears a single pewter goblet.

They start to chant, each word rasping out as though pulled from a dry throat. A green, bitter scent cuts the air—foxglove and yew—the kind of plants that steal breath and give power. Then the figure raise its eyes, a woman's eyes, and focus on me, the purple in her irises like polished amethysts.

She reaches for the pewter goblet and lifts it high. "You have done well, sisters. This is our largest gathering yet. I am pleased, and so is our master. Welcome…to acceptance." Her gaze sweeps the circle. "To vengeance." She spreads her arms wide. "To immortality. All the things heaven has denied you."

Her voice softens, almost tender, like a hand offering sweets before tightening around the throat. "We will teach you our ways, beyond mere hair tonics and soaps, I assure you. No one will laugh, belittle, or steal from you again. All we ask is tribute to the master and your sworn devotion. Together, the scorned, the ugly, and the forgotten will rule God's world."

The chant picks up again, and the chorus of voices arouses dust and smoky fumes. Words accelerate, my heartbeat with them, until every rib throbs.

The woman holds a goblet in one hand and a blade with the other. Thick eyebrows shadow eyes outlined with heavy, black wings. Dusky lipstick accentuates full, exultant lips while pale skin stretches over high cheekbones.

She approaches, robes trailing behind her. The spectators in the circle, Noelle among them, turn their faces away. Her cloak swallows the light as she swoops over the boy, dagger raised, and clutches his good wrist. He barely jerks as she slices downward, and blood oozes into her goblet. A soft moan escapes his lips, but his eyes remain shut.

I can't help. Can't—his wrist, the blade. I don't know his face and the relief at not knowing him is acidic.

The witches won't let me go after this. My parents will hear from the authorities that they found my dead body in the river with my eyes cut out.

The woman with the purple eyes strides away and slices her own palm. A few drops fall into the goblet before she passes it to the first person in line. They press the cup to their lips—pause—then hand it off. Each figure in the circle drinks. Some shudder. Others stay still.

The purple-eyed woman lights candles around the room and motions to Jane, who inclines her head, hurries down the stairs, and returns with a hot iron. She touches the tip, and a cruel smile distorts her lips.

Each person in line extends their arm, and they thrash as the iron presses against their skin, but none scream. As the last person is branded, the purple-eyed woman twists her wrist, and pulls her sleeve back to reveal several blackened symbols. "Welcome, brothers and sisters," she said. "You have been given the power. Now it is left to you to acquire the knowledge, which we, the Mekori, are here to share."

Something shifts in the air. The candles dim, and a strange sensation crawls beneath my skin.

The boy twitches and goes still.

The purple-haired woman's upper lip curls, but her eyes move past the boy and land on me.

She takes a step in my direction, holding the knife aloft. "I'm sorry, child, but you weren't invited to this party."

"Stop." The voice calls from the stairway—Professor Reeve's deep tones. "Jennet!"

The third name. The third sister from the letters.

Jennet glares past me. "What are you doing here?"

The ropes around my wrists loosen, and I'm able to pull free. I whimper as I rub my wrists, and two strong arms encircle me, almost protectively. "I'm taking the girl. You have no right to kill her."

Reeve's arm slides beneath my knees. The ground falls away. My head lolls against his chest, hair brushing his jaw.

He found me.

He's taking me away.

I'm not going to die. I'm not—

"Is this her?" The woman draws herself upright, wiping her blade on her robe. "Fascinating." She studies me like I'm something pinned under glass. "Take your offering, Reeve. But cross me again and I'll slaughter you where you stand—whether she dies today or tomorrow makes no difference to me."

He shifts my weight in his arms and touches his neck where my tree pendant hangs on a silver chain. "You can't kill me."

Jennet's eyes narrow. "Where did you find that?" She spits at his feet. "Lying thief. How long have you had it?"

"I didn't steal it."

"It's mine. I don't care where you got it. That necklace was mine from the beginning. And you said it was lost."

"How can it be yours? You can't even touch it."

Jennet shows her teeth. "The moment that comes off, I'll slit your throat."

He turns his back on her and carries me down the stairs, his mouth a hard line. The silver tree hangs from his neck, and I have half a mind to snatch it for myself.

The professor sets me down at the bottom of the stairs, and holds my elbow. I glance back to the silent form on the floor and stop. That boy won't last much longer without medical attention. "We can't leave him."

"The kid? He's already dead." Reeve's voice is a hiss. "Trust me, I know dead."

He drags me forward. The bell on the door chimes, and frigid air nips at my nose as we stumble out onto the sidewalk.

A shrieking laugh follows from the open window. "Watch her, Reeve." She says his name with an exaggerated sneer. "Watch her closely."

The professor yanks open the door of a black sedan parked along the roadside, scowling. I drop into the passenger side, legs weak. He gets in after me, fumbles to fasten his seatbelt, and starts the car. As he backs out, his hands shake on the steering wheel. We turn off Mill Road, and Professor Reeve flips on jazz music.

I examine my own unsteady fingers and count each breath. Despite the mellow saxophone, every muscle in my body clenches. They killed a boy right in front of me.

Snow sprinkles the roads outside, but all I see is red.

"I told you to go home," the professor says.

"I know."

"I'm doing my best to protect you," he continues. "But I can't do this again. You have to leave. Surely after this, you wouldn't be so stubborn as to ignore me a third time."

I avert my eyes. "I'll go. I…I promise."

The lines on Professor Reeve's forehead smooth.

I take a deep breath, steadying my voice. "Can you tell me one thing?"

He glances at me and looks away. "I can try."

"Why haven't you gone to the police?"

A bitter laugh bursts from his lips. "The police can't protect you from the Mekori."

"Who're the Mekori?"

Professor Reeve only shakes his head. "Briony, I'm willing to do anything I can to protect you, short of something stupid. I know you don't know me very well, but I haven't maintained many contacts through the years. Though you may view me differently, you're the closest thing I have to family. You're all I have. Please go home. Now that you've grown up, I'll keep in contact."

I turn away.

Family calls occasionally. He never did, and it's a little too late.

"Robbie died the same way that boy did, didn't he?" My voice breaks as I say it.

I'm glad Julian never witnessed the witch ceremony.

"Maybe." Professor Reeve pulls into a McDonalds. "Let's get you something to eat." He doesn't ask what I want but orders a Quarter Pounder with orange juice at the drive-through window and passes it over.

Reeve watches me take the burger, and runs a finger absent-mindedly over my necklace, tracing the outline of the tree.

I take a hesitant bite and set the hamburger down.

"I need my necklace."

"You don't." He lets go and puts his hand back on the wheel.

"I can't leave England without it."

He gives me an odd look. "I'll ship it to you."

Yeah, right.

"Told you I'd go, and I plan to. But I need my necklace. It's the only piece of my past I have."

His eyes flash. "You heard Jennet. The minute she learns I've taken this off, she'll come looking for me."

Still, I shake my head. If it truly offers protection, I could use that, too. "I'm sorry, but I need it."

His mouth presses into a flat line, but he unclasps the necklace from around his neck.

I hold out my hand, palm up.

He scowls as he hands it to me.

My fingers wrap around it, and suddenly the car doesn't feel so small or so dark, like the shadows have lost their teeth. "Why can't Jennet touch it?"

His eyes linger on my fist. "It was hers once. That's all I know," he says.

Does that mean she's related to me, too? My head hurts just considering that. "How did you know to find me?"

"I keep a close watch on you, as well as Jane. If I didn't, you'd be dead in a dumpster, not sitting next to me drinking orange juice."

I suppose I should be grateful.

I close my eyes to shut out the image. "Just take me home."

"Rubbish first."

I scoop up the wrappers from my lap and hand him the empty orange juice cup. He stuffs them into a bag, and stows it on the back seat floor. "I'll drive you to your hall. You should be safe inside the gate. But my protection will only last a day. I'd book a flight tonight if I were you. Those witches have been hiding in plain sight for years. They know how to keep secrets, and you're a loose end."

Witches.

He said the word aloud, so there's no doubt what they are.

He reaches over, touches my cut wrist with gentle fingers, then draws away with a quiet sigh. "I'll come and visit you in Colorado, if you'd like. We can talk about your ancestry as much as you want."

I turn away.

I can't think about that right now.

As soon as he drops me off, I flee to my room and lock the door behind me. An eerie silence squeezes the walls from all sides. I cover my face with my hands, slide to the floor. Hot tears burn the corners of my eyes. In every dark place, there's a cloaked ghost, hands extended to the sky. Gray stone walls grow from the ground, marked with scorches, and, above my head, hangs a single noose.

CHAPTER THIRTY-TWO

LIGHT CREEPS INTO the sky as I stumble into the bathroom. My head aches, and my eyes stare back with bruised circles. Every noise woke me—rattling pipes through the walls, a squeak outside the door. Every time I closed my eyes, the nightmares returned.

The boy who died—I should see his face in the news soon. On posters, maybe, plastered all over the school. They'll show his grieving family and the life he left behind.

I shuffle into the bedroom, pop ibuprofen into my mouth, and dig into my savings for the first return flight home. I'll have to find a new job in Colorado. If the flower shop doesn't rehire me, maybe my dad's lumber business will have an opening.

My hands shake as I empty the room of my stuff and toss clothes into a suitcase, tears splattering on my shirts. The potted ghost orchid will die soon without proper watering, but I can't take it with me. Wish I could. I lift my mattress to reveal the book from the graveyard. The eye below the tree stares back.

I'm leaving danger behind, but I stuff the journal into my backpack, anyway.

The absence of a phone feels odd, like being stuck outside the flower shop without keys. I need a ride home from the airport but can't call Sadie or Mom to arrange it, or to give them my flight information. No way I'm going back to the cosmetics store to get it, though.

Instead, I send a quick email.

I should send Julian a message, too, or go see him in person, but I can imagine his disappointment. He'd try to convince me to stay.

Reeve can figure out any arrangements that need to happen after I leave.

I try not to think about what might become of Noelle while I ride the bus and then a train to Heathrow Airport, but during the wait at the terminal for my flight, I sit in the chair facing the jet bridge and her betrayal returns for another punch.

She abandoned me, knowing full well what they would do.

I board the plane and stare at the back of a seat the entire way to JFK airport and on to Colorado. Dull gray with black stitching, old fingerprints on the faux leather, and a green smear that looks a bit like a booger. The sound of the AC overhead is my only company, and the occasional cough and crying baby. The AC hits my arms on full power, making my little hairs rise from the cold.

"Not gonna watch anything?" a woman watching chick-flicks asks.

I shake my head without looking at her.

As I wait for my mom at the Denver airport, waves of people disappear down the walkway toward the parking lot, or head to baggage claim, until the steady stream thins, and the hall empties to lifeless carpet. Vacant.

I close my eyes and open them again, half-hoping to find Julian standing on the empty carpet. He's not here, and won't ever come to Colorado. Why would he?

Someday I'll find someone as smart and kind as Julian. And Julian will move on.

I wipe my face on my puffy coat.

If I told Mom my suspicions about the witches on Mill Road, she'd send me to a psychiatrist rather than a special needs school. Anyway, I made the right decision coming home. There's safety here. A world without witches.

My mom pulls up in the passenger pickup lane a few feet away and gets out, a hesitant smile on her face. "Welcome home, hun." She helps me load my bags into the back of our old Ford. "You're being quiet." She ducks into the front seat. "Why'd you come back?"

"Just ready to be home."

Mom wraps an arm around me and gives me a quick squeeze. I stare dully out the window, at the mountains' blue-gray peaks, capped in snow. The leaves have all but fallen, recent rain turning them a rotten brown.

She starts the car and we leave the airport behind.

Mom tells me about Sadie's latest boyfriend, and her new bathroom cabinets. The jagged mountains grow, and the familiar river rock and logged walls of my home appear around the bend. The air smells of pine needles, so I roll up my window.

Mom pulls into the driveway.

I drag my suitcases across the pavement, down the stairs, wave at my little brothers, and lock myself in my room in the basement. My potted plants are gone—Sadie's caring for them. My old duvet is spread across the bed, embroidered with sunflowers, just as I requested on my eighth birthday. I've loved it for years, even though sunflowers are more weed than flower.

The sunflowers belong here more than I do.

I fish for copies of Austen novels to take me away and stop. Austen will take me to England. Time for a new favorite author.

The doorknob jiggles, and my dad's voice filters through. "Briony?"

I wipe my nose. "Yeah?"

He lets himself in and gives me a long hug.

"You hated it, then?" he asks.

"Can we talk later?"

He nods, and leaves, just as I ask, and I shut the door before he can ask more questions. He'll worry, but everything will go back to how it used to be.

I grab a book about high society in New York—one I've been meaning to read—and sprawl on my bed. I open it to the first page and start with stories of high society women living in brownstones. But then those brownstones become terraced houses, like the ones in Burnley.

I open my eyes—don't remember closing them—and it's dark.

The first rays of dawn peek through my blinds, highlighting the grass and rusted playground. My breathing slows a little.

There are no witches here.

I sit at the upstairs kitchen table and stuff my mouth with toast, dig up a bag of chocolate chips, and munch on the two together. I should look for jobs today. If I crack open my suitcase, I have a whole set of dress pants to choose from to wear for interviews, but I don't want to open my bags.

My eyes water, and I quickly rub them dry.

Sun shines in my eyes from the east window so I shift to the left, just as my dad strolls out of his bedroom, circles the counter, and pours a bowl of cereal. He looks just the same, like his beard hasn't had the chance to grow. Like I was barely gone a week. "You're up early. Excited to go back to school?"

I pop another chocolate chip into my mouth. "Not really."

"Called yesterday, and they said you could sit in on your old classes until your paperwork goes through."

"Thanks," I say. "I'll go now, then."

"Oh…okay."

Returning to school is inevitable. I grab my car keys, head out the door, and drive to the parking lot, where Subarus and pickup trucks fill the rows. Some with empty ski racks. The slopes don't have enough snow for the ski season to officially start.

It's been a couple months since I was here last and walking in feels like walking backwards.

I head to my first class. Then the second. Teddy sits across the room, but I avoid looking at him. My teacher, a woman who says, "makes sense?" every time she finishes an equation, no matter how many confused looks she gets, gets up and puts her dry erase marker to the board. She writes a series of numbers, her writing slanted, hurried, and borderline sloppy. Then more numbers.

Has Julian tried calling? Never told him I lost my phone. He probably went to class, and I wasn't there to sit by him. No one else likes to sit in the far back corner like Julian does. Where the backs of everyone's heads are visible.

"And that's the Quadratic formula. Makes sense?" the teacher says.

I rub at my face and groan inwardly.

When class ends, I avoid everyone in the hallways and make it through my first few days without incident.

Same schedule. Drive. Put my books in my locker. Sit through class. Listen to lectures. Students pass in homework that I don't remember being assigned.

This is a story I finished, a book I closed. I'm not supposed to revisit it, but here I am.

Until Friday, the morning of my fourth day back.

I'm sitting at the breakfast table when there's a knock at the door. My dad stands to get it, and the door swings open to Teddy.

I nearly spit out the eggs I'd stuffed into my mouth seconds ago.

Teddy smiles the same smile that used to make my heart race. It's the smile that had me waiting by my phone countless nights. It's the smile I hoped I'd never see again.

"Hey," he says.

He could have talked to me at school.

My dad looks between us, a storm brewing in his eyes.

"I'm sorry, Mr. Delwood," Teddy says, "but can I talk to Bree really fast?"

"From right here, sure," Dad says. "Where I can watch you."

Teddy looks past him, almost like body language and social cues aren't things he understands. "I tried texting you," he says, "but you never answered. Can I drive you to school?"

I only look at him.

Teddy steps forward, and Dad steps forward, too. "Look, I'm sorry about the way things ended, but Lynn and I broke up, and I heard you're back. Thought we could go out. How long'll you be here? Wanted to catch you before you're gone again."

My heart pounds in my chest.

This feels so familiar, but it's like watching an old movie of someone else's life. I know the lines, the ache, the way my chest used to tighten when he said my name. But now? There's nothing left—just an old echo fading into the hallway.

I fought for him in all the wrong ways. When I finally learned how to fight for myself, I left.

I stand, hesitate, and hurry down the stairs.

"Bree?" Dad shouts.

My little brother, Henry, pushes his way through the door from the basement and clings to my waist. "Don't leave again," he says. He's short, but brawny enough to make a hug borderline painful.

I squeeze him tight anyway.

I don't have the money to buy a plane ticket. Even the wiser half of my brain says I need to stay, but the smarter choice isn't always the right one.

As soon as Henry releases me, I run to a computer, pull up the flower store's phone number, and dial it with our home phone that Dad keeps around for the business.

"Can I have my old job back?" I ask Steph the moment she answers.

"Bree?"

"Yeah, it's me."

Today, if you want." She sounds relieved, like managing her own shop without me has been the biggest pain of her life. I'm glad she felt my absence.

"I'll be there."

After my shift, I walk into the living room, the TV flashing ads, with no one sitting on the couch watching them. I stride past and hurry to my room in the basement, where I pull the purple book from my backpack.

If I'm going back, I need to know how to use it.

I have an odd notion to try unlocking the latch with my necklace, and it falls open easily, like it's been waiting for me to figure this out.

"Oh!"

On the first page, there are sketches of the moon. A paragraph written in archaic calligraphy. Black-and-white pictures as fuzzy and indistinct as the stars.

Strange words shift and move across the page as indistinguishable illustrations creep from the corners and curve into paragraphs. Then the words sharpen to recognizable patterns and letters.

The pages flip beneath my fingertips.

Spells. Astrology. Symbolism involving plants, animals, humans, and metals. The power of the planets creates metaphysical power, while the connection of humans and animals have other unique properties.

But how does this protect me?

I read until my eyes burn.

There's something missing.

A bang interrupts my lonely musing, and my brother, Henry, plows in holding a stitch in his side. "Bree, come upstairs. You've got to see this."

I follow him up to where Mom watches the news. Usually, my brothers lounge on the bean bags, a shared bag of Cheetos between them. Today, there's only Henry and no Mom.

"Mom left the TV on. She kept watching the news to make sure you're okay. She wanted you to come home, but Dad said no. She tried not to call. Now that you're home, guess she doesn't need it."

Burnley Boarding School takes over the screen. "But what're you showing me?"

"It's that place you went to school," Henry points to the headline. "Look."

Teen missing! Search Intensifies.

The boy I watched die? I scan the description.

The police have yet to find a body.

I want to shrink, curl into a ball. Instead, I run for my backpack, yank my computer from an inner pocket, and search the web for news articles.

Parents of students at the nearby boarding school are calling their children home. Headmistress Chelsea Craig, who was just last year accused of dividing students into honorary classes based on favoritism rather than merit, and ignoring students with disabilities entirely, has been summoned to questioning…

Until the culprit has been caught, students should not be out after dark, and everyone should walk in pairs, never alone.

No names.

I close my browser window and shut my laptop.

Even if Julian, Noelle, Mika, and Eser are fine, they're in the midst of it.

I can't afford to go back, but they need me.

The doorbell rings and Henry rushes to answer. "Hey, Sadie," he says.

She walks in with her usual effortless grace and crosses the room to squish me in a hug.

"Have fun in England?" she asks, voice light but careful as she steps away.

"Yeah."

"But you decided to finish the year here?"

"Um, yes."

"Missed you."

"Missed you, too."

"Dinner," Dad shouts from the kitchen.

I hurry in his direction to avoid any further questions, sit down at the table with a bowl of spaghetti, and stir it so the red sauce makes satisfying swirls. Just a couple plane flights away, the students at Burnley Boarding School are sleeping.

"Briony?"

I meet Sadie's gaze.

"I said I pooped in someone's mailbox, and it didn't get your attention. You didn't even ask how I managed it. What's wrong?"

"Did you really?"

She waves a hand. "That's beside the point. Why did you come home?"

"Because Reeve told me to," I say.

Not because he didn't like me, didn't want to get to know me, or because my grades weren't good enough. He was worried about my safety. But there are hundreds of other students there, all in just as much danger as I was.

Sadie leans against her chair and nods. "Okay. That's it?"

I shrug and sit in silence for the rest of dinner. When everyone's done, I walk around Sadie and put food away, do the dishes, wipe down the table, and wait for Sadie to go downstairs. Then I plop down in front of the TV.

I focus on the noise, the dialog. Waiting to laugh. Instead, I see Mika floating in the river. Noelle. Julian.

If something happens and I'm not there to prevent it, I'll never forgive myself. I could call and tell them—tell anyone—but they won't believe me. I wouldn't believe me.

Footsteps creak across the floorboards, and my mom's gentle fingers scoop the remote from the couch. "It's almost five," Mom says. "Did you sleep at all last night?"

I blink.

"Think so?"

Mom raises an eyebrow, and leaves me there, a chasm opening in her absence.

Light enters the room without brightening it. The scent of cooking bacon wafts into the living room, but it only makes me sick. The black TV screen stares back. It's been off for hours, and I can still see the footage of Burnley Boarding School.

The witches know who I am. They'll come for me the moment I return, just as Professor Reeve warned.

Someone coughs from the doorway. Sadie surveys me, a strand of hair tucked behind one ear. She's wearing overalls, a fad I tried once, until a boy at school told me I looked like an Oompa Loompa. Maybe I'll borrow them sometime.

She drops an envelope on the side table.

"What's that?" I ask.

"A plane ticket."

I stare at it in amazement.

Sadie heaves a deep sigh. "I didn't pay for it. Dad did."

My eyes are glued to the envelope at the edge of the table, still sealed.

I never fully unpacked my bags, except to stuff jeans in them and to toss the old dress pants. Mom can drive me to the airport, and I can be back in no time at all.

But am I insane? Jane, Ellen, and Jennet might have a ceremony prepared just for me, and I'd walk right into it.

Julian doesn't know why I left. With my phone gone, I don't have his number anymore, nor does he have any way of contacting me. He heard news of his friend's death, and then found me gone only a few days later.

And then Noelle. Noelle was my first friend at Burnley, and she left me for dead.

I pull at my hair. Pressure pushes from all directions, rumbles in my skull.

I can't abandon Julian, so I rush to where Mom is teaching simple addition and subtraction with plastic teddy bears, my brother whining at her side.

"Can you drive me to the airport?" I ask, out of breath.

Mom musses my brother's hair, sets the tiny teddy bears on the coffee table, and smiles. "Let's go."

Mom parks in the drop-off zone of our small-town stucco airport with a sloping terracotta-red roof and taps me lightly on the shoulder. "Before you go, I want to ask you a favor."

My hand hovers over the door handle. "Yeah?"

She takes a deep breath. "I know you see me as Mom first. I know Sadie is way more fun to talk to—"

"I call you all the time."

She holds up a finger. "You called a handful of times. Look, all I want to say is, I want to be a friend to you as well as your mom, and I want to be part of your life wherever you go. I want to hear about the things you care about, even if it's another mother. I want to know if you're struggling, and if you're not."

I never meant for her to think I went to England to find another family. Searching for my biological family was to learn who I am and what I'm capable of. Life moved too fast before, but England showed me I can move with it.

I give her a one-armed hug, and she holds me tight. "Call more, promise?"

"I will."

I pull away, reach for the door, and pause. "There's someone I want you to meet—if he'll still talk to me. Will you come visit?"

Mom's eyes light up. "Just tell me when."

CHAPTER THIRTY-THREE

AFTER I LAND IN Heathrow, I file past the flight attendants and into the terminal, muscles tensed, prepared to shove past anyone in my way, even if that won't make much of a difference. I take deep, calming breaths as I navigate through passport control, grab my bag from the carousel, and step outside. The air is heavy with cut grass, exhaust, and the faint burn of cigarette smoke from the taxi stand. It smells the same as before, like I never left, and he's close.

A weight lifts from me.

The train to Burnley comes and goes on time. I stare out at fields of heather, grateful for the soft greens and purples, and miss my stop. Typical. So I wait again at the next station to go back. When I'm finally delivered to the school grounds, I drag my suitcases down the hall to my room at the end, just as I did on my first day.

When I left last week, I didn't tell the administration office. Now my door stands open, yawning into darkness. I definitely closed it.

Someone either ransacked my room, or they're here, waiting for me.

I glance over my shoulder, but the hallway is empty. Just dark black, vintage floral wallpaper and gold sconces. I steady my breathing and inch toward the doorway to look inside.

Noelle sits on the mattress, her hair even longer and thicker, her acne all but gone, but deep shadows ring her eyes and climb the bridge of her nose.

For a heartbeat, I can't move. It's like seeing a ghost I never meant to forgive.

She turns her puffy eyes and makeup-stained cheeks toward the open door. "Briony? You're still here." She leaps to her feet and throws her arms around my neck. "Please," she sobs, "please forgive me. I didn't know. I promise I didn't. I thought you'd gone back, and it was my fault." Her voice wobbles as she grips me by the shoulders. "I've been checking this room every day since that night. I didn't know what to do when it happened, I swear, and I didn't drink from that cup."

She pretended to be my friend, looked me in the eye, then melted into a crowd of murderers. Or murder accomplices. My first friend here—the one I risked everything for—was no friend at all. "They tried to kill me, Noelle, and you stood across the room and watched."

"I—I know. I'm sorry."

"I needed you."

Noelle's eyes shine with tears. "I didn't realize what I got myself into. But when I realized what was happening, I did the only thing I could think of." She reaches into her purse, draws out two phones, and offers both to me.

One is my own phone, its weight still familiar in my hand.

"What's the other for?" I ask.

Noelle unlocks the screen and plays a video—hooded figures

in a circle of black. My stomach twists. I can't breathe. The night floods back. Jennet's knife, the blood, the salt.

I don't want to relive this.

Noelle lifts her arm to reveal the angry welt from Jennet's hot iron—an elemental star, a sign so hauntingly familiar, it makes me shudder.

"I have proof," she says.

A knock echoes from the door, and Noelle makes no move to get it.

"Are you expecting someone?" she asks, her voice half-choked.

"No."

The knock sounds again, louder this time. My palms sweat as I crack the door open. It's Professor Reeve again, without his hat, black eyes narrowed to slits. My pulse jumps before my brain catches up, and I'm not sure if it's from actual alarm, or conditioned fear.

I should have expected this.

Maybe he's got a tracker on me, but the best way to do that would be through my phone, and it's been here the whole time. The thought unsettles me to my core.

"What are you doing here?" A muscle twitches in his jaw. "I thought you went home. Must I buy you another bloody flight?"

"How did you find me?"

Could he be watching my room? The thought makes my skin crawl.

"You didn't answer my question."

"Professor Reeve, I'm grateful for you saving me from that cosmetics store, but I understand the danger. And I've got a plan."

"Do you really?" he taunts. "How do you know what you truly understand and what you don't?"

I try to close the door, but he grabs my arm. "What do you

think you're doing?"

I jerk out of his grasp. "I could say the same to you."

The tendons in his neck stand out beneath his collar.

"I belong here, Reeve," I say. "I came back for my friends. You warned me about witches. I'm going to get rid of them."

"Get rid of them?" He laughs, the sound edged with hysteria, and I almost pity him. "Look, come to my office. We can talk about this."

"I'm not going to your office, and I'm not running away. Have a great day, Professor."

This time, when I shut the door, it closes with a click, and I rest my forehead against it.

Noelle casts me a furtive look.

"What?" I ask.

"Why does he stalk you the way he does? It's almost—"

"Creepy?" I stuff my wallet in one boot and my phone in the other.

Noelle, still pale, raises her hands to form a picture frame. "I wouldn't mind him showing up at my door. But yeah, he's hotter when he's not yelling."

I shake my head, a laugh pulling at my lips. "I'm glad you can still find humor at a time like this. Let's get going. We've got to pin down Julian."

When I open the door again, I check to make sure Reeve isn't still there. The hallway is empty. Relief floods me—sharp and shaky—and Noelle follows me into the hall.

CHAPTER THIRTY-FOUR

I KNOCK ON JULIAN'S dormitory door and wait, though no sound comes from inside. Certainly, none of the racket I heard last time I came.

"Is he home?" Noelle asks.

"I don't know."

He never responded to my texts.

I sink to the doorstep, and Noelle slumps beside me, her fists tucked in her armpits, knees bent. She flinches with every passing headlight, like she half-expects to be dragged back to the cosmetic store's attic.

"What now?"

I exhale, and my breath swirls in the dark, foggy air. "We wait, I guess."

"For how long? It's freezing."

Noelle makes a good point, though I don't want to say so. We can't stay here all night, and I have no idea how dangerous riding the bus is, or being here, out in the open. "Let's text Mika then."

"I left my phone at home. I don't want to see how many times the women at the cosmetics store call. I jump every time my phone lights up." Noelle shudders. "Briony, I'm scared."

Noelle might have let me die that night at Mystic Cosmetics, but giving me this footage is a risk. I'm not sure I can forgive her just yet, but I do feel sorry for her.

I squeeze her arm because there's nothing else to do. "It'll be okay." Rather than see Noelle's fear swimming in her eyes, I avert my gaze. She has as much reason to be afraid as I do. Maybe more. "I'll call Mika."

I call but only get a voicemail, so I shoot a text off and wait for an answering ping.

"It won't be okay," Noelle says in a soft voice. "They'll kill me the moment they find me."

The police may not believe us, and if I go to Professor Reeve, he'll tell me to run, but Julian will help. He'll try, at least. "We'll figure this out, I promise."

Noelle buries her face in her knees. "How?"

"Julian knows people, and Mika will get back to us soon."

More than anything, Julian will listen.

I should say something to make her feel better, but instead I say, "Let's make this right."

Noelle wipes a tear from her cheek.

The night dissolves when headlights slice across the parking lot, revealing a brown Mercedes with chipping paint.

I stand on wobbly legs, half from the cold, half from the thought of seeing him again.

Noelle grips the railing. "Is that his car?"

"I think so."

"Thought it'd be nicer," she says under her breath.

I smile a little.

Julian gets out and waves as Silas pulls away, probably to get another coffee. No matter how late it is. As Julian nears, he reaches in his pocket, pauses, and looks up. "You're back," he says. He says it flatly, like he's trying not to sound like it matters.

I can't mess this up. "Julian, I need your help."

"What do you mean?" His expression stays blank, his flat smile practiced.

"Can we go inside?" I ask.

He frowns but leads us into his dormitory.

Noelle rubs her arms. While the shag carpet and bookshelves haven't changed, at least the flat has heat, though gusts of cold follow us inside.

Julian nods toward the couch. "Please."

I hover for a moment before lowering myself into the sofa's cushions, where Robbie's sock smell still lingers, and tuck my hands under my legs. Noelle curls up at my side. Julian takes off his jacket, hangs it, and sets his backpack down. Then, still standing, he studies us with a crease in his brow.

I take a deep breath. "I'm sorry about Robbie."

His face doesn't move. Not even a flicker. "Thank you."

"I'm sorry I didn't call."

He blinks.

Get it out.

"I…" I lick my lips, and the words I planned to say spiral into oblivion. "I know you're wondering why we're here so late. Robbie—"

Julian's face darkens. "Died just before you left."

"Yes," I say. "He was killed by witches at the cosmetics store on Mill Road."

Julian stares past me, and I can't tell if he heard.

"I went to their store and stumbled on a witch ceremony. They were initiating new followers by sacrificing a boy. I watched it happen." My voice cracks. "And I'm certain they did the same to

Robbie. I know how this sounds, but it's real."

His eyes focus on me. "You were there?"

No questions. Not even a skeptical eyebrow.

"Yes, but I got away. It's why I left. I was afraid they'd come after me."

Something shifts in his expression—the hardness gives way to something else. Deep furrows cut into his brow as he scans my face.

"It's true," Noelle says from her place on the couch. "They hook you with promises, offer to teach you how to make their products, and force you to do what they say. Then they brand you." Noelle holds out her wrist, showing Julian the burn. "I backed out when they tried to kill Briony."

Julian glances at the burn and then looks away. "You were right to go back to America, Briony. It might be best if both of you go."

When I rehearsed this moment, I imagined his response a hundred different ways, but I didn't think he'd pull a Professor Reeve.

I clench my fists. "I'm not leaving again."

He opens his mouth, but I interrupt before he can even begin.

"It's not an argument." I tug the journals out of my backpack and pass them over. He stares at my hands before taking them.

"Professor Reeve gave me these when I first arrived. Told me I was in danger, and I should read them to discover why. He also told me to stay away from you but refused to give a reason. You're welcome to read them."

He leans in, one hand on the first page.

"I highlighted the important parts," I continue, "so you don't have to read them all. Maybe you'll see something I don't. They're littered with references to women with the same names as the women at Mystic Cosmetics."

I spent the whole flight going through them, so I could point out which parts Julian should read, mostly the ones that mention the Mekori.

Noelle cranes her neck as Julian sits, the edge of his jacket brushing my knee. I shiver as he lays the printed pages on his lap and leafs through them. "A sword," he murmurs—so softly I barely catch it. "And a ghost in a lake." He twists the cross on his chain again, his wool shirt unbuttoned, his sleeves rolled up to his elbows. My eyes follow the line of his shoulders, the way his fingers trace down the page. I force my attention back to the text.

Noelle drifts off. She probably hasn't slept in days.

I watch Julian move to the journals I didn't highlight, the ones signed by Guido. Until that's all he's reading. His knuckles whiten on the paper. Then he starts them over again.

I'm about to direct him back to the important sections when he hunches over the words. "Guy Fawkes?"

It sounds familiar.

I peer over his shoulder. "Where?"

He points. "Right here. The man on the horse, going down the hill. It says his name is Guy Fawkes, but he goes by 'Guido.' The Guy Fawkes you always hear about went by 'Guido,' too. It's the Spanish version of his name."

I remember Guido, but I must have overlooked his other name.

Noelle opens an eye. "What about Guido?"

I'd ask the same question.

Julian's face flushes. "I've been researching him for months, at the Botanic Gardens even. I've felt a connection to him for a long time, ever since I first heard his story as a child. Always wondered why people burn him every year. I feel the stories about him are incomplete, and Old Palace Yard is part of it. These writings could explain so much."

"But what does that have to do with the cosmetics store?"

Julian's face falls. "Probably nothing." He continues to read and doesn't glance up.

Noelle coughs, and he jumps, his hands clutching the pages. He scans the room, inhales, and returns to his reading without so much as a grimace. At last, he straightens the stack and hands them to me. Though he doesn't smile, his forehead smooths. "This version feels right."

Had I known he'd take such an interest in them, I'd have shown Julian the journals sooner.

I grab my backpack and zip them safely inside.

"You think the women at the cosmetics store are the same women?" he asks.

"I know they are."

"But why more followers? What's the point?"

Should have thought of that. "I don't know."

He rubs his temple. "Why did Professor Reeve give you these? He could have told you to avoid the witches and might have turned them in himself. He never gave me these journals, never even mentioned them."

Wish I had the answers. "It bothers me, too."

"I've given you my thoughts," he says, "but what do you need from me?"

Before I came, I pieced together the beginnings of a plan, just the framework, and hoped Julian could fill the gaps. "I thought with your knowledge of the school and staff, and with your dad's connections, you might advise us."

He rests his chin on his palm. "Give me a night to think on this. We can talk in the morning."

"Thanks for believing us."

His mouth twitches. "You're about as mad as I am, which isn't saying much." He hesitates. "Will you be safe? Do you need a ride?

I can call Silas."

I pick up my bag. "We'll be fine." The witches won't dare come after me if we stay where crowds of people are, and Professor Reeve will protect me. At least on campus. He seems to know where I go before I arrive.

"You're sure? You shouldn't be out there alone."

I stand. "Really, we're fine. It's not far."

"If you're determined to walk, I'm walking with you."

A gentleman even when I'm sure he'd rather not be.

"Sure."

Julian leads us to the door and walks behind us, a silent figure, hands at his side, one finger twitching. His eyes dart across the buildings, even the cars. Noelle wraps herself in her arms and glances over her shoulder at the zebra crossing.

"Will you be safe walking back?" I ask as we reach the double oak doors of Birdie's Court.

But he's busy studying the empty hallways and doesn't answer.

Then he slows to a stop, hands stuffed in his pockets like the first day I met him. "You should be safe from here," he says, and takes a step back.

"I'm sorry," I tell him before he can go. "Really."

He tilts his head. "I'm glad you felt you could talk to me."

I want to tell him I didn't come just for help. That I missed him. But his leather shoes are already turning away.

"I always could," I whisper.

Noelle drags one hand on the banister as we climb the stairs.

"He cares about you," she says, voice wistful.

"What?"

"I always wanted someone to look at me like that."

My heart skips a beat. "Oh."

We separate in the hallway, and I let myself into my room,

head for my suitcase and dump my stuff at the foot of my bed so the purple book tumbles across the floor.

Each page is formatted like recipes, as if it's a cookbook listing food I've made a number of times. The ingredients are muscle memory. Except I don't remember making them.

I memorize every page, pound it into memory, though the outlines are already there. All I have to do is put the recipes back, like sliding books onto empty shelves. Dusting the edges. Organizing them by color.

I go to close the book but pause on the first page. Scrawled in the middle is one word.

Remember.

CHAPTER THIRTY-FIVE

M ORNING ARRIVES BLEAK and cold, the greeting of November. The nip in the air is the promise of snow. A change in season. Change always comes colder than I expect, and I'm not ready for it.

I wrap a scarf around my neck and meet Noelle at the bus stop. She's in gray-brown sweatpants with a sweater, which, for her, is underdressed. We ride to Julian's dormitory, and Noelle stands at the front of the bus, gripping a pole tight, knuckles pale. The shadows beneath her eyes are even deeper.

I touch her shoulder, but she shrinks away.

The tree pendant of my necklace is cold as I twist the chain tight against my neck, let it dangle, and pick it up again.

I should say something to boost her courage, to comfort her, but I don't feel courageous.

The bus stops, doors creaking open. I follow Noelle off, and we walk to Julian's dormitory, same as the night before. I knock, and my knuckles are still against the smooth wood when Julian opens the door.

For a second, I forget why we're here. He looks half-awake, hair tousled, sleeves rolled up, and I hate that a single glance from him can still undo me.

Dropping my backpack, I sink into his threadbare sofa. It still smells faintly of coffee and his cologne.

Julian eyes Noelle. "Neither of you looks like you slept."

Noelle bends over to grab a notebook from her purse. "Let's just get this over with."

Julian spreads a bunch of heavily marked papers on the floor. "I have some ideas, but you first."

Noelle stares at Julian's writings. "You can read those scribbles?" She wrinkles her nose.

"Glad to see you back," Julian says.

She wilts as Julian twists the papers sideways. "At the proper angle, my writing is perfectly legible, thank you. Some might even call it artistic."

Noelle simply clamps her lips shut.

"We can warn the dean of the college in an anonymous letter," I start. His eyes catch mine and linger, and my brain blanks. Focus. This isn't about him. This is about getting through the next hour without everything falling apart. "Or submit an unsigned article to the school newspaper."

"Good ideas." Julian picks up a square note card, the typing barely visible from the other side. "But how about something more direct?" His expression gives nothing away.

"Such as?"

He shakes the note in his hand. "There's an event going on this week. Burnley School is inviting local businesses to come in to post jobs, pitch careers, or talk to students about potential futures." Julian draws out a catalog of names. "I called this morning, and the events director gave me this list of attendees. Mystic Cosmetics is on here. They're looking for part-time associates, and at least one owner plans to attend."

"Of course you know the director—"

Noelle stops herself, and Julian continues as if he didn't hear.

"I asked if we could highlight my dad at the event for his work with the town council. Some of it directly relates to local businesses. Told the director that having an important person there would boost attendance, and I'd be more than happy to invite my dad myself. My dad never says 'no' to being openly recognized. Plus, students can ask him questions. He'll be a prestigious career advisor and might even bring internship opportunities to the table. The director loved the idea."

Noelle's brow pinches. "Yeah, so?"

She has a point.

"Why do we need your dad?" I ask.

"So we can expose them at the event. It's being broadcast and there'll be an MP there. With solid evidence, they'll have to launch an investigation into Mystic Cosmetics. You have proof, right?"

Evidence with our names attached. The Mekori will know exactly who filmed the rite. Cold hands squeeze my chest, and I struggle to breathe. Noelle bites her lip.

"Yeah," I say.

Noelle hands Julian her phone, with the video already pulled up and ready to play.

He takes the device in one hand and rotates it so it's not upside down. "What is it?"

Noelle only rocks on her heels.

My stomach coils in a dozen knots, but I manage to say, "It's a video, but warning—it's rough."

I pull on wide-leg corduroys—dress pants 2.0—and for once, they actually suit the occasion. Or at least, I hope I do. I grab my coat and go.

The door opens, and Noelle stands there, her exhaustion hidden beneath coverup. She smiles too quickly, like she's hoping I won't notice the shadows under her eyes.

Her room looks like a magazine spread—everything spotless, that heart-shaped frame of a puppy probably still waiting for her back home.

She fiddles with the threads of a loose knit sweater. "Bought this when I got here," she says in an offhand way. "It doesn't get this cold where I'm from, not very often."

I shrug on my coat. "Ready?"

Noelle leans against the wall and looks away.

I could let her off. Tell her she doesn't have to do this. But for the students at this school, this is life and death, and she involved herself. "It's time." I usher her into the hall.

We descend the stairs, the scent of old wood and chalk dust trailing us. Footsteps echo off the stone, as if the walls themselves are listening. Outside, fog breathes over the cobblestones. The bus squeals to a stop, the top open, spiral stairs leading up to it. But it's too cold, so I opt for the first floor and Noelle boards behind me.

We sit across from each other, Noelle lacing her fingers over her lap.

I give her what I hope is an encouraging smile.

All we have to do is show up, hit play, and survive.

We ride to the career fair building—a stately brick structure with tall windows and a clock tower. Inside, someone's tried to modernize it: polished concrete floors, industrial fixtures, walls of glass that let in cold light. The heating struggles against the high ceilings. I hate it already.

We take the elevator up and step into a wood-paneled hall where corporate meets academic. Framed photographs of influential philosophers line one wall—their faces overlaid with muted colors, names engraved on brass plaques beneath. Tables are scattered across the floor with navy tablecloths, each one displaying company logos that feel out of place in the scholarly setting. Students move between them, backpacks on shoulders, phones in hand, consulting handouts and business cards. Near the back, a handwritten note taped to a carved wooden door reads "Special Guest."

"What now?" Noelle asks at my side.

I suck in air that reeks of new paper, fresh out of its packaging, and bleach. "We find Julian."

With Noelle in tow, I press through the crowd. A sign above a booth sways over the others, with lists of various careers for students to consider. Global engineering, project services, manufacturing, electronics, history.

"Do you see him?" Noelle asks.

"Not yet."

But a pulse in my veins tells me he's close.

A crowd forms around a bend of tables. Rather than typical signs and advertisements, this table has cauldrons with steaming concoctions, glass beakers, and scales. Ellen's blonde curls stick to her flushed skin, a sheen of sweat on her brow as she stirs a concoction that bubbles over onto the tablecloth.

She keeps herself busy and ignores the crowd, but as I approach she looks up and scans the room.

My stomach drops.

Intermixed with the students, but rising above them, stands Julian—polished and untouchable—facing the blonde witch like all the others. He has one hand in the pocket of his tweed jacket.

In his other hand, he holds pamphlets from the cosmetics store.

Join our support group…

Ellen's gaze locks on him as well.

I'm tempted to reach out and grab his arm, but clench my fist at my side instead.

He turns and smiles. Then makes his way toward me. "I'm ready," he murmurs, loud enough for only me to hear.

"Then let's go."

I avoid looking at Ellen as Julian motions for Noelle and me to follow him and ushers us out of the crowd to the side of the hall. I stick close. Near the door with the sign, he turns to Noelle. "We'll film in here. Can you wait by the lift for my dad? Just tell him we'll start soon—award, student questions, all that."

"Sure." Noelle makes for the doors and doesn't look back.

As soon as she's gone, Julian guides me into a small auditorium. The door shuts, and the noise outside muffles.

We're alone, save for a projector, empty rows of chairs, a podium, and a laptop.

He gestures to the laptop and projector. "All look okay?" he asks.

I study the soft brown of his jacket, the way his sweater pairs with it. He looks classy, like fine wine paired with old historical texts. Light freckles on his nose. Faint lines that crease around his mouth. The intensity of his eyes when he's thinking hard about something.

Julian takes a step back. "We have a few minutes. We can fix it."

"It's fine." I tear my gaze away.

"Can I ask you something real quick?"

He wants to bring up the night of the dance. Or when I abandoned him and left for Colorado. Maybe he's concerned our plan won't work.

I can't decide which is worse.

"Ask me what?" I drop my purse on a seat by the door.

He steps closer. "In the room, you looked upset. But only for a second."

After all he's done and all he's about to do, maybe I owe him. Still, the walls seem to press in from all sides, and I falter before I begin. "I fought Noelle on bringing you to the cosmetics store. Not because I thought Ellen would bother you, but because…"

He's watching me closely, breath ghosting across my cheek, strands of hair falling across his hazel eyes, eyes that see too much.

My fingers knot and unknot like they can undo the words building in my throat. "I…I like you. I suppose."

The words taste like a confession and a mistake all at once.

Julian lifts my chin, tipping my face toward his. "You suppose?"

I'm not sure what to do with my hands, so they hang stiffly at my sides. "Okay, I like you a lot. But I'm not in a fancy program. I wouldn't have been able to get in under normal circumstances. I was failing my classes at home, and Professor Reeve opened up this new special program for struggling students, and my parents hoped it would save my grades. It's why I came here in the first place."

"Is that all?"

I meet his eyes. "Think so."

"Thank you," he says.

Simple, like the period at the end of a sentence.

He wraps his arms around me, one hand pressed to the small of my back. His touch is firm, anchoring. Not even a tremor, and I breathe easier too. For a moment, we're both still. Time folds in on itself.

I smile. Because maybe we can be like the vines that rise from the earth—always reaching, always learning, tangled but growing toward the light. A lifetime together. Or many lifetimes.

And suddenly, new memories flood in.

Running through the graveyard, the woods, across bridges. Always running.

Not my memories.

I want to cherish this moment, rather than let my nightmares pollute it. My fears and insecurities.

He leans in slowly enough that I could stop him. I don't.

His lips part my mouth, and my hands tremble as I cling to him.

He's solid in a way the rest of my world isn't.

"Never leave me again, Briony." He kisses me lightly on the nose.

The door creaks open, and Julian takes me by the hand as a man steps into the room, leading a second man in a stiff, black suit, so straight his back might be a headstone. Sharp cheekbones, gray hair, and a long nose. "Here's where you'll be speaking, Lord Bristol. I really can't thank you enough for coming," the first man says as the door closes behind them.

Lord Bristol's eyes fix on my hands, intertwined in Julian's. His face remains smooth, unperturbed. "Lovely to see you again, Briony. I was just telling your shadow to make itself comfortable."

I squeeze Julian's hand tighter. "Lord Bristol."

"We've got you scheduled in an hour," Julian says. "But we'll start in twenty. We recorded a video to introduce all the startups. Where's the girl I sent to get you? The video's on her phone."

Lord Bristol cocks his head. "If she's gone, I'm sure she's in good company."

"I told her to wait for you by the lift."

"She'll turn up eventually. They all do."

The man who brought Lord Bristol steps forward. "I found Lord Bristol by the elevator alone. I didn't see anyone else."

"Maybe she went to the bathroom?" I ask.

Julian shakes his head. "Thank you, director. We'll take it from here." As the director leaves, Julian turns to his father. "I'm going to look for her. Can you wait here for a few minutes with Briony? And Briony, can you get everything ready?" He points to the stool. "I'll be back before we start."

She's just gone to find a drinking fountain, that's all. Not everything is a worst-case scenario. Not all endings are bad.

But my hands are slick with sweat as I set up chairs and start the laptop and projector. The start time nears. Students wander into the room to find seats. Lord Bristol sits at the front of the room and puts his fingertips together. The room fills, but Julian doesn't reappear.

Every minute without him tightens a thread around my ribs.

Lord Bristol watches me with the interest of a doctor observing a slowing heartbeat. Waiting to see how long I'll last. And, maybe, hoping I do.

He checks his watch, and I pretend not to notice. I straighten a few more chairs and align the next row. We need to start soon. Someone has to lead the presentation.

He checks his watch again, this time tapping the glass with one long finger, his gaze cutting to mine.

I look between him and the door, my heart a block of ice.

He stands before the microphone. "Good evening, all. I usually meet people under…quieter circumstances. But thank you for coming to join me today. I trust the air is suitably still for the occasion."

I shove open the door where a smaller crowd of students linger at the tables outside, none resembling Julian or Noelle.

I break into a run, shoes slipping on the polished floor, breath catching sharp in my chest. Past the booth with the Mystic Cosmetics sign, currently unoccupied. Cauldrons and chemistry tools cleared from tabletop. No crowds. Just a few unknown faces.

Outside the elevators, I shove people aside. Mouths move, heads turn. I storm into the bathroom, kick in every stall. I shout Noelle's name.

Then I stop cold at the elevator's closed door, pivot, and take the stairs.

My heart is pounding feet.

I skip several steps, my insides lurching as I round the last corner. At the bottom, a body lies crumpled and broken, a leg twisted backward, the neck bent, familiar brown eyes popping. Noelle's name reverberates up and down the stairs as a scream tears from my throat.

Her pupils catch the stairwell light, bright enough that for a second I think she's still there.

I stumble down the rest of the steps, dropping to my knees and reaching for Noelle's soft hair. Blood clings to my fingertips, a vivid red, the metallic scent a familiar reality. As is the fading heat of Noelle's skin. My fingers burn as I hold her.

The world blurs.

I search Noelle for her phone, and find only empty pockets. Someone planned this.

Bringing Noelle was a mistake. I shouldn't have allowed Julian to send her away. Should've had him wait at the elevator instead.

Julian!

I scan the area, but the landing is empty, save for Noelle. The relief at not finding him is eclipsed by the terror of knowing he's gone. And I could find him dead somewhere else.

I rush back up the stairs to the room with the projector, and a stunned hush greets me, the seat beside Lord Bristol still empty.

"Happy Guy Fawkes Day!" Lord Bristol is saying to the audience, completely ignoring my rapid breaths. The fact that I'm half crying, half choking, every inhale sharper than the last. Like my body is trying to claw back the life that left Noelle.

"Remember, remember the fifth of November. Gunpowder, treason, and plot. If you know the history around the Gunpowder Plot—"

My toes go cold. The words hit like déjà vu. I've heard them before, but not here—not now.

Remember.

I press my palms against my ears.

Remember. Remember. Remember. Remember.

Fire crawls up stone walls. A noose. Words engraved into the rock. Yellow eyes. A judge standing outside the door. "Briony," he jeers. Except that's not my name.

A rift deepens inside me.

Remembering hurts.

Without a word of explanation, I snatch my purse from the chair where I left it and flee. Down the stairs, over Noelle's too still body, out the door, and into the frosty night air. Tears sting, then freeze on my lashes.

A figure parts from the shadows, blonde hair hanging in sheets. Ellen smiles, mauve lipstick dividing over white teeth. A hint of lilac clings to a dusky dress with draping sleeves.

My breath clouds in the cold between us. In the light, she looks carved from glass.

She extends her hand and opens it to reveal a black origami cat perched on her palm.

"For you."

CHAPTER THIRTY-SIX

ELLEN'S SMILE THINS.

I snatch the paper and crush it in my fist. "I know what you did."

"I killed your little friend." Ellen's voice is maddeningly calm. "Not that she was much of a friend."

My throat locks. Noelle laughing in the dorm. Answering my calls when I need help. Waiting for me in the dining hall. I'll never speak to her again.

"Why?"

Ellen only looks at me, pale and unsympathetic. "I would think it obvious. You, however, I need not kill. You'll manage that on your own." A nod to my fist, where I still grip the origami cat. "Consider that a hint. Julian deserves at least that much."

The taste of metal floods my mouth as I squeeze the origami cat, feel the paper wrinkling beneath my nails.

"What've you done to him?"

Ellen's eyes glint. "You're quick to point fingers, aren't you? You remember what happened?" Her voice lowers to a purr. "You do remember. James Altham came, and you folded. Even Jennet expected more from you."

I hold my face still, but her words hit bone, and the truth buried within myself rises.

She clicks her tongue. "My sisters are watching, and my duty is to them first. Hurry, little witch, if you want to get there in time." A sharp turn of her shoulders, her dress flaring as she strides off. Her heels echo in the still night air.

I unclench my fist. Two words glow in white, cursive letters on the deceased origami cat.

Moorhill Cemetery.

A graveyard in the middle of the night? It could be a trap. Also, it's my only lead.

I shove onto the first bus, then a train bound for York. The windows rattle. Stations blur. Buildings and trees fly past, dark contours against the stars. My chest hollows with each stop.

At eleven years old, my parents reshaped my world, told me my whole life was built on a lie. Adoptions papers instead of arms that held me the day of my birth. Now I'm a child again, sitting alone on the battered seat, surrounded by strangers, moving farther from Burnley and the river that framed my window.

Who am I?

I've been orphan, misfit, quiet failure. Bree. Briony. Marguerite.

My fingers tremble over my wrist, but I resist scratching. Instead, I pull the purple book from my purse, still there from when I showed Julian, and flip it open.

A feeble light shines from beneath my scars—the same elemental star the Mekori burned into Noelle. I move my arm away from the book, and the mark fades.

The spell cracks something deeper than the earth—it cracks open memory.

Stone floor. The walls of a prison cell. Fingernails tearing skin. Blood inked with meaning. The mark refuses to disappear no matter how hard I scrape. The pain, the responsibility, the realization of who I am.

Alice Grey was a witch with the sole responsibility of protecting her little brother, Hugh, but she failed, and Hugh was lost.

I am Alice Grey.

The name slides into place, heavy and whole. It weighs on my shoulders, but it's also freeing. And at my side is Guido.

Images cascade: He's dancing—just the two of us in a cottage in the woods. A crackling fire in the hearth. Hugh's yellow eyes watching. A wilted rose; happiness in Hugh's eyes as he disappears into the trees alongside Julian, a gun slung over Julian's shoulder, his knee-high boots almost covered by the length of grass.

Julian's mouth against mine, honey on his breath. His hands in my curls. His knife. His betrayal.

Guido. Julian. The same soul.

Iduna, the white witch, arrived at my cottage, dressed in purple, lavender scent, branches weaving through her hair. She charged me with the protection of my brother, of the future of the world, and offered the tree necklace as protection.

I was still a child myself.

She pressed a hot iron to my wrist. My knees buckled, but I didn't scream.

"A seer hath foretold that thy brother, Hugh, shall defeat the Mekori," said the White Witch. "If the Mekori should find him here, they shall bend all their power to his destruction. Thou must needs be ready. Master thine own craft of witchery, that thou mayest rise against them—for surely they will come."

"The Mekori demand sacrifice of blood and bone," said the White Witch, loosening her hold on my hand. "I require thy freedom."

The wound healed, and my days filled with learning spells. I grew herbs, discovered alternative uses for plants. Always afraid.

Until Guido came, and the Mekori followed.

I was alone in my little cottage in the woods, my father gone, my grandfather unwilling to acknowledge me, and my half-brother napping in the other room, unaware of the danger. Every night, I watched the swaying trees, flinching with each shape that moved.

Jane saw me with Judge Altham in the alehouse, and told Jennet of my association with him, fearing I would ruin their plans to steal Altham's money. When they investigated me, they found Hugh at my cottage.

Guido noticed Jane flitting through the trees on his daily rounds through the woods. But it wasn't Jane we should have feared. We overlooked Altham and his jealousies, which the Mekori used to further their own ends.

During my seven years in prison, Altham visited every year.

Knock, knock, knock.

The door squealed on heavy hinges.

Altham filed in alongside the Mekori—witches with red hair, blonde, and black.

Jennet stepped forward, the rest waiting in the lantern light, which cast yellow crescent moons on each of their faces. After years of living in this squalor, I didn't smell the must that grew in the cracks anymore, but I could see it in Altham's scrunched nose.

Jennet gripped my hair in her fist as I shrunk away from those purple eyes. "Where is he?" Jennet demanded.

"I don't know."

Years of visits. Years of suffering. Jennet's fist in my hair. Prison walls dripping. Altham's jealousy weaponized.

A house turned gallows, its circular tower as tall as the trees.

Ropes strung from rafters, looped over my head. My feet dangling. Flames licking skin. A silver cup of Guido's blood.

Judge Altham became a necromancer, and with his initiation, the Mekori placed a curse that would bar me from seeing my brother again. A curse that has followed us throughout time.

James Altham lost his money, position, and reputation, and sought the power that came with the ability to change one's appearance, live forever, command the devil and raise the dead. To be chief among necromancers. For this power to become his, the Mekori required him to sacrifice an innocent and demanded he continue that sacrifice eternally. I was a target for the Mekori and an obvious sacrificial choice for Altham.

We find each other. We kiss. Altham begins to age. Rather than risk a step closer to death, he kills us. Over and over and over.

So, I am reborn, forced to remember my oaths just as Altham kills me.

I never search for Hugh, because I don't remember him until it's too late.

I never live a full life.

One lifetime ago, James Altham, tired of a vendetta long fulfilled, offered the best compromise he could. When I could offer no information on my brother, the Mekori lost interest and ceased their involvement in Altham's sacrifices, which allowed Altham to keep our agreement a secret. The agreement prevented me from meeting Guido, negated the kiss, and postponed my death as long as possible. It should have worked, but I broke my end of the deal.

Iduna's voice whispers from memory:

Protect him, Alice. You have everything you need.

The grimoire glows in my hands. Images shift, pages rewrite themselves. Illustrations form and words morph into fresh letters. I grip the pages so tight, my fingers ache.

To bless a sick child with health.

Instructions follow the label. The words don't teach so much as remind. The patterns—the pull between objects, liquids, and celestial spheres—they're already there, waiting to be recalled. The knowledge tingles as it returns.

I haven't held this book in ages, but it knew me when I visited my grave. It knew to return.

I flip to the last page.

Understand the laws to command them.

A shiver runs the length of me.

The spells in magical texts aren't learned so much as traded. Knowledge for memories. Knowledge for humanity. Some knowledge can be stored in magical objects, such as this book, available to download by magic users later. All at a price.

There's more here than I have time to read. More than I learned during my years in that cottage in the woods, but I only have a train ride to prepare. Fortunately, I've already made the necessary trades. This knowledge is mine.

The train slows to a stop, and I shoot to my feet. The doors open, and I sprint to a street smothered in snow, leaving blackened footprints behind. Frost bites my toes, and each breath comes in ragged bursts.

I don't slow until night unfolds its wings, and I reach a pillared entrance with skeletal white stones. The pumpkins at the base are rotting, some caving, mold growing in patches. Spindly branches rise to the sky where the moon glows red. Its crescent shape, color, and position are all wrong for the spells I'd hoped to use.

Gravel crunches beneath my feet as I pass a towering crypt housing the remains of someone wealthy or famous, and search for any opening large enough to hide a person. Or two. But there's only me.

The trees to the left sway in the breeze, snow fluttering to the gravestones. More stones to the right. Moorhill Cemetery was the only clue Ellen gave, and there are many places to hide.

I scour the tombstones, even following the same lonely row down to my own stone. Except it's gone. An open grave yawns instead, fresh dirt heaped at the edge. I back slowly away, throat tight.

Reeve warned me:

Beneath the earth and tombstones at Moorhill Cemetery are mounds of piled bodies. A past incarnation lies among them. I will remember her, if no one else will.

Marguerite. My grave. My bargain.

I force my breathing to calm. Altham won't let Julian die alone. He needs both of us.

I run toward the tombs, then behind them, where the path narrows, and the stars sit in hushed silence. Their positions are unfavorable, but I'm glad they're there, watching.

Rows of tombstones stand erect, pale as bones. The path stretches on, past trees and graves, until York's lights vanish. A hedge rises, tall and unnatural. It blocks off half the graveyard. It wasn't here before. It wants to keep me out.

I touch the leaves and they crumble into ash. When I push through, the thicket melts around me, turning into a brittle tunnel, until I break through the other side, only to face another wall of hedges.

To the left, a path stretches on, disappearing into the gloom. The other side does the same.

The hedge seals behind me, trapping me in a maze, and the leaves regrow, hardening into something cold, glinting, like silver blades that suck the warmth from my fingertips.

Run.

You'll never make it. A voice curls inside my skull. *You haven't used these spells in hundreds of years.*

My brain will blank and I won't remember a thing, even my own name. And I could fail again.

I run faster.

Dead birds sway from higher branches, eyes missing, ribs exposed. They scream with high-pitched calls.

Turn. Turn. Dead end. Skeletons peel from the hedge, ribcages tangled in the vines. They block the way back.

One slumps, jaw rasping:

"They called it sin, your secret shame. They broke your bones and cursed your name. Deny the mark—the pyre will tell—the name you thought your flames could quell."

I lift my glowing wrist, elemental star up.

"Witch," I whisper.

The skeleton cocks its head.

"Witch," I repeat, louder.

The skeleton's teeth clatter, laughing, some teeth still intact. Then the skeletons retreat back into the hedges, the vines swallowing them.

I sprint past them, back into the depths of the maze, but the maze shifts. Instead of a right turn, it's now a left. I slow, heart pounding, and turn in a circle. There are ravens all around. One with three eyes watches like he knows the ending already. Everything is dark and mildewed, dead and dying.

Vines lash at my wrist, and I pour life into them until they blossom, but as soon as they release me, they blacken again.

I keep going.

Another dead end. A pool, surface smooth as a mirror, but

stinking of rot. Like algae left out for weeks beneath the sun. I stop at the edge of it, and my own face stares back. My reflection fractured into a hundred selves.

I stumble back from it, but when I turn around, skeletons crawl toward me. The water stirs, laps against the ground at my feet, and a woman rises. She wears a hooded cloak, long hair, ghostly white. Like a marble statue, she turns slowly to face me.

"Where calm waters hold the past, and fears lie buried in the dust. Gaze deep, and what you seek may show, the path your soul must yet go."

That ceramic face waits, head bowed.

Fears buried in the past—the endless faces of the lives I lived. This is who I am. Maybe accepting that is where I must go. Into calm waters.

I gaze at the water at the ghost's feet, my reflection disrupted by ripples. And leap into it. I drop, my stomach hitting the bottom of my thorax, until crisp grass smacks my knees. My breath whooshing out of me.

I stand in an empty meadow, a stone arch looming like a sentinel. Stairs claw up its side, while gnarled branches lace over emaciated stones, dusted with snow.

My lungs seize, crushed by the wind's frosted fingers.

I have burned beneath stones like these before—a cloaked figure drinking my blood, Guido's body crumpled and still beneath me.

The circle has closed.

A hooded person stands beneath the arch and raises their arms over a fire, chanting with old, rhythmic words. Wind sends spirals of smoke into the sky.

I step forward and a branch cracks beneath my foot.

The chant quiets. Then the hooded person raises its head to

reveal a cleft chin, square jawline, and the black, wavy hair of Professor Reeve. Except his eyes are dark circles, his skin stretched tight over his gaunt, haunted skull.

Seeing his face brings clarity. It's just as it was before. The Mekori haven't bothered to witness my death in centuries. They'd rather sacrifice students instead, expand their following, and revel in my torment, until they finally find the person they really care about. Tonight's sacrifice is to continue the cycle.

"Hello, Altham," I say.

CHAPTER THIRTY-SEVEN

"ALICE." THE WRINKLES around his mouth deepen. "You remember now. Good. Then you must remember the promise you made."

I promised I wouldn't come back. "I remember," I say, though the memory scrapes like broken glass.

James Altham circles his ritual pyre, footsteps fast and erratic. "You ignored everything I said. What else could I have done short of killing you the moment you arrived?"

"You could have let me be."

"Look at my face. I'm vulnerable." He claws at his bony cheeks. "Lord Bristol is just waiting to usurp me. He's almost done it already. And what will happen if Bristol kills me?" He shakes his head. "It's only the devil waiting on the other side. He owns me now, whatever I do, and this gives me the power to keep my position. I'm done chasing you, Alice. I don't want to kill you. Honest, I don't."

He kept his end of the bargain, but it's not enough.

"I postponed this as long as possible," he continues, stooping to take off his socks and shoes. He shows me his purple-veined feet, all the toes missing.

Bile climbs my throat, and I turn my face away.

"It's not just your flesh I sacrifice, and I'm out of toes. It'll be my fingers next, and when I run out, it's over for me. I hoped you'd remember before it was too late. Every time I delayed, I hoped it meant I could kill you one less time. Every time I saved you, I hoped you would see my devotion and return it. You thought I saved you. We were family already, and so close to having everything I wanted."

No matter how hard he tries, I'll never love him, and I'll never respect him.

He glares across the flames, shadows cradling cheekbones. "I told you of the curse once, and you turned on me; ran to your lover instead. I couldn't let that happen again."

"Let Julian go."

He scoops up a bundle of Marguerite's bones. "You were supposed to live your life and listen to me," he says to the bones. "You can't blame me for how things turned out." He drops them into the fire where they crack and spit embers.

A soft moan issues from the bubbling cauldron. Then it comes again, but this time, it comes from overhead, from the top of the stone arch, where the steam curls and spirals into darkness. And casts dim light where waves of red hair stick out of the stones, his body likely sprawled over the peak.

Julian?

"Run to him," Altham says with a resigned sneer. "At this point, it changes nothing."

I race toward him, up the slippery stairs, sliding until I'm crawling to the top of the arch where Julian lies on his side, arms shackled behind him, his hair matted with blood. His eyes are open and staring, but as I fall to my knees, he twitches.

"I'm here," I murmur. "I'm here."

He blinks and looks up at me, the ghost of a smile touching his lips.

I claw at his cuffs, reaching for vines to grow into them and break them, but there's no life to draw from.

Magical chains spring from the stone and arc toward my wrists. I dodge the first set of chains, but the second set catches my arm and jerks me backward, dragging me against Julian.

If it ends here, I hope the grimoire will reappear in my next life and give me another chance.

Below, Altham feeds the pile of wood beneath us and raises his hands. The fire flares, and the heat burns the hairs on my legs. His pale lips crack as he looks up and smiles.

The temperature drops even further, until even my nose hairs freeze. The air turns dank, and dark shapes swirl overhead. Voices whisper, and leering faces grin and then vanish as vile spirits swoop and careen away. They tie Julian down, scraping their fingers against the rocks as they stretch for me.

A cold, hard resolve builds a glacier around my heart, around the last vestige of my sympathy. Altham made a deal with the devil long ago, and it's time he faces it.

I reach for Venus and the moon, innocence and childishness, brightness to defy the dark, and allow it to fill me. There's nothing physical to link the planets to, no plants to draw from, no witches to make a connection with, so I harness the energy and let it pass through my core. It's not as strong as I would like, but the spirits withdraw, their wrath just out of reach.

I keep the pressure as a barrier, blinding them and keeping them at bay. The effort sucks my strength, but I don't release the spell because as long as they can't touch us, and can't return to Altham to alert him, something is working.

Below us, Altham pulls out a knife and slices his finger down to the first knuckle. I wince as he screams.

His pain is a distraction, and it won't last. He usually hangs me next.

I focus my power on the manacles that secure my wrists, looking for a symbolic weakness to bend what is strong. When I lived in the cottage in the woods, I used the soft malleable stalks of plants for this, but there's only melting snow. Instead, I throw the black piece of paper from Ellen on the ground. It absorbs the moisture and curls in on itself.

"Paper soft, Mars is strong, loose my chains, play along," I chant.

Paper is soft, malleable. It should work.

The manacles don't change shape.

I'll make the metal brittle then.

"Neptune, furthest from the sun, icy cold would help a ton." Too bad the skeletons and ghosts can't give me a lesson on poetry.

I direct the cold into my manacles, but the ice burns my wrists, and I cry out from the pain.

On the grass below, Altham pushes himself to his knees, clutching his hand with the missing finger, and groaning.

Julian stirs, his jacket gathering water. Sweat beads down his forehead as he lets loose a low, sickly chuckle.

I squeeze my eyes shut and focus on the lock and every mechanism inside it, rather than the entire manacle. When the pain doesn't come, I smash the metal against the stones, and the manacles tumble from my wrists.

I gasp in air but push the triumph back. We're still a long way from escaping.

Altham staggers to his feet and hunches over his cauldron, but doesn't look in our direction.

Julian's eyes widen, but I hold a finger to my lips as I break his manacles as well. I waver, and Julian holds me upright, his grip tight on my elbow. Steadying.

I crawl down the makeshift stairs and Julian follows, his steps silent as a prayer. Then he crouches behind the stones at the bottom. Altham whispers to his fire, holding his bloodied hand against his chest, eyes popping. The flames burn brighter, growing bigger, though the light turns to smoke and shadow.

Then he stands straight and pulls his hood back. The gray in his hair fades, rough strands going sleek again, jawline sharp.

My legs tremble, urging me to run, but I draw energy from the deadened grass beneath my feet instead. The grass heaves a great sigh. There's not a lot there, but it's something, even if my heart winces at the waste. The grass dies as I transfer its energy to the ground beneath Altham's feet.

The spirits hound the barrier I maintain, but my magic holds.

Julian ducks behind a stone column and I make the grass grow taller to conceal him.

Altham looks up and listens. Then stumbles as he takes a step, only to find vines reaching around his ankles, curling up his legs. He tries to tear himself free, but they only tighten, and the effort of maintaining them makes me gasp for breath.

"You can't hide from me." Altham holds out his hands and inhales. "I sense your vitality."

He reaches for the fire and his fist re-emerges with a ball of flames. Fire floats above his palm. Then he pauses a few feet away from the cauldron, like he's unable or unwilling to go further, and levels his gaze to where I am.

A chilly breeze ruffles my hair.

"I'm not hiding," I say.

The fireball in Altham's hand flickers. "Decided to fight back this time, huh? Well, if you're dead within minutes of each other, I can take care of you first." He flings the fire.

I wobble on a loose stone as I sidestep. Another fireball singes my hair. Several hit my leg at once, and the pain scorches down to my ankles, leaving my pants smoldering.

Altham steps closer, hands shaping another flicker of light. "I'm a lot more powerful than anyone gives me credit for. Even more powerful than most witches, though my sacrifice was greater for it. Certainly more powerful than you."

Julian rolls out from behind the arch, crouches low, and picks up a rock. I only catch a flicker of movement, barely a whisper, as he starts toward Altham. Before the necromancer can notice, I call out, "I hope it was worth it."

The fire in Altham's hand shrinks.

"You know it wasn't," he says.

Julian is right behind him, stone in hand, arm cocked, ready to throw. Altham extends a hand and bends his fingers, like he's squeezing life from the air.

The ground creaks.

Then a hand touches Altham's shoulder. Altham turns, and Julian meets him with a punch to the face, rock still in hand. As Altham clutches his nose, Julian snatches a knife from Altham's belt and stabs his side.

Altham's back arches. He coughs. Blood spews from his lips and he smiles, leering with red teeth. "I'm immortal, fool." He shoves Julian, and I'm too far to grab him before Julian trips over a gravestone.

With a grunt, Julian hits the ground.

Cracks snake through the dirt, and skeletal hands burst through. Worms hang from loose threads of hair. Snow falls from barren skulls, and clothes crumble to dust. Skeletons climb from open graves. They grasp Julian by the arms, their outstretched fingers dragging him into the dirt.

Julian disappears beneath grasping hands. The sound that tears the air isn't his this time—it's mine.

Altham raises a fist.

Legions of empty eyes turn. Pressure builds, and tremors wrack my knees as skeletons stalk toward me, the closest one with gray curls clinging to its skull.

Bones grate, wind howls.

Evil faces, devoid of life, stare up at me as if they expect me to join them. As if I already have.

I close my eyes and plant my feet. Rather than zombies, I picture water flowing through the dirt, across the bones. Wind. Plant roots and worms. The setting sun. The molecules that create water, that power the substance. The pull of the moon.

Cool, bony hands clutch at my wrists. Daggers rake my skin, and teeth bite into my shoulders. Blood runs in warm rivulets down my forearms.

Julian's hoarse, breathless shrieks come from somewhere beneath the pile of undead. His face replaces the images of water, but I squeeze my eyes tighter. Moon, worms, water, sun.

Power pulses in my blood, down to my fingernails.

"Bones, they groan, Worms, they eat, Water feeds, and Light is heat. Wear away, groan no more, Burrow deeper than before," I chant.

My voice is strange, but the language that tumbles from my lips is stranger.

Silence presses as the earth, wind, and snow obey. Water trickles from the ground and creates pools at the skeletons' feet. Worms crawl, mold blossoms, flowers grow, and boney pores widen to tunnels for wind to whistle through. Something slimy wriggles against my leg, but I force myself to stand still.

Buried scenes come rushing back: James Altham before he was handsome.

When he strung me up, barely alive, from the top of a tower, the three Mekori witches stood around him. One carried a bottle of ashes—the remains of Guy Fawkes. Another held a pewter chalice and dagger. Altham drank my blood, and Ellen used an iron to sear the mark of a necromancer, a black skull, on his wrist.

The teeth and jaws that bite my shoulder slacken. Dirt blasts my cheeks, and a piercing scream forces my eyes open.

Altham's clothes and cape remain intact, but his skin peels from his limbs. His face twists with shock and pain. His body fights to reform while magic disintegrates him. Lurching sideways, he takes a gasping breath. "You can't do this forever. You and I both know you're a terrible witch."

The energy dies, the grass dead in every direction. The glow fades from my fingers. I have nothing more to pull from, and the minute my magic goes, Altham is in one piece again, like nothing I'd done mattered.

CHAPTER THIRTY-EIGHT

I WRAP MY FIST around my necklace.

When the door of my cottage opened, and my father entered with Altham, Hugh escaped. Guido wrestled against the ropes binding his hands. I tossed seeds beneath the moon and begged the sky for help, but while the sky twinkled with stars, the moon's light shone cold on my skin.

I didn't plan for nights with a dark moon and what little power I had, I'd used on Guido.

So, when the guards tackled me to the ground, I had no way to drive them off. James tied me up and led me to the tower, where he stole my necklace and set me aflame.

Julian emerges from a pile of skeletons and punches one in the skull so its head snaps back, stabs another, runs, and lunges for Altham, burying the knife in his side and wrenching it back out. Altham stumbles as he's jerked sideways.

"End this now," Julian says. He points the knife at Altham and waits. "Give it up."

My hand goes to the tree pendant that hangs from the chain around my neck, but suddenly Altham is standing beside me. He links his arm in mine and jerks me toward him. Except when I look, my own face stares back.

Julian blinks, shakes his head.

My jaw moves, no matter how hard I try to keep still.

"Did you ever tell her?" Altham and I speak with two identical voices.

Julian takes a step to the left, knife still raised. "Tell her what?"

"Why you came to Lancaster."

Three more steps.

"She should know," we say.

"Excalibur."

"Why Excalibur?"

Julian's face remains smooth. "It's a tool. To rid our government of the evil that had infiltrated it."

"Just the government?"

Julian takes another step. "Necromancers."

"Just necromancers?"

Julian lowers his knife.

"We're the same, are we not?" we taunt. "Earn Excalibur and kill us both."

My back is stiff, heart in my throat.

Julian raises his chin, then his knife and I'm taken back four hundred years. Standing in front of my father, a man who only cared about my usefulness, and Guido, the man I hoped could love me. But, instead, pointed a blade at my heart.

He stares at us, and I at him.

Dozens of deaths and nothing has changed. I'm still a witch.

My mouth goes dry.

"I can't." Julian throws the knife, blade first, into the dirt.

A swallow hard, gulping down my relief.

Then a loud thump draws our attention—the very place I

fell to after meeting with the ghost and jumping into her pool to transport here. A gleaming, silver sword, the hilt carved with horses, knights with pikes, and ghosts. The very echoes of battles fought for life and death.

The ghost over the small pool who gave me a riddle. The witch bound to the bottom of the lake. The Lady of the Lake.

Altham's hold over me slackens, and I work my jaw in relief.

Julian glances between us and the sword.

I shove Altham away and step between him and Julian.

"You used this necklace as a talisman the first time you burned me alive, but do you know what it really is?" I dangle the pendant for him to see.

His eyes—my eyes—narrow.

Even Jennet, the head of the Mekori, didn't know he had the necklace, not even when he bound his immortality to it with her curse. She didn't know until she saw me wearing it.

The necklace once belonged to Jennet, but she was banished from it. She can't touch it or harm it, which is why the necklace protects the wearer. Iduna, the white witch, gave it to me.

James's connection to me and Julian thrums against my fingertips, like a heartbeat, as I clutch the pendant. It's love and it's misery. I focus on the necklace's chain, the symbolic link between the three of us, and as I break the metal, the magic unravels.

James Altham lets out an anguished scream as his likeness to me fades and he's a man again, hair brittle, cheeks sagging.

Before he can fully recover, a knife hits the ground at Altham's feet. He stoops to pick it up, his fingers wrapping the hilt.

"My mercy," Julian says.

"What? Want me to kill her for you?" Altham asks. Despite looking ready to collapse into a pile of bones, he gives us a cruel smile. Then launches himself, not toward Julian, but toward me.

I dodge his knife, stoop to dig up a clump of mud, and throw it straight into his eyes. Altham claws at his face, and Julian's already lunging forward, sword arcing. His attack forces Altham to turn back and face him.

Altham catches Julian's sword on his blade's edge, spins, and catches Julian's second blow. But his movements, once unnaturally fast, slow, like every step costs him a year of life.

Julian waits for Altham before returning with his own counter-moves. Each cut with the sword is methodical, until Altham slips over the icy mud. Julian kneels, sword pointed upward, so Altham, caught unbalanced, falls onto the point. His body jerks, and he heaves a sigh. Then slouches and goes still.

A set of yellow lights in the trees blinks and goes out.

I gasp as Altham's hold over me vanishes, and stumble forward, falling to my knees beside Julian. A soft gust stirs Julian's hair. He could kill me, too, but I stay where I am, knees and hands in the dirt. Just breathing.

He turns his head, looks past me.

The cauldron still smokes, but no one stirs it. The danger is a black spot in the snow, a memory, a scar, just like the tower where I died the first time.

"He's gone," I whisper.

After so many lifetimes of being hunted, I'm free. Or, at least, as free as I can be.

I offer Julian my hand, and he pulls himself upright and dusts off his pants. His face is pale, and his eyes are still wide. Blood covers his arms and legs from fresh bite marks. He's seen many wars, but none waged by ancient swords and the undead.

He holds Excalibur in his hands and flips it over, studying the illustrations. Runs a finger over the lady, the ghostly witch, of the lake. "The sword hasn't gone," he says in surprise. "I half-expected it to disappear."

Altham's black cloak lies on the sodden ground, perhaps with its own counter-aging spell. I pick it up, and one pocket puckers. So I reach inside and draw out a page that matches the style of the other journal entries Altham gave me.

—1604—

There has been much talk of the Samles-bury witches in Pendle, at times called the Mekori. I watched them a good while ere I dared approach.

My career had tottered on the stroke of a pen since my quarrel with the king. All that I held dear was gone. My money was gone. My wives denied we were ever wed. My name became the rags that barmaids used to wipe the floors. And worst of all, Alice still refused me. Nothing remained but to win back what I had lost and end my torment.

I plied my craft into their affairs and found proof of true witchcraft. They had already been accused of sorcery by Jane's father-in-law, the Jesuit priest. The village hag, known as Demdike, would swear to peddling potions in league with them, though I know there is not a drop of witchery in Demdike's blood. I might have brought this information to the king and had my losses reversed, but a grander prospect opened to me.

I had real witches at my fingertips, not mere pretence.

I came to Jennet's house with the threat of conviction in my pocket. She answered the door and led me down the passage, past Jane's children as they pressed their backs to the wall, and into the larger room beyond. I had thought Jane the head of the Mekori—I was mistaken.

When the door shut, Jennet turned upon me. "Thou meddle'st in powers far beyond thy ken," she said. "All magic springs from me. No mortal may slay me: no fire, no hangman's noose. Nothing thou threaten'st shall hold sway."

Ball, her black-feathered raven, swept in through the open casement and settled upon her shoulder.

"Thou must pay for thy conversion."

"Conversion?" I laughed as if she meant to christen me. "Doth the devil give baptisms?"

"Mock me not." Jennet's violet eyes flashed. "I know why thou hast come. Know'st thou the price?"

"What price dost thou mean?" I asked, though she had already guessed my intent.

"I demand coin and blood."

A few gold coins and a cut of the palm — such things I expected. "And after this," said I, tasting the air, "as a necromancer shall I command the devil and his spirits? Shall I master the dead, as the tales say? Shall I be handsome and deathless besides?"

"Thou shalt have such power as thou cravest, after the initiation is complete — after thou hast drunk the blood of an innocent, burned it, and eaten of the ashes."

"Drink blood?" I had not foreseen this, but I could manage. "I will do it."

"There is more. One innocent shall not suffice. Thou must do this again and again, for every lifetime. Thy innocent shall be returned to thee each time her life ends, and the sacrifice must be made anew."

No single soul would be too great to serve, and lifetimes are long. I could make this endure. "That doth not deter me."

Jennet tilted her head; the raven on her shoulder mirrored the motion. "This innocent must never taste of love. Alice must never know the joy thou didst steal from her, lest thou die in her stead. Thou didst sunder the love once — thou must do so again."

"Alice?" I asked.

She spoke the name as one who read my thoughts. How else should she know? Jennet paced about me, slow and deliberate. "Alice is the obvious choice."

I coveted this knowledge — the power to read another's mind, to know when they plotted ill so I might punish them; to be rich again, yet greater — impenetrable, undeniable.

A smile warped Jennet's lips. "Thou shalt be all that thou desirest. Fairer women than Alice shall fall before thee."

I could see it. "Is it worth the price?"

Jennet paused, the raven cawing softly from her shoulder. "I shall meet thee at Malkin Tower with the innocent. Fail me not."

She led me from the room, and I set forth to do what must be done. I have become what I

> *was meant to be. My remorse for Alice will ebb, I am certain, and others shall take her place. She and Guido are dead; I live forever.*
>
> —*James Altham*

Some curses end in death. Mine began with it.

James Altham will never bother me again, and I'll go on living the life he stole from me. The lives he stole.

Julian glances at the letter over my shoulder, but his expression doesn't change.

I give him an inquiring look, and he shrugs. "I always suspected my connection to Guy Fawkes. Honestly, I don't think I ever fully forgot. Maybe that's why he sent me to live with necromancers—to torment me more. But it didn't fully hit until he called you 'Alice.'"

I fold the page up and slide it into my pocket, but don't take my eyes off him.

"You never told me," he says.

The accusation hangs between us.

We've never remembered long enough to have this conversation.

I search his expression for disgust and fear, but his face is only somber. "I never wanted to be a witch."

I never wanted to hurt him.

He looks away.

"It still bothers you, doesn't it?" I ask.

Firecrackers disrupt the black sky in the distance, and Julian stares upward. "You're everything I swore I'd destroy." He gestures to the explosions, the sparkling flames falling towards us like wilting flowers. "Now there are bonfires instead of burnings. Effigies instead of witches. I thought I was doing the right thing."

Remember, remember.

When I reach for his hand, he flinches.

I brush my fingers lightly along his jaw. "They don't know you."

He huffs a breath—a rough, bitter sound. "I couldn't care less what they think." He catches me by the waist, fingers hooking into my belt loops, his touch steady and warm. "Forgive me?"

"Only if you take me to another dance—and leave your dad at home."

He laughs, but the sound is shaky. Uncertain. And I wish I could pick up my bags again and move across the world. Leave the past behind. Far behind. An ocean behind.

But the past always follows, and the only answer is to stay.

CHAPTER THIRTY-NINE

THE WHITE-TIPPED CANDLES flicker uselessly against the November gloom. Even the priest's voice can't fill the emptiness. Students fill the rows of seats—students who never knew Noelle.

Noelle's entire family attended the funeral at a church near Burnley Boarding School, except for a little sister who was too sick to come. After the service, her family plans to send her body to Florida for its final burial in the family cemetery.

Noelle deserves to be alive—not shut inside polished wood that reeks of varnish and grief. The hearse, draped in flags, looks small against the ageless stone and fields of muddy, dying grass. It shrinks as it moves down the endless road out the gate.

Attendants carry bouquets out the church doors, no less lovely than the ones I arranged at the flower store in Colorado. When they pass on either side, gray skies dull the colors. They'll wilt by morning.

Warm fingers slip into mine, and the hollow in my chest eases—just a little.

"I'm sorry, Alice."

The taste of salt lingers on my lips.

"Can I take you home?" Julian asks. "Or somewhere to get your mind off this?"

I exhale slowly. "No. I want to remember." I want to remember everything. To cling to the moments that will pass and fade from memory before I can reclaim them.

Julian squeezes my hand. "Are you leaving, then?"

"In a few minutes."

"That's not what I meant. Are you going to stay at Burnley after your mum comes?"

Iduna's face materializes in my head—lavender eyes and branches in her hair. The White Witch. She probably thinks I'm dead, but if she finds out I'm not, she'll expect me to find her. I glance down at my wrist, at the scars covering my witch tattoo. The grimoire brought the mark back for a moment, but it faded again. I'll have to renew it, as well as my vows.

"I'm not sure," I say.

I could stay while I search for Iduna. The witches on Mill Road haven't vacated. They're still there, luring students into their store. Whatever happens, I have a duty to Burnley Boarding School, so long as the Mekori are nearby.

When I checked my phone, the recording was gone. Deleted. So much for proof.

The Mekori have no reason to go, so why would they? I have to give them a reason, but I can't do that without regaining the full power I once had.

"I need to find someone," I say.

"Who?"

"Someone I knew a long time ago."

"Where are they?"

"I don't know."

Julian raises an eyebrow.

Even when we lived in the cottage and Iduna came to visit, I didn't know where she came from. "I'll figure it out, and I promise I'll tell you everything I know."

Wish I could bring Noelle back, but I can't. I can, however, look for Hugh. I have to discover what happened to him. With his affinity for immortality, he might still be alive, though I squash the hope before it sprouts leaves too green. Iduna might know more.

"Will Iduna help with the murder investigation?" Julian asks.

"I doubt it."

They found Noelle at the bottom of the staircase. I can't stop picturing it—her hair against the stone. The police locked down the building, interviewed students, and posted security guards on every corner of campus. However, the police are no closer to solving the missing persons case, though the case gained more attention when a highly esteemed professor, Reeve, disappeared, too.

Many students have been called home by their parents. My parents haven't called, but they don't live here and might not have seen the news yet about Reeve, though I'm sure they will soon.

The Headmistress has been swamped with unwanted media attention. No one's seen her in days.

Julian tugs me toward Mika and Eser, standing beside the church doors, waiting for us. Mika waves, and Eser turns—perfect sweater, perfect posture. Of course.

Mika nods.

"Do you think there's a chance we could ever be happy? Like those days in the cottage in the woods?" he asks.

I study Julian—the gold in his hazel eyes, chestnut hair catching the light, the steady way he moves. The kindness of his smile. The strength of all the years we've endured together.

With or without a curse, I'll chase him through lifetimes, but

I'll never be content until I've redeemed myself.

I can't lie to him, so I say nothing.

My lips rehearse the vow I made all those years ago as we walk down the aisle of the school's church. A reverent hush settles over us. The room's all carved wood and stained-glass windows—as old as my story. The nave showers the room with rainbows.

When we step into the courtyard, the spires are silhouetted against the low sun, spilling color across the sky like paint. Every hue glows flawlessly, as flawless as the moment—Julian's hand still in mine.

I want a normal life, too, but I also want my brother back. And I'm all he has.

"I, Alice Grey," I repeat under my breath, "accept the blood of the witch tree, the source of all magic. I am the protector of my brother, and I will not fail again."

Let's Be Friends

If you enjoyed this book, please leave a review so other readers can find it! One line is plenty!

Follow me on
Instagram: @brookeclonts
TikTok: @brookeclonts
Website: brookeclonts.com

For early access to deals and announcements, subscribe to my mailing list at www.brookeclonts.com.

ALSO BY BROOKE CLONTS

Empire of Glass and Stone

ACKNOWLEDGMENTS

Thank you to my beta readers—I've had many over the years and I'm immensely grateful for every one of them. Thanks so much to Rachel Lopiccolo for helping me keep the content true to the history that inspired this tale (check out Rachel's books on the witch trials). And thank you to Kelley Riegert, Fiona McLaren, and Kim Autrey, my editors, for polishing it! And Seth Weinheimer for convincing me not to throw this book in the trash after more than ten years rewriting and revising it.

ABOUT THE AUTHOR

Brooke Clonts was born in Salt Lake City, Utah. Her passion for writing started as a kid when she spent most of her time hiding in her bedroom with a book. Her cousin recommended she try writing, and it became her obsession. She has a degree in exercise science she's never used, is a self-taught software engineer, left her job to run her own businesses, and is a wife and mom to the most beautiful boys in the world. She often writes late at night after her sons go to bed. But her stories follow her all day long.

SECOND
STAR PRESS